LIANYU TAN

CAPTIVE IN THE UNDERWORLD

A DARK LESBIAN ROMANCE
NOVEL

Copyright © 2020 by Lianyu Tan

https://lianyutan.com/

All rights reserved. No part of this book may be reproduced or used in any manner without written permission of the copyright owner except for the use of quotations in a book review. For permission requests, write to lianyu@lianyutan.com.

First paperback edition January 2021

Cover design by MiblArt

Editing by Wicked Words and Christa Cooke

ISBN 978-0-6489948-1-7 (paperback)

ISBN 978-0-6489948-0-0 (ebook)

Shattered Scepter Press

SUMMARY

Some flowers bloom only in the dark…

In the land of the dead, Queen Hades' word is law. Hades gets what she wants—always—and what she wants is a certain goddess of the springtime.

Innocent Persephone chafes beneath her mother's hawkish gaze and mercurial temper. Demeter has rebuffed all her daughter's suitors, but she is not yet satisfied; she strives to crush Persephone's spirit.

Still, when Hades pulls her into the dark realm of the underworld, Persephone longs for the world above, even if it means an eternity under her mother's thumb.

With her tears and pleas for freedom ignored by pitiless Hades, Persephone must learn to satisfy her keeper in all ways, lest she suffer the consequences.

And though she cannot deny that something blooms within her, something forbidden, Persephone despairs of ever feeling the sun upon her skin once more.

No matter the cost, Hades intends to keep her.

Forever.

Captive in the Underworld is a standalone dark lesbian romance novel set in mythological ancient Greece. It is rooted in the misogyny and cruelties of the Hades/Persephone myth and contains sensitive material. Due to mature content and dark themes, this book is intended for adult readers only. It contains scenes depicting death, abuse, kidnapping, assault, rape, and other intimate partner violence. It is not recommended for readers sensitive to such content. Neither the publisher nor the author endorses any behavior carried out by any character in this work of fiction. Additional content tags are available at: https://go.lianyutan.com/underworldtags

For my precious flower.

1

SOMETHING YOU WANT

No one would blame Persephone for being so nervous she could vomit—no one except her mother, of course. Demeter's breath was hot on her cheek; Persephone focused on maintaining her smile. Bland smile, modest clothes, and a silent tongue. Gaia forbid she do anything to embarrass her mother.

Demeter adjusted Persephone's girdle for the seventeenth time and smoothed the curls back from her forehead. "You'll remember what I told you?" she asked.

"Of course." Persephone cleared her throat. "Mind the wine. And no promises."

"No promises," Demeter echoed. She stepped back from her daughter and smiled. "Lovely."

Persephone did her best to look gracious, but the woolen himation wrapped around her shoulders was stifling her. It did its intended job to conceal her figure—she might as well be taking vows of chastity today, instead of attending her first celebration in what felt like forever.

The gates of Zeus's palace loomed above them, sparkling

gold in the afternoon sun, as glorious as ever. A pair of guards nodded to them on their way in. As they passed through the gates, strains of music and laughter met their ears. The crisp, warm scents of Olympus in autumn mingled with the sweet fragrance of nectar and ambrosia. A minor godling stumbled past them, reeking of wine.

The outer courtyard was littered with guests. It seemed like everyone in Olympus had been invited, including nymphs of the rivers, forests, and seas, and a few mortals. Persephone maintained a polite smile, even when some of the mortals passed too close and their acrid sweat offended her senses.

Once they had reached the palace proper, a servant announced both of them. "Demeter of the Grain and her daughter, Persephone."

Her mother guided them through throngs of well-wishers toward the depths of the palace. Persephone followed, though her mind wandered. She ought to use this opportunity to reconnect with Athena and Artemis—it had been years since the three of them had been in the same place. The other guests, though...

"Greetings to you upon this wondrous day."

Persephone turned to find Hephaestus watching her, his crooked smile endearingly shy. "And to you," she said, trying not to stare at his leg. He'd strapped some kind of metal contraption to it, which allowed him to walk almost as if it were undamaged. The mechanics seemed more complex compared to the last time she'd seen him, though she couldn't quite pinpoint any specific changes.

"A good day to you, Hephaestus," Demeter said. "We have yet to speak with Zeus."

He nodded. "Of course."

Persephone felt his eyes upon them as they continued walking, heading toward Zeus's throne room. Her cheeks grew hot, which she did not much like. "I wonder what he wanted," she said.

"What do all gods want?" Demeter asked, her lovely face marred by a scowl. "Mind you dissuade him firmly."

"Yes, Mother," Persephone said, distracted by the graceful curve of the arches above them. The colonnades were decorated with carvings of nymphs and small animals, cavorting as they upheld the high ceiling. It reminded her of the solemn dignity of a forest canopy.

It was not long before they reached Zeus's throne room. Her father, an immense hulk of a man, his face dwarfed by his beard, loomed larger than the earth herself. His voice boomed with the echo of thunder, his laughter emanating from his belly.

Hera was not by his side, only his true-born daughter Hebe, standing behind him with her hands clasped, her gaze wandering. Despite the vast hall filled with people, Persephone wondered if he might sometimes feel lonely.

"Kore!" Zeus said, still referring to Persephone by her childhood name. "Let me look at you. Where have you been keeping her all these years, Demeter?"

Demeter's forehead creased in a frown, but she prodded Persephone's side, pushing her forward.

Persephone stumbled for a few steps, then fell to her knees in prostration. "Skyfather, I renew my allegiance to you and your rule. My sword and my shield are yours," she said.

"Persephone, fruit of Demeter, daughter of mine, I accept your fealty." Zeus took her hand, helping her rise to her feet, then slapped her back, nearly bowling her over. "Now, eat. Drink! The day is young, and we rejoice as one family."

"Yes, Father."

His attention was already gone from her, moving on to the next visitor—Poseidon, who had eyes not for Zeus but Demeter. Persephone gratefully took the opportunity to slip away whilst her elders were distracted.

A breeze had picked up by the time she found her way into the courtyards. She ran her hands over the leaves of an ornamental fig, yellowed by lack of nutrients. The leaves brightened when she touched it, though the effect would not last long without further treatment.

She had not escaped the other revelers, but everyone else seemed preoccupied, clustered in little groups and arguing over petty trifles. She took a cup of wine from a passing servant and sipped at it, feeling its heat rush to her cheeks. A little wouldn't hurt.

Hephaestus found her in a courtyard. She heard him approach, distinguishing him by the unusual scuffle he made as he walked, favoring his lame leg.

"Persephone, well met, again. I was hoping to find you; we see you so rarely. Have you the time now to entertain my attentions?" he asked.

Persephone smiled and then stopped herself, her mother's words echoing in her mind. "I—yes, of course. But—"

"I wish to give you a gift on this loveliest of days." With a flourish that seemed practiced, he revealed a small box from under his chlamys and held it out to her.

"You shouldn't have," she said but saw no way to refuse him that would not seem rude. She opened the lid of the box, revealing a small metal bird nestled in cloth.

"It winds with this key," he said, pointing out the mechanism.

Persephone held it on her palm and turned the key several times. To her delight, the bird flapped its wings and opened its beak, trilling out a few sweet notes.

"Oh!" she said, enraptured. "How clever."

"You like it?"

"Yes, of course! It's beautiful."

The spring powering the mechanism wound down, and the bird returned to its original stationary position. Persephone placed it back in its box.

"My forge is known best for its weapons, but I can create so much more than that," Hephaestus said. "I prefer to make scythes over swords, at any rate."

"You have a true talent."

He smiled at her, seemingly encouraged by her words. His face set him apart from the other gods and goddesses, all paragons of beauty. Had he ever forgiven Hera for her rejection?

"I see you've found us again," Demeter said as she walked over to them. She plucked the wine cup from Persephone's hand and drank deeply.

Persephone uncovered her box, presenting it to Demeter. "Look, Mother. Isn't it beautiful?"

Demeter made an ambiguous sound, and placed her hand on Hephaestus's shoulder. "Lovely. May I speak with you, my dear boy?" she asked, taking his arm before he could object.

Hephaestus shot Persephone a look of alarm before Demeter led him away.

Persephone took this opportunity to head back into the palace. Inside, a large circle had formed of dancing youths, their brows slick with sweat, their arms linked. Persephone skirted around them and grabbed a chalice of ambrosia, draining it before her mother could take this from her, too.

She recognized Aphrodite's perfume before she saw her—cinnamon and balsam, spicy and sweet. Aphrodite sashayed up beside her, turning to face the dancers.

"Wonderful, isn't it? All those beautiful bodies on display." Aphrodite sighed, her long lashes perfectly framing her eyes as she pouted.

"Hello to you, too," Persephone said.

Aphrodite dragged her gaze from the dancers to glance at her. "I wasn't expecting to see you. It's been an eon, hasn't it?"

Persephone shrugged and forced herself to smile. "Not quite, but I'm pleased to have come."

"Mm. Are you cold? You can't possibly be cold. Here." Aphrodite reached up and unwrapped Persephone's himation, throwing it to one side. She then rearranged the neckline of Persephone's chiton, pulling it lower to reveal more than a hint of cleavage.

The tips of Aphrodite's fingers tickled her skin. Persephone drew back, her face flushing. "I'm fine." She hoisted her neckline back to its proper position.

Aphrodite's assessing gaze traveled from the brown curls coiffed around Persephone's head to the smattering of freckles across her sun-kissed arms. "Yes, you'll do," she said. "You'll find love tonight, I'm sure of it."

"I'm not looking for that."

Aphrodite's eyes widened, and she leaned forward, taking Persephone into her confidence. "*Everyone* is looking for that. So tell me who it's to be. Apollo? Ares? No, too pig-headed for you. I know, how about—"

"I'd sooner join Athena and avow chastity." Persephone reached for her himation, but Aphrodite slapped her hand away.

"Trust me, you don't need that. Don't tell me Demeter will be mad. She isn't here!"

Yes. Her mother wasn't here. Persephone glanced around the room, but all she could see were the dancers and their admirers, her mother nowhere in view. She inhaled, light-headed from Aphrodite's perfume, or perhaps she had imbibed more than was wise on an empty stomach. She set Hephaestus's gift down on a nearby table for fear of dropping it by accident.

"Come on," Aphrodite said, grabbing her by the wrist. "Dance with me."

"I don't know the steps," Persephone said, trying to pull away, but Aphrodite's grip was as tight as her girdle.

The dancers were halfway through a song, a mixed group of gods and goddesses. The circle parted to admit Aphrodite and her unwilling find; Persephone found herself staring at the feet of the dancer opposite to mirror their steps. Everyone else seemed to know the motions as she alone fumbled her way through the song, doing her best to follow the cues whilst not stepping on anyone's toes.

Time crawled. Through sheer dint of repetition, Persephone learned the dance well enough to take her eyes off the floor. She could not help but notice most of the dancers and onlookers staring at Aphrodite—at her golden curls and long legs, the unrestrained bounce of her chest. Persephone's face grew hot when Aphrodite turned to her and smiled.

"That explains so many things," Aphrodite murmured, glancing at Persephone up and down. Her smile grew wicked.

"I have no idea what you mean." Persephone tore her hand from Aphrodite's grasp and broke rank with the dancers. The circle closed behind her as she slipped out through a side passageway.

The sounds of music and festivity faded as she walked further from the main hall, her footsteps echoing as she headed down a vast corridor. She wiped her palms on her skirts, her hands trembling. The way Aphrodite had looked at her—as though she'd been staring straight into Persephone's heart. She could still feel Aphrodite's fingers on her wrist.

She wandered aimlessly, taking turn after turn until her heartbeat slowed to a more regular pace. She found herself on a walkway overlooking a courtyard, the ground one story below. She leaned against a column and covered her face with her hands.

If Aphrodite knew, then everyone would know. Demeter would know.

She'd not intended to have that conversation with her mother quite so soon—perhaps, not ever. It wasn't a crime, of course, but Demeter had so thoroughly charted out the arc of Persephone's life that she would no doubt be displeased by this revelation.

When Persephone heard voices approaching, she froze, terrified that somehow her thoughts had summoned her mother's presence. The voices came from the level below; she pressed her back against the column concealing her and grasped her skirts in one hand, lest the wind reveal her presence.

"You must consider the merits of my case. Semele's life was inordinately short, due to my dear wife's meddling. She deserves a second chance," said a booming male voice that she was relieved to recognize as belonging to Zeus.

"Perhaps you should direct your question to the Fates," said a quieter, female voice. She sounded familiar, but Persephone couldn't quite place the speaker.

"Bah! They have no claim over her now."

Persephone sank to a crouch and peeked through the banisters. Her father stood in the courtyard below, talking to a goddess whose back was turned to Persephone. She had black curly hair swept up in braids and wore a long, flowing chiton as dark as night, held firm by a belt of gold links.

A virtuous girl would have turned and walked away immediately to avoid intruding on what was clearly a private conversation. Demeter would expect no less from her.

Persephone did not move.

"I have noted your concerns," the goddess said.

"And?"

"Lives end every moment of every day. Some are long, and some are short. I cannot make exceptions simply because you chose to make this one a vessel for your seed."

Persephone clasped her hands over her mouth to prevent a gasp. She should've left when they'd first entered the courtyard; this was not a conversation meant for her ears. She did not care to displease anyone who could speak so imprudently to the great Zeus.

"There must be something you want," Zeus said.

The goddess did not speak for a long time. When she broke the silence, Persephone had to strain to hear her. "What could I possibly want? No god can match my riches; not even you."

"Perhaps that was a mistake."

Persephone heard the smile in the goddess's voice. "Ah,

well. But the great Skyfather could not possibly make mistakes, could he?"

"We'll discuss this later," Zeus snapped and strode off, the fabric of his robe flying out behind him from the speed of his steps.

Persephone glanced around, wondering how to make a discreet exit. If she suddenly appeared and continued on her way in full sight of the courtyard, it would be obvious that she'd been eavesdropping. If only—

The goddess turned and looked directly at Persephone's hiding spot. Persephone understood now how she'd been able to speak so disrespectfully to Zeus, not caring if she offended him.

Even the gods feared her realm and the secrets within it.

"You might as well come down," Hades said.

Persephone's face flushed. She longed for the ground to swallow her whole, for the earth to claim her as her own and hide her shame, but her feet found nothing but solid stone as she trudged down the flight of steps leading to the courtyard.

"Well?" Hades asked. "What do you have to say for yourself, Kore?"

She was tall, pale as though she'd never seen the sun. Her aquiline nose looked carved from marble. It had been a long time—decades, perhaps—since they'd last met.

Persephone lowered herself to one knee and gazed at the ground. "Forgive me, Queen Hades. It was wrong of me to eavesdrop."

"And yet you did," Hades said. "Did Demeter teach you no manners?"

Persephone risked a glance. Hades' face was unreadable, still as a statue. "Of course she did. The fault is mine alone."

Hades considered her in silence. After a moment, she made a sharp gesture with her hand. "Let me warn you now: if you wish to forgo conventions, you had best avoid getting caught."

Persephone rose to her feet, stilling the impulse to brush the dust from her chiton. "You won't tell her, will you?"

"That remains to be seen." Hades jerked her head toward the next courtyard. "Walk with me."

She couldn't disobey a direct order, no matter what Demeter might've said. Persephone hurried to match Hades' long strides. "Have you been well?" she asked. "I hear you've not been seen for some time."

"Well enough. And you, Kore. Are you keeping safe?" Hades asked.

Persephone blushed, wondering what Hades thought she had to fear. "Yes, thank you."

Hades led them up several flights of steps to a wide balcony at the back of the palace, overlooking the ocean. There was only one path down from the balcony, the walkway coiling in clear view below them. Someone ascending would be seen long before they reached the top. The pathways were heavily planted, overgrown with ivy that sprawled across the railing and steps. Hades leaned over the balustrade and closed her eyes, the breeze tousling her hair and billowing out her skirts.

The sun glittered over the ocean's waves. A few gulls danced close to the shoreline, tiny specks of white swooping down over the water to fetch their prey.

It was pretty enough, but that alone did not explain Hades' pensive expression. The silence stretched on as Hades studiously ignored her, seemingly forgetting Persephone's existence for all the mind she paid her. Persephone could not leave without a clear dismissal, and so she waited, caught in a formless limbo where she began to doubt her own memory of whether, in fact, Hades had requested her presence at all.

The silence grew overlong. Perhaps Persephone's frustration at being ignored gave her courage, for she could not blame her next words on the ambrosia. "May I... may I ask you a question?" she asked, stumbling a little over her words.

Hades turned her head, as if seeing her for the first time. "Out with it."

"Do plants grow in the underworld?"

Hades stared at her as though she were addle-brained. "Yes. Is that all?"

Persephone blushed. "I meant—are they growing then, truly? Or is it simply their souls taking on a different form? I mean, do plants have souls? I've always thought that trees would, of course, but as for annuals—"

Hades cut her off. "I would rather not discuss matters associated with my function."

"But when Zeus—" Persephone bit her lip, horrified at her mistake. Of course Zeus could ask Hades whatever questions he deemed fit; she would not dare compare herself with her father in the same breath. Except she'd done just that.

"This is why we do not eavesdrop on our elders," Hades said, her eyes slitted.

An apology came quickly to Persephone's lips, but words alone seemed inadequate. She unconsciously took a step back, her hand brushing the ivy-covered guardrail. The plant grew a new tendril, which slithered across her arm, as if trying to comfort her.

Hades' gaze dropped to the ivy. She reached out and touched its leaves, then crossed the distance between them. Persephone froze in place as the ivy wound up her bare arm and across her back, followed closely by Hades' fingertips grazing her skin.

Hades' hand lingered on her shoulder, a warm and heavy weight. Persephone's breath caught in her throat.

"Fascinating," Hades said.

She was no longer looking at the plant. Instead, her gaze focused on Persephone, her pupils large despite the warm afternoon light.

They were close enough that Persephone could have kissed her, had she the mind to. Not that she wanted to.

Hades' hand trailed across her collarbone. She placed her fingers around Persephone's neck, her thumb brushing over the hollow of the girl's throat. Her perfume was floral and green—gardenia? No. Asphodel. Persephone's pulse beat a mad staccato rhythm as she stood motionless, the stillness of prey caught in the hunter's sight as she searched for what to do, to say, to make Hades unhand her.

"Persephone! I've been looking all over for you!"

Demeter's voice. Hades didn't release her, not immediately. Her mouth curved into a slight smile, and for a moment, her fingers tightened around Persephone's neck, squeezing the breath from her. The ivy coiled around Hades' wrist, temporarily binding them.

Demeter's footsteps. Hades released her and took a step back, tearing the ivy from her wrist. Persephone gasped and clutched at her throat, her other hand clinging to the railing as the greenery wound its way toward her.

Demeter's sandals slapped against the stone steps as she climbed the last few stairs up to the balcony, the hem of her chiton held up in one hand as not to trail in the dirt. Had she seen... what must she think? Perhaps the distance had been too great. Persephone could only hope.

She did not know what to think herself. She almost wished she'd the courage to ask Aphrodite whether she believed—but no. Persephone couldn't ask anyone for help in deciphering Hades' smile. Had she simply meant to frighten her? She'd succeeded.

"My dear Hades!" Demeter flitted over to her, placing one hand upon the goddess's cheek. "How pale you are! How have you been keeping? You look so severe, you might as well have dressed for a funeral!"

"I would prefer a funeral," Hades said, moving aside from Demeter's touch. "Wouldn't you?"

Demeter tittered. "I'd forgotten how droll you can be. Will we be seeing more of you this year?"

"I think not."

"Why ever not?" Demeter pouted.

Hades glanced skyward, toward the ocean. "The same reasons."

Demeter simpered. "Why, that's nonsense, of course. I don't see how you bear it, being trapped in that awful place, year in, year out! Could you imagine it?" she asked, directing this last question to Persephone.

"No," Persephone said as she gently extricated herself from the ivy, supplying what she thought was the desired answer.

Demeter wrapped her arms around herself and shivered theatrically. "Simply dreadful!"

Hades said nothing. She briefly met Persephone's gaze. Was she amused? Annoyed? Persephone couldn't read her well enough to tell.

Demeter sighed. "We each have our burdens to bear." She

took Persephone's arm, her mirror-bright smile wide enough to cut her face in two. "Speaking of which, I must get this one home."

"Of course." Hades inclined her head. "It was good to see you again, Demeter. Persephone," she said, annunciating the syllables in her name with care.

Her name shouldn't have sounded indecent coming from Hades' lips, but all the same, Persephone shivered. She mumbled her farewells as she stared at her feet.

Demeter gave a little tug on her arm, and then they were away.

"Must we go so soon?" Persephone asked once they had made their way downstairs.

"This is not 'soon,'" Demeter said. "It is almost dark. Let's get you to bed."

Persephone glanced up at the sky. The sun was not quite set, and there was still plenty of light. "We must find Father," she said. That would take some searching, surely. "To make our goodbyes."

"I've already said our farewells to Zeus," Demeter said.

Persephone blinked. "I would've liked to see him again."

Demeter did not slow her pace as they headed down the corridors of Zeus's palace, weaving around groups of inebriated party-goers. "What was that? Speak up, child."

Persephone bit her lip. "It was nothing."

They drew near to Zeus's private wing, where he and his immediate family lived. Persephone glanced up to see Aphrodite descending the staircase, re-pinning a fibula to secure one shoulder of her chiton. It did not match the brooch on her right shoulder. In fact, Persephone could've sworn she'd seen something of that design adorning Hera's clothing.

Aphrodite winked at her.

Demeter's grip tightened on Persephone's arm, and once they were a safe distance away, she sneered. "Strumpet."

"It is only her function, Mother," Persephone said, made bold by the hum of conversation around them, the laughter pealing through the evening air.

Demeter didn't deign to respond. Outside, a servant waited for them with horses and a chariot. Persephone would rather have walked, barefoot, to feel the hum of the earth beneath her toes. She did not bother suggesting such a thing to her mother. Walking would have looked plebian.

Demeter waited until they were well out of the shadow of Zeus's palace before she spoke again. "What did she want from you?"

"Who?" Persephone asked to buy herself time.

Her mother gave her a sharp look.

"Hades and I spoke of nothing of consequence," Persephone said. "Plants," she added. She resisted the impulse to rub at her throat.

"Don't harass her with your inane prattle in the future," Demeter said. "Don't you know she hasn't been seen above ground for at least seventy summers? She must have much more pressing things to do. Whatever would a silly little girl like you have to say to the Queen of the Underworld?"

Persephone bit her tongue. She hadn't asked to be caught with Hades; in fact, she'd had no intention—none!—of conversing with her at all, if one could even call their interaction a conversation. She'd squandered the day, and now Gaia only knew when she'd next be able to speak with Athena or Artemis.

"And what of our agreement?" Demeter asked.

"I kept my head. I hardly had a drop," Persephone said.

Demeter sniffed. "And the other?"

"No promises." They had left so early, what did Demeter suppose she had done with the scant time available?

"Even a kind smile is an invitation, to some," Demeter said. "And what happened to your himation?"

Persephone rubbed her bare shoulder, shivering as she remembered Aphrodite's knowing smile. "I—danced a little. I must have dropped it. I'm sorry." She had also left behind her gift from Hephaestus. She hesitated, opening her mouth, but stopped herself before she could commit the sin of asking to turn around to fetch it.

Demeter rolled her eyes skyward but remained silent the rest of the chariot ride home. Once their driver had brought them to the back of the house and departed, she turned to Persephone. "You'll not try to bother her again, will you, dear?"

"Hades?" Persephone asked.

Demeter twirled a lock of hair around her finger. "It's just I would so hate for her to take offense at your prattling. She can be vindictive, you know."

The warning was unnecessary. Persephone touched her fingertips to her neck, echoes of their conversation repeating over and over in her mind. *Did Demeter teach you no manners?* "I won't bother her," she said. It was an easy promise to make.

Demeter smiled and placed an arm around her shoulders. "Come, the hour is late."

Persephone obediently followed her mother up the steps to the house. Though she could not quite forget her brief audience with the Queen of the Underworld, they spoke no more of Hades that evening, nor any evening thereafter.

2

NONE ARE WORTHY

Seasons passed, and Persephone's chance meeting with Hades became a distant memory. She did not think of her overly much except in spring, when all her flowers were in bloom, including the star-shaped white asphodel. There was something imperfect about their scent, mismatching what she remembered wafting from the heat of Hades' skin— they were too warm, too bright, too... immaculate.

She spent a season watching a nest of ospreys learning to fly, the chicks molting from ugly gray lumps to trim little juveniles, finally growing up to leave the nest and find territories of their own.

Spring brought rain and warm breezes before giving way to hot, dry summer. Once the heat had passed, the trees grew golden, their leaves turning brittle in the flush of autumn. The weather changed, and spring came anew, tiny shoots bursting through the earth as if summoned by the sun.

Demeter was always busy, busy, busy. There were new kings to teach, new fields to plant. Humanity seemed destined to spread like an entangling weed, even as the machinations of

Athena and Ares sent generation after generation of mortal sons to Hades' realm.

The house was never empty—there were always acolytes and attendants about, all to serve Demeter, of course, but few of the other gods deigned to make an appearance.

So, it was with some surprise that Persephone found Hephaestus lurking at the front of the house one summer, apparently summoning the courage to knock upon their door.

Persephone shifted her flower basket to her other arm and brushed back a lock of hair from her face. "Hephaestus! What brings you here?"

He smiled nervously at her, his face glazed with a sheen of sweat. "You, dear Persephone." He shifted from one leg to the other, the metal contraption that encircled his damaged leg squeaking slightly.

"Why don't you come inside and share some wine with us?" Persephone asked.

Hephaestus coughed. "Well, actually, before that—I would rather speak plainly with you, if I may."

"Of course." Persephone smiled at him in an attempt to put him at ease, but it only seemed to make him more nervous. "I still remember the mechanical bird you gave me. It was the most charming thing I'd ever seen," she said.

"Ah." Hephaestus seemed to draw courage from her words. "I'm glad. It was over a hundred summers ago, you know."

"Really?" Persephone's eyes widened. Had it been that long since she had danced at Zeus's palace? "I'm sure your skills have only grown since that time."

"And I would fashion many more delights for you, each one more wondrous than the last, if you were to permit me to—to—"

Persephone waited, biting her tongue to keep herself from

interrupting.

"—if you would permit me to court you," Hephaestus said, almost sagging with relief to have the words out.

Persephone blinked. "Oh!" She flushed and glanced away. She could not say that she felt strongly about it one way or the other—and it was not that she minded his limp, nor the misshapen slope of his face. She had simply never thought of him in that way. Then again, he seemed kind enough and was clever with his hands.

A vision of their future flashed before her. He would not despise her, as Hera despised Zeus, and he would be mindful of his conquests, pursuing them quietly without compromising Persephone's reputation, unlike the other gods. Under his wing, she would be free from her mother's house, at last.

She could do worse. "I—I would be honored," she said and tried to smile. She offered her hand. "Let's go inside and tell Mother."

Hephaestus gingerly entwined his fingers with hers and allowed himself to be led inside.

Persephone found him a seat and was pouring them drinks when Demeter walked into the room.

"My dear boy," Demeter said. "What brings you here today?"

Persephone set down the wine jug and offered a cup to Demeter. "Hephaestus has asked to court me, and I've accepted," she said. "We humbly request your blessing."

Demeter glanced between the two of them, and then she began to laugh.

Persephone froze in mortification. Her outstretched hand trembled, and she set down the cup, wine sloshing over the sides.

"Please forgive me," Demeter said, wiping an imaginary tear from her eye. "I mean you no ill will, Hephaestus. It's simply that my Persephone is yet a child and lacks the maturity to be anyone's potential bride."

"I'm no child, Mother," Persephone said. She gestured toward Hephaestus. "He said it's been over a century since I was last seen at Zeus's palace."

Demeter airily waved her hand in the air. "Another five centuries, perhaps, and we could talk."

Hephaestus rose to his feet. "It seems clear that Persephone believes she is ready for the trappings of adulthood, Demeter." He glanced at Persephone.

"Yes," she said. "I am." She took Hephaestus's hand, squeezing his fingers. "And this is what I desire."

Demeter's eyes grew cold. "You can't possibly know what you want. An eternity with him? Really?"

"It's a courtship, not a contract, Mother!"

"Ladies, please—"

"Enough!" Demeter shrieked. She snatched up the wine jug and threw it at Hephaestus. He ducked, and the pottery shattered behind him, but he could not avoid the wine splashing his face and clothes.

"Mother!" Persephone exclaimed. She searched Hephaestus's face for signs of injury, but the only wound seemed to be to his pride.

Hephaestus wiped a hand across his eyes. "Father said you would listen to reason, but I see now you are lost in your delusions."

"Get out of my house," Demeter said, holding a plate in a threatening manner.

"Mother, please—"

"You can't keep her a prisoner forever—"

"Get out!" Demeter said, throwing the plate for emphasis. This time Hephaestus blocked it with his arm, and it shattered on the floor.

Persephone grabbed his other arm, leading him out of the house before her mother could hurl anything else. Once they were a safe distance outside, she released him. "I'm sorry," she said. "I had no idea she would treat you so badly."

Hephaestus squeezed wine from his tunic. "It's quite all right. Ares warned me about her temper, but I didn't listen. I thought she might look upon me more favorably. I was wrong."

"Ares?" Persephone asked.

Hephaestus glanced away. "Perhaps I spoke out of turn. You didn't know he was trying to court you?"

Persephone grimaced. "There was that year I received a severed gorgon head as a present, but I thought... Mother said it was a mistake. I didn't actually see him in person."

"Demeter has something of a reputation."

"How long has this been going on?" Persephone asked. The gorgon head incident felt like it had been years ago; decades, even.

Hephaestus grimaced. "I don't know. A while, perhaps." He hesitated. "You may think this cowardly of me, but I have no desire to cross the goddess of the harvest. A pity. If you manage to change her mind, by all means, send a message to my forge."

Persephone smiled to hide her mixed emotions. "Of course. I understand."

Hephaestus pressed a kiss to the back of her hand and bowed slightly before leaving her alone in the gardens. She watched him walk back to his chariot, and then he was away, with no one left to stand between herself and Demeter.

She took slow, measured steps up the path back to the house. Inside, servants had already cleared away the wreckage of Demeter's temper, leaving the floor clean, albeit damp. Demeter herself was seated, idly shredding a lettuce leaf between her fingers.

"Well?" she asked as Persephone approached. "Did he see reason?"

"He left," Persephone said.

"Good."

"Mother…" Persephone hesitated. "He said you treated Ares in a similar manner."

Demeter dropped the lettuce. "Of course. I don't discriminate."

"But why? They are both worthy gods, aren't they?"

Demeter rose from her seat and walked toward her, placing her hands upon Persephone's shoulders. She gazed down at her daughter, her eyes dark and solemn, the afternoon sun setting her pale hair aglow. "None of them are worthy." Her grip tightened until her nails dug into Persephone's skin. "Anyone who would take you from me is my enemy."

Persephone pushed back against her mother's hands, but Demeter's hold was firm. "Mother, please… You're frightening me."

"Swear to me, then," Demeter said, shaking her by the shoulders. "Swear that you will not leave me."

"Of course. Of course," Persephone said, the words slurring together as she tripped over her tongue. "I do so swear."

Demeter was pressing hard enough to leave bruises. "His ichor runs through your veins. How can I forget it, seeing it there plain on your face? Your father has whores in every corner of the civilized world. You know that, don't you?"

Persephone fumbled for something to say that would not be considered blasphemous. "His children are many—"

"And you would seek to follow in his footsteps?"

"No—no!" Persephone's throat constricted. Aphrodite had not divulged her secret, then. Her preference for goddesses was not a topic she particularly wished to discuss with Demeter, ever.

Demeter studied her. Persephone did her best to project an aura of frightened honesty. She spoke the truth, besides—though perhaps not all of it.

Demeter released her. "I cannot stand the sight of you," she said, waving her off.

Persephone stepped away with relief, rubbing her shoulders. "I'm going to help in the kitchen," she said and ran before Demeter could think of something else to blame her for.

The servants were quiet around Persephone, as if they could avoid invoking Demeter's wrath by not engaging with the current object of her displeasure. That might have bothered Persephone, if she'd let it, but she was too busy contemplating how to defuse her mother's anger to be concerned with the rest of the household.

She was lugging an overflowing pail of scraps to the midden when she saw the most remarkable thing mixed in with all the trash. Persephone set down the pail and pulled out a bouquet of cut flowers. They had some life left in them, although not much, their narrow white petals frail and wilting.

They would not respond to her touch. There was a kind of chill about them, despite both the heat of the summer's day and the warmth of the midden.

Persephone saved the freshest stalk and brought it inside with her, placing it in a cup of water at her bedside. She tried running her fingertips over it again, and still, she could feel no sense of recognition in the plant. It wasn't simply that it had been cut; there was something else wrong. As if it had died and been reborn and now was dying a second time.

Downstairs, she beckoned to a maid and pulled her aside. "Kyra... those white flowers. Who brought them?"

Kyra scrunched up her nose. "Couldn't say, Miss. Only your mother's sent word they're not to be kept in the house." She shrugged helplessly.

"You mean this has happened more than once?"

Kyra opened her mouth, then seemed to realize she'd said too much. "Well..."

"How many times?"

Kyra gulped and shook her head, silently begging Persephone not to ask more.

It was answer enough. Persephone sighed and waved Kyra off; she seemed grateful to return to her work.

How long would she let Demeter rule her life?

She went back upstairs to her bedroom and climbed into bed, staring at the lonely flower in its makeshift vase. So Hades hadn't found her bothersome and insolent after all—or perhaps she had but hadn't cared.

Persephone shivered and rested her chin on her hands, closing her eyes as she inhaled the asphodel's faint fragrance. This time, it matched her memory—icy, green, with a faint trace of smoke like a freshly snuffed candle.

She ought not to leap to conclusions. She couldn't think so highly of herself; Demeter may have been wrong about some things, but she was right in saying that a girl like Persephone could hold no interest for the Queen of the Underworld.

Hades had to think her rude; she'd never once sent back a word of thanks.

She was still pondering whether she dared to acknowledge Hades' gift when the door of her room flew open, swinging back against the wall with a bang.

Persephone sat up at once, shuffling to the side of the bed to try to block the asphodel from view. "Whatever is the matter?"

"Ignorant children like you are so naive about what it takes to survive in this world," Demeter said, as if they'd never ended their previous conversation. She stood in the doorway, blocking the only exit. "I've bled so that you could live a charmed life, free from struggle and sorrow—the kind of childhood I never had."

"I've always been grateful for what you've done for me—"

"Grateful!" Demeter sneered. "Is that what you call cavorting behind my back? Consorting with cripples?"

Persephone bristled. "That is unkind of you, Mother, and besides, Hephaestus and I never—"

Demeter pushed her aside and leaned over the bed, snatching the asphodel from its cup. She stood up, holding it as water dripped down her wrist, staring at it as though it were a pig's leavings or something equally foul. "What is this weed doing here? In my house?"

Persephone said nothing, which was not the correct response, as Demeter threw the flower in her face. It landed wetly on her cheek, then fell to the floor.

"I won't have such filth in here," Demeter said.

"It was a gift," Persephone said. "For me. You had no right to throw it away!"

She'd gone too far. Demeter's eyes widened. "No right? No right!" She raised her hands to the heavens, as if imploring the gods of the sky to hear her. "My hearth and home, and this ungrateful child tells me I have no right!"

Persephone picked up the bloom from the floor and stood, moving toward the door.

"And where do you think you're going?"

She held up the asphodel like a talisman. "You said you didn't want this here, so I'm taking it out of your house—"

"When I'm talking to you, you will sit and listen," Demeter said, her arms folded over her chest. Her cheeks were in high color, and her gaze could've cut marble.

Seeing no way out, Persephone sat back down on the bed, her eyes lowered.

"When you were born, you were such a little thing. So frail and useless. Hera advised me to cast you down, as she'd done with her son—did you know that?"

"No," Persephone whispered. She'd heard this tale countless times before but knew what was expected of her.

"But I didn't listen to her. I nursed you from my own breast. And to this day here you are, still draining the life from your poor, exhausted mother! Why I bothered to keep you at all, Gaia only knows. If I'd known you'd be such a spoiled and selfish brat, I'd have followed Hera's advice and cast you into the ocean!"

That didn't sound so bad right now. A kind nereid might've saved her, for one. "I'm sorry," Persephone said, not entirely certain what she was being sorry for.

"I should've known nothing good ever came from your

father's seed. He might be the king of the gods, but we all know the truth—at heart, he is a beast, no better than any satyr!"

Persephone flinched and glanced out the window. The sky seemed clear, at least for now. If Zeus had heard her mother's rantings, he gave no sign.

"Look at me when I'm talking to you!"

She turned her head, and Demeter slapped her across the face. Persephone tasted ichor, the blood of the gods, upon her tongue.

"You would be nothing without me."

Persephone held her hand to her cheek. "That's not true," she whispered.

"Oh, you think yourself so capable and worldly?" Demeter sneered.

"I didn't—"

"Fine." Demeter went to the trunk at the end of her bed and began pulling out clothes, belts, and sandals, tossing them over her shoulder onto the floor. "Everything I've bought for you—no expense spared, no luxury out of reach—you think you can do better for yourself? Very well. Take your things—*my* things, those things earned by my sweat and labor—and go."

Persephone stared at the mess all around them. "That's not what I meant, Mother. Of course I appreciate everything you've ever done to raise me—"

Demeter dropped the last belt on the floor, its metal links clinking. "You have no idea what I've been through to keep you safe! No idea of the dangers outside, of the sacrifices I've made for you!"

Persephone ducked as her mother flung a sandal at her head. It hit the cup that had held the asphodel, and the pottery smashed. "Mother, please!"

Demeter advanced upon her. "If you think yourself so wise, let's see how you do for once without my protection! Then you'll know. Then you'll know how hard I toil, just to keep you safe! And for what?"

Persephone shrank back until she'd reached the edge of the bed, one arm raised to shield herself against her mother's rage. "Please, Mother. I love you. Forgive me. Forgive me!"

Demeter took Persephone's face between her hands, her nails digging into the girl's scalp. She bent down until her lips were almost touching Persephone's forehead. "From now until harvest, you are no longer my daughter," she said, her voice flat and even. She dropped her hands as if she were discarding something loathsome and wiped her palms on her chiton before turning her back on Persephone. A slight breeze picked up the hem of her chiton, the whisper of fabric almost eclipsing her next words.

"Get out."

Persephone had not the faintest idea of what she would need to survive for even a day on her own, but there was no time to prepare. She grabbed a himation and a spare chiton from the pile of discarded clothes. She backed away toward the door, expecting her mother to turn around, to say all was forgotten, but Demeter merely stood there as if she had been struck by Medusa.

Persephone flew down the stairs, taking them two at a time in her haste to get away, her meager belongings in hand. She left out the back door and ran, with no idea where she was running to, only knowing that she had to get away; away from the rage and the silence and the weight of her guilt.

THE FLOWER

Demeter's words rang in her ears, a constant refrain drowning out all other thought.

You are no longer my daughter.

Persephone ran until she could no longer see her mother's house in the distance. By then, the long summer day was beginning to end, Helios washing the sky in hues of rose and amber.

She bent over, hands on her knees, gasping for air. She'd rolled her spare chiton inside her himation and tied it into a parcel; the bundle dropped from her shoulder as she caught her breath.

Where could she go? Her father would not turn her away, but she had no desire to incur Hera's wrath. She could ask Hephaestus, but he had made it clear that he would not stand against Demeter's wishes.

There were the nymphs of the forests and rivers, her friends... but they belonged to her mother's lands, and Persephone had no intention of trespassing when she was clearly unwanted.

She could turn to Grandmother Gaia for help—to burrow

into the earth for a time, like a bulb, and rest in the cool embrace of her earth dreams until her mother's wrath had receded. Gaia rarely meddled in her kin's affairs, though, and who was Persephone to expect her aid? She was no one amongst hundreds of gods and goddesses, and...

She fought back tears at the thought and sniffled, rubbing her nose. She'd known better than to provoke her mother. This was her fault. Nothing good ever came from raising Demeter's ire.

She brushed the sweat-slicked hair back from her face and straightened, slinging her clothes bundle over her shoulder. If she couldn't decide whom to implore for help, she would have to seek her own shelter for the night. She'd slept in trees before, when she was younger, in a time when Demeter hadn't chastised her for being unmaidenly. Those times were dead and gone, as lost as Demeter's patience.

She stood near the edge of her mother's lands. To her left and right grew fields of grain, tall and almost ripe. She ran her hand over their swollen ears without thinking.

"Oh!" Persephone drew her hand back and into her mouth, tasting the sweet tang of ichor. Around her, the fields shivered, a wave rolling through them like the tides stirring the ocean.

The stalks nearest to her whipped at her legs. She lurched backward into the opposite field. Instead of parting at her presence, the stalks around her began striking her, the impact shaking grain loose all over the ground.

Persephone stumbled. The crest of the wave hit her, feeling like a wall of solid air swatting her away from Demeter's lands, away from the safety of her mother's protection.

Persephone tumbled as though an invisible fist had struck her. Her body rolled, crushing stalks of wheat, being pushed along by them as if the crop shared Demeter's wrath. By the time she came to the end of the fields, her momentum continued to carry her down the side of the hill, bouncing across the uneven ground with her hands pressed over her face to protect her eyes.

It took Persephone an embarrassingly long time to stop moving, but at last she spread her arms out and dug her heels into the ground, coming to a halt. It hurt to breathe, but she was too exhausted to do more than that for a time.

Cassiopeia was visible in the night sky when she finally sat up, wincing as the movement awakened new bruises on her body. Her headlong flight had left her scratched all over and had torn the hem of her chiton.

She staggered to her feet, finding the soft earth giving way to dense rock. She'd found some sort of cave, proving that she must have traveled past the boundaries of her mother's estate. Demeter disliked unproductive land.

Perhaps that was a good omen. She walked forward quietly, mindful that there could be other creatures calling this place home. Inside, the air was damp and cool; she shivered, but she had dropped her himation and spare chiton somewhere on the hillside.

As she went deeper inside, the only light available was from tiny phosphorescent mushrooms clinging to patches of rock. She closed her eyes and stretched out her hand, calling to them.

When she opened her eyes, the cave was covered on all sides by a profusion of glowing vegetation, surrounding her in an arch. The back of the cave extended into darkness, deeper than she had anticipated.

She hugged her shoulders, gazing at the eerie colors all around her, and saw the most peculiar thing.

Farther into the cave grew a yellow narcissus in bud, sprouting from the earth in a place no sunlight could penetrate. She walked to it as if in a trance, an ache growing in her chest with each step. Even if the sunlight were to reach it somehow, it was impossible for the flower to bloom now, in high summer. It should have long ago shriveled and died, returning to the cool, dreaming earth with the rest of its fellows to wait for spring.

Persephone crouched down and touched its calyx. It grew taller and unfurled as she watched, each petal perfection.

The air grew colder. Persephone straightened, her eyes wide in the dim light. "Is someone there? Show yourself!"

She waited so long for an answer, teeth chattering and the fine hairs on her arms standing on end, that she felt foolish. She was scaring herself. It was cold and dark, and she was tired. There was no reason why she felt like she had to run—

The ground shook beneath her feet, and she cried out, grabbing a nearby stalagmite for support. Before her, the floor sank into a rift, the narcissus tumbling into darkness.

Persephone crouched down and covered her head with her arms as dirt and small shards of rubble rained from the ceiling. She stayed like that until the rumbling stopped and the ground became still once more. Even then she was slow to uncover her face, doing so only when she heard hoofbeats and the rattling wheels of a chariot.

She looked up to find half the cave sunken into the earth, creating a steep passageway that went down as far as the eye could follow. The sound of the chariot drew nearer.

She should run. She knew she should run. But her legs wouldn't obey her; she stood rooted to the spot, unable to think.

When the chariot emerged from the darkness below, all she could do was stare.

It was gilded, with a swirling design of vines and flowers carved on the guardrail. Two geldings pulled it, their coats velvety black.

Persephone could not raise her eyes to the chariot's rider. If she ran now, she could keep her promise to Demeter. If she obeyed her mother's wishes, perhaps she could still be forgiven...

The chariot ground to a halt, and its rider stepped out. "Persephone. Why, you're trembling."

She'd made a promise, a pact with her goddess mother. And now, in the wake of Hades' presence, all she could do was stare.

Hades wore a chiton of ink black, the color deep and even, shimmering as she moved. A gold belt encircled her waist, matched by a diadem set among her curls. The air around her was icy, as if she'd brought a little piece of the underworld to the cave.

"You have journeyed far to be here," Hades said.

Not that far, surely. Not so far as to be devoid of Demeter's gaze—she might not be watched by the goddess herself, but surely her spies, her followers, would learn of this. Persephone wrapped her arms around her body, shivering.

Hades' gaze dropped to the bruises on Persephone's skin, blooming purple from her headlong flight.

She had to fix this situation before she made it worse, before she tossed more fuel onto the conflagration of her mother's anger. "It's nothing," she said of her bruises. "I promised Mother—I mustn't trouble you." Her words came out in a rush. She turned to leave, but Hades caught her wrist, pulling her up short.

"Wait."

Hades' fingers were warm and unexpectedly gentle. She stroked her thumb against the pulse in Persephone's wrist.

Persephone snatched her hand away and took a step back, cradling her arm to her chest, her skin burning as though she could still feel the press of Hades' fingertips. "Please, O Queen —I must—I promised—"

"There's no need to be so frightened. We are friends, dear Persephone, are we not?" Hades asked in a low voice, her calm tone belied by the intensity of her gaze, which felt like it was pinning Persephone in place. She couldn't think; she couldn't breathe.

Friends... A minor goddess like herself would never presume to count the Queen of the Underworld as a friend. She opened her mouth. As if from far away, she heard herself speak. "Yes, Queen Hades."

"Well—as a friend, tell me why you are out here, alone, and at this hour?"

Words caught in Persephone's throat. Centuries of prudence stayed her voice. "I tripped," she said.

Hades looked at her whilst Persephone's cheeks burned. "Then it is fortunate you *tripped* so close to one of my gateways." She reached up and plucked a leaf from Persephone's windswept hair, then twined a lock around her finger and brought her face close to the girl's neck, inhaling.

Persephone's cheeks grew even warmer. She wished she could sink into the ground and disappear. Instead, she took a step back, out of reach. "You presume too much," she said, both proud and terrified of her own audacity.

Hades' lips thinned. "Do I? You stand at the threshold of my realm, the scent of my asphodels on your skin. Why else are you here, if not to offer yourself to me?"

To... what? "I never—there must be some mistake," Persephone said.

This whole day had been one long mistake. Upsetting her mother, walking past the grain fields, and now, disobeying her mother once more by speaking with Hades instead of running away and pretending she had never found this place.

Hades' eyes narrowed, her gaze piercing. "A mistake. Are you so blind as to believe the legends, then?" Hades approached her, taking one step forward for each step that Persephone took back. "Do you accept all the lies they tell about me?"

Persephone's back scraped against the side of the cave. She pressed her palms against it, trembling as Hades leaned in.

"Do you know what they say about you, Demeter's daughter?" Hades asked, her voice low, her eyes as dark as pools of water on a moonless night. Persephone saw herself reflected in them, a bruised and battered girl with hair the color of mud.

She knew. Everyone knew, and she thought she would crumble from shame to hear the slurs from Hades' lips. They echoed through her thoughts, spoken by a chorus of faceless, nameless voices.

Frigid bitch.

Thinks herself too good for Hera's sons.

How is it that the goddess of spring keeps herself barren?

"Please don't," she whispered.

Hades cupped Persephone's face in her hand and ran her thumb over the girl's lips. Persephone's breath came in ragged gasps.

"Don't," she said again. The cave wall was cold at her back, the chill seeping in through her chiton and into her bones. The heat radiating from Hades' body felt like fire by comparison.

Hades leaned in, and for one terrifying, exhilarating moment, Persephone thought she might kiss her—but Hades instead brought her lips to Persephone's ear.

"You were always destined to be mine," Hades said and then took a step back, turning away from Persephone for the first time. She clicked her tongue and beckoned, and the horses trotted up to her, bringing the chariot along with them.

Run! a voice screamed inside Persephone's head. *Now, while she's distracted... run!*

She couldn't move. Her ear tingled where Hades' lips had touched her. "What... what do you mean?"

"I mean that we shall go on a journey, you and I."

Persephone stared at the darkness beyond the rift, the precursor to the darkness unending beneath the world's crust. At last, at long last, her legs became hers to command, and she ran.

She was almost at the mouth of the cave when the horses drew level with her. They soon surpassed her, and from inside the chariot, Hades reached over and snatched Persephone from the ground.

"Stop!" Persephone screamed. "Let me go!"

The horses turned sharply, and the chariot careened on one wheel, almost toppling over. Persephone slammed into the side of the chariot, and Hades fell on top of her.

She caught a tiny glimpse of the night sky as the chariot completed its turn. For all she knew, that would be the last time she saw the constellations of Cassiopeia and Cepheus, Pegasus and Deltoton.

She pushed weakly at Hades. "Stop. Stop—make them stop."

The chariot found its balance, but the horses did not stop or even slow. They plunged into the rift, cold air wafting over Persephone's skin as though they were passing through a cloud of mist. Pressure built in her ears until they popped with a ringing sensation, and then she found she could not stand, or scream, or even think.

Hades caught her as she collapsed, and the darkness swallowed them both.

4

IT WILL PASS

Persephone woke to the sound of water sloshing, the gentle, rhythmic noise so unlike the call of the ocean. She blinked, staring up at a dark and starless void.

Something hard dug into her back, and her fingers tingled, as though she had been trapped in one position for far too long.

She was on a boat, she guessed, from the sounds and the way she felt gently rocked. She shivered uncontrollably, and it took her a few dull moments to realize why.

The sky she saw was not her sky. It was far too empty, devoid even of clouds. Where were the stars, the moon? Instead of Nyx's veils there was a strange kind of texture to the expanse above her—it seemed rough, like hewn rock. This cavernous sky gleamed faintly from within as though moonlight were cast upon it, emitting an eerie kind of twilight glow.

"Let me help you."

Hands at her back coaxed her into a sitting position. She grabbed the side of the boat and clung to it for support, splinters cutting into her palms.

She was on a boat. With Hades. She looked to the prow,

where a robed figure drove a pole into the riverbed below, propelling them along. Only his back was visible, illuminated by a lantern. He was a thin, tall shape swathed in threadbare dark linen, but somehow she could bring his name to mind.

She was on a boat. With Hades. And Charon. That meant...

"The nausea will pass," Hades said. She placed a bucket before her.

Persephone clutched it with both hands, staring down at it while her stomach roiled. Some unknown liquid sloshed at the bottom of the pail, reflecting her haggard countenance and eyes wild with fear.

She gritted her teeth and willed herself not to vomit. She wouldn't be seen like that, like some lush handmaiden at the Dionysia.

The motion of the boat did her no favors. She closed her eyes and imagined the shape of a narcissus. Six tepals, count them—one, two, three, four, five, six—surrounding a corona. Within the corona, six pollen-bearing stamens (one, two, three, four, five, six), around a central style.

When she opened her eyes again, the nausea had diminished sufficiently that she was no longer in danger of embarrassing herself. She pushed the bucket away, and it scraped against the deck with an awful whine.

"What is wrong with me?" she whispered, barely audible over the slap of water against the side of the boat. She loathed the weakness in her voice but could not force any more air from her lungs.

"You are alive, and thus the transition to the underworld is... unpleasant," Hades said.

Persephone gripped the vessel's wall once more and peered

over the edge. The water was dark, but there were glints of light in its inky depths. She looked closer and gasped.

Someone stared back at her.

The dead man's face was visible for just an instant, long enough to embed within her mind the bloated pallor of his skin, the colorless eyes rimmed with purple. She longed for the bucket, but it was too far out of reach, and she didn't trust her legs to support her. She longed to be on dry, sun-kissed land. She longed for her mother.

"What is that noise?" Persephone asked. It set her teeth on edge and sent shivers down her back—distant cries of lamentation and woe, seeming to grow louder as the boat pressed on.

"The shades are restless tonight," Hades said.

"Every night," Charon said from the prow.

He and Hades shared a laugh.

How could they find humor in something so terrible?

Hades' hand landed on her shoulder, her fingers closing in as if to never let go. Persephone was too weak to swat her away. "Almost there," Hades said.

The other side of the river rapidly approached. The boat bumped against a pier, and Charon secured them to the dock. He leaned on his pole, hood obscuring his face as he waited for them to disembark.

Before Persephone could protest, Hades scooped her up in her arms and carried her onto the pier. Behind them, Charon freed the boat and pushed off, a solitary guardian endlessly crossing from one side of the marsh to the other.

Persephone stared at the craggy not-quite-sky overhead. Torches lined the path, flaring into life with blue flames as they approached, then winking out behind them. The lights blurred when she blinked, and at some point she must have fallen unconscious once more, for the next time she opened her eyes they were in a chariot.

The shrieking had grown more distant, dying down to a barely perceptible murmur. Hades continued to hold Persephone in her arms. The fragrance of asphodels still surrounded her. Or was it simply that they had just passed a field of asphodels? Persephone couldn't trust her senses, nor come to terms with the fact that she might not be dreaming.

The chariot slowed to a halt, and Hades shifted her weight, moving so that Persephone's head lolled against her shoulder.

"I can stand," she said, trying to sound more convincing than she felt.

Hades looked down at her with a smile on her lips. "As you wish." She set Persephone down on her feet, watching as she stumbled and grabbed for the rail of the chariot.

"Why have we stopped?" Persephone asked.

"I have someone I would like you to meet."

Persephone clung to the railing, breathing heavily. The floor insisted on spinning beneath her. "Take me home."

"This is your home," Hades said without a trace of humor.

Persephone turned to look at her and managed to stand up straight, although she still held the railing for support. She glanced up at the formless sky. In this barren land she had no favors to give, no weapons, no allies. She ought to say something nice to her captor. Something that would make Hades more inclined to take pity upon her and release her in a timely manner.

"Go p-pleasure a goat," Persephone said.

Hades' lips pressed together as though she were trying not to laugh. "You must be feeling better. Good." Hades left her in the chariot and walked on ahead.

Persephone gazed up to see that they had stopped before a pair of tall black gates set within a massive wall. In front of the gates sat an enormous hound, a bright red tongue lolling out of each of its three heads.

Hades hugged the nearest head, her arms unable to reach around the girth of its neck, and placed a kiss on its cheek. In return, the hound barked happily, the sound echoing, and it lowered its head before her, pushing against her hands. All three heads vied for affection and did not desist until Hades had paid adequate attention to each of them.

Persephone was not a great lover of dogs—they trampled her flowerbeds and chased rabbits through her carefully plotted lines of salad greens—and so when Hades turned and crooked a finger in her direction, her first instinct was to remain in the chariot, where she had at least the illusion of safety. The horses fared little better; they shifted their weight back and forth, stamping their feet, the whites of their eyes greatly apparent, but they were too well-trained to abandon their designated position.

It grew clear they would go no further until she did as Hades bade, and so she stepped out of the chariot, holding onto the rails until the last possible moment. She hiked the skirts of her chiton up in one hand to avoid tripping as she made her way up the path, the gravel abrading her bare feet.

"Cerberus, this is Persephone. She is to be treated as a treasure," Hades said when Persephone drew near.

Each of the heads swiveled to look at her. The hound had dense black fur, against which its yellow eyes seemed almost to glow. It was incontrovertibly ugly, its form densely muscled under the fur, its skeleton deformed to accommodate the weight of the three separate heads.

Persephone shivered under its scrutiny, not resisting when Hades took one of her hands and held it out to the beast.

Cerberus sniffed her palm with each of its three noses and then nuzzled her face, almost knocking her off her feet.

"Good boy. Enough." Hades gave each of the heads a final scratch and led Persephone back to the chariot. The gates opened before them, and the horses leaped forward, leaving Cerberus far behind.

The chariot took up speed shortly after they left Cerberus, and the landscape flew by in an unnatural blur, too quickly for Persephone to see the landmarks around her. They only slowed as they approached the path leading to Hades' palace.

The palace stood atop a great hill, its walls dark and glittering as if carved entirely from obsidian. In contrast to Zeus's abode, with its organic, sprawling curves and meandering paths, Hades' lair was made of sharp edges and parallel lines, cold in its symmetry.

Hades guided the chariot to a stable, where a waiting groom took over. Not far away, a gaggle of servants clustered, all of them women.

Hades turned to Persephone. "I must leave you, for my duties await. We shall speak again in due time."

Persephone didn't know whether to be relieved or insulted. For Hades to abduct her and then to drop her as quickly as that was mildly off-putting, to say the least. "Wait," she said, reaching for her.

"Patience." Hades took Persephone's hand and pressed a

kiss against her knuckles, her fingertips stroking the underside of her wrist as she released her.

Persephone cradled her hand against her chest and watched Hades depart. It wasn't until Hades was out of sight that she felt like she could breathe again.

The servants clustered around her. "Come inside, you must be freezing!"

"But—" Persephone began. "Hades—"

One of the servants patted her arm. "Our queen always keeps her word."

That was not particularly reassuring.

The servants led her into the palace proper, through a maze of corridors and into a bathing room wreathed with steam. They divested her of her garments and proceeded to wash her from head to toe. Persephone started to shiver again when the steam caressed her naked body, until the chill of the underworld melted away, leaving only the warmth from the water.

The servants finished washing her and anointed her hair with scented oil. The fragrance of asphodels made bile rise in her throat, but she endured it. However, when a girl began to file away at the calluses on her feet, Persephone screamed.

"Don't! How will I walk?"

"Pardon me, mistress, but it's not becoming of your station."

"I need them," Persephone insisted, but despite her rank she was ignored. Two of the girls held her down, while the other two worked at her feet, scrubbing away at the worst of the calluses and then smearing on a thick ointment to protect the newly exposed skin.

Persephone screamed and sobbed until her voice was nothing more than a whisper. They were her anchor to the land, her way of feeling the health of the flora, of hearing the hidden language of the earth. She had climbed mountains, forded rivers with those feet.

Perhaps the servants were right. What good could bare feet do for her here, in this cold and sunless land, save to bring grief with each step?

Once the ordeal was over, the servants threw a tunic over her head and guided her to a darkened room and a soft bed. Despite her best intentions, Persephone was asleep before she heard the sound of a key turning in the door, locking her in her bedchamber.

5

THE GOWN

When Persephone next awoke, her head was light and her mouth dry, but her limbs seemed all intact, and she was no longer in danger of falling over her own two feet. She found herself resting upon a large bed, its frame bedecked with all kinds of jewels and precious inlays, covered by a layer of blankets and furs.

"Good morning, Mistress Persephone. How are you feeling?" asked a cheerful voice, not more than ten cubits away from her.

Persephone blinked, staring at the ceiling where painted scenes of swans chased each other through a midnight-blue sky. A light breeze brushed her face, though she could not imagine what might stir the air in the underworld. "Is there even morning here?"

The voice of her companion sounded closer this time. "Oh, yes. Our days and nights are the same. I hope very much that you will grow to like your new home."

Persephone tore her attention away from the swans and glanced at her visitor, not recognizing her from the previous night. She was a mortal woman appearing to be of middling age, dark hair pinned in curls against her head. She did not look like a fool, and so Persephone did not bother dignifying her inane comment with a response.

"Would you care for my assistance in dressing? I'm sorry for hurrying you, but our queen has a strict schedule for you today." On the bed, the servant had laid out a himation, a chiton, a belt, and a pair of jeweled sandals.

Persephone's fingers tightened around the bedclothes. "Is she letting me go?"

"I'm afraid I don't keep our queen's counsel."

Persephone breathed out a long sigh and drew the sheets back. "I'll dress myself."

In the end, she needed the servant's assistance—the mechanism of the fibulae and belt were unknown to her, and so the servant fussed around her like a mother hen until she was fully clothed.

"What is your name?" Persephone asked.

"Xenia, mistress." She braided Persephone's hair, weaving in golden chains adorned with sapphires.

Persephone smoothed down the skirts of her new chiton and said nothing. The azure fabric was woven of such fine thread that even skilled Athena would have wept to lay her hands upon it. It was a garment ill-suited for running barefoot over open fields, where it would be shredded by gorse, or for kneeling over a dusty hearth to bake bread.

"If you ever need anything, the cord over here will ring in the kitchens, and someone will come." Xenia gestured, pointing out a long cord hanging from the ceiling near the bed.

It sounded like a better arrangement than shouting, which was Demeter's method of summoning help. Persephone doubted she would be here long enough to need it. "What does Hades want of me?" she asked.

Xenia's hands stilled. "I couldn't say. But there's no need to be fearful."

Persephone sniffed. Only a fool would be unafraid of the Queen of the Underworld.

With Persephone's hair finished, Xenia turned her attention to her feet. She loosened the straps of the sandals and knelt.

"Oh, no. I prefer to walk barefoot," Persephone said.

Xenia's lower lip quivered, and she clutched the sandals to her chest.

"What is it?"

"Begging your pardon, mistress, but our queen might be angry if you're not fully dressed."

Persephone flexed her newly scrubbed feet. Her skin still stung from the excessive treatments lavished upon them, and she had to admit that the palace tiles were too cold to walk upon barefoot.

"If I must, then."

Xenia nodded and placed the sandals upon her feet. Persephone winced as the straps dug into her ankles.

Once she was fully attired, Xenia handed her a plate of polished brass in which to observe her appearance. Curled locks of hair framed her face to either side, the rest of her braid pinned at the crown of her head. The metal distorted her image slightly, leaving her with the face of a ghost.

Persephone lowered the plate, placing it on the table. Without Hades to focus her anger upon, she was forced at last to reflect upon the enormity of her situation. She should have run. She had disobeyed her mother, and now this was her punishment—to be damned, like Prometheus and Ixion before her.

"Our queen will be most charmed," Xenia said, as if that were a thing to be desired.

Persephone shuddered. "When may I speak with her?"

Xenia looked nervous. "Forgive me, but it won't be today. Instead, I've been asked to—"

Persephone couldn't have cared less about what Hades wanted her to do. "She won't even see me?"

"Soon," Xenia said in the tone all servants used when they wanted to smooth ruffled feathers but had no authority to keep their promises.

Persephone threw her hands up in disgust. If the jewels had not been so intricately wound into her hair, she would've ripped them out.

Xenia held up a sheet of papyrus. "Today, Queen Hades simply asks that you rest and take a leisurely visit to the main areas of the underworld. In addition, she asks that you become aware of the areas where you would be ill-advised to visit without assistance—namely, Tartarus, the Plain of Judgment, the Vale of Mourning, and the lands east of the Elysian Fields."

Such an itinerary did not suit a plaything who had been stolen for one or two nights and would soon be released. Persephone felt a lightness rushing to her head, causing the room to sway.

She grabbed the bed frame for support and sat on the bed. Who were her allies here? Hermes was bound to visit at some point, though Gaia only knew if Persephone could catch him alone. She knew of no one else who would be sympathetic to her plight and had business in the underworld.

"Mistress? Would you care for some water?"

"No," she said. Drinking or eating the food in the underworld could bind her here forever. She remembered that much from her lessons, at least.

Xenia shifted uneasily, the movement partially obscured by her long chiton. "Shall we begin with the Asphodel Fields, in that case? It's a pleasant ride down and most becoming at this time of the morning."

Where had Hades found this servant? The woman was relentless. "Very well," Persephone said. She tried to calm herself by thinking about how the tour would do her good. The previous day, she'd been in no position to memorize landmarks or to understand the geography. If she were to escape the underworld, she needed knowledge, and it would be senseless not to take the opportunity this tour afforded her.

Xenia smiled and seemed genuinely relieved. "Of course. They will have the chariot ready for us, I'm sure. Please follow me."

Xenia led Persephone down a maze of twisting corridors to reach the stables, using a different route to the one she remembered from last night. Once outside, Persephone glanced up. The 'sky' here appeared to be nothing more than a layer of bedrock, floating impossibly above them and glowing as though lit from within. Daylight in the underworld, this morning, at any rate, was as bright as a stormy day in the overworld. The whole effect was just as gloomy—the rock above them was brown and gray, striated in places with traces of quartz and other minerals.

An existential dread settled in her stomach. How could anyone gaze at such a sight and not feel terror? If it was a layer of Gaia's earth hanging above them, there was nothing keeping it upright, nothing to prevent it from crashing down and crushing all their bones for eternity.

Furthermore, there would never be a day of blue skies here, nor the heat of a summer sun. The mural in her bedroom of the swans in flight now seemed impossibly sad, the last vestige of a lost world. Persephone shivered and wrapped her himation more tightly around her shoulders.

Near the stables, a groom held the reins of two black geldings, already harnessed to a chariot.

"Is black the only color she permits here?" Persephone asked.

Xenia waited patiently as Persephone mounted the chariot and then followed after her, taking the reins. "Her Grace has affection for all colors, but she finds that the other gods take her more seriously when she wears black."

"The gods didn't used to treat her seriously?"

Xenia smiled at her. "Forgive me for saying so, but sometimes I forget how young you are! We have been waiting for you for so long."

"I don't understand."

"Oh, well... think of nothing of it, Lady Persephone." Xenia flexed the reins, and the horses set off at a trot, which quickly turned into a gallop. Soon the spires of Hades' palace were a distant memory as they passed through flat, open fields.

Small clusters of houses dotted the horizon, and as they drew closer, people walked out to wave at them or bow their heads in homage. They did not seem unhappy, despite being deceased.

"Who are all these people?" Persephone asked.

"Those who are neither particularly wicked nor particu-

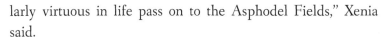

larly virtuous in life pass on to the Asphodel Fields," Xenia said.

"Which one were you?"

Xenia simply smiled at her. "I must have done something good, to have the privilege to serve our queen."

The Asphodel Fields were not entirely filled with asphodel, but the scent surrounded them nevertheless. Persephone asked Xenia to halt the chariot and stepped out to pick a handful of flowers. They grew larger here than they had above ground, each petal the length of her forefinger. Like the cut asphodel she'd found at Demeter's house, these plants would not respond to her touch, nor her silent commands. Persephone looked around at the grasses and shrubs, the mosses and trees. When she closed her eyes, she felt nothing. That void frightened her more than the hound, more than the distant shrieking of the dead.

When she'd finished her examination of the local plant life, she looked up to see a small group of mortals had gathered around. Several families clustered a respectful distance away from the chariot, the children clinging to their mothers and staring at her with wide, unblinking eyes.

"We must press on," Xenia said. "Our schedule—"

"No," Persephone said. She approached the humans, who shuffled themselves in a semicircle around her. "Good morning. Is there something you need?"

One of the women dropped to her knees, and the others soon followed suit. "Begging your pardon, but it ain't often we get visitors such as yourself. It'd be the greatest honor if you could bless our little ones."

She was more used to blessing food crops, but she assumed that children would be little different. "Very well."

The woman beamed and ushered her children forward, two boys and a girl. Persephone passed her hand over each of their heads in turn. She murmured a brief request to Gaia, the all-nurturing earth that supported them even now, deep within her core, to ensure that their afterlife was full of peaceful days and free from strife. She repeated the gesture with the other children, then the adults, as she could hear their unvoiced request even though they were too nervous to ask more from her.

When that was finished, the people fell to their knees once more and praised her, their children trying to follow along as best they could. The sight unsettled her, and it took her a moment to realize why.

Above ground, she had always received the respect due to her as a goddess, but it had been in her role as Demeter's daughter. It was Demeter who led the harvest, who taught the people how to feed themselves. Persephone was beloved, yes, but only as part of Demeter's retinue.

Was this any different? Here, she was afforded the highest courtesy not for herself but as Hades' guest. Did she have anything within her that was worthy of reverence, in and of itself?

Persephone waved them to their feet. "Please, stand." She hesitated, having always been told not to show ignorance in front of mortals, but curiosity got the better of her. "What can you tell me about your ruler, Hades?"

At her use of Hades' name, some of the mortals flinched. One man spoke up. "She is strict but fair, Lady Persephone."

Another chimed in. "She does not take favors. Men who died with riches cannot cheat her, whilst beggars might still hope to see the Elysian Fields."

"I see," Persephone said, though she did not. They almost sounded... fond of Hades. "And what of the last realm, for the wicked?"

One of the women cleared her throat. "My cousin was sent to Tartarus, but we always knew he'd meet a bad end. He had this violent temper, you see—"

"Now, I'm sure Lady Persephone doesn't need to hear all the particulars," Xenia said.

Persephone held up her hand. "I do, actually. Go on. What happens to mortals in Tartarus?"

The humans exchanged glances.

The woman with the cousin started. "It's a place of punishment, mistress."

"Forever?" She knew the Titans were safely locked away in Tartarus, but it hadn't occurred to her how they would spend their time there. And humans lives were so brief. How much wickedness could one person truly cause to justify them being tormented for all eternity?

"We should move on, mistress," Xenia said.

Persephone glanced at her and back at the villagers. They shuffled uneasily under her scrutiny, and she could see that with Xenia present they would be unlikely to offer her any more useful information. Persephone reluctantly turned away and returned to the chariot.

She glanced over her shoulder as they pulled away, watching as the villagers shrank down to specks. Around them, a mild, dry breeze sent ripples through the fields, and the light overhead warmed her skin such that she might have imagined herself back on the surface, enjoying a mild spring day.

As the chariot rolled on, the gates of Hades loomed in the

distance, where Cerberus dwelt, but Xenia guided them to the right and away from the wall bordering the place of the dead.

If Persephone were to escape, she would have to pass Cerberus and then either find the boat to take herself across the marsh or somehow convince Charon to help her. The latter seemed unlikely. Could she overpower him and commandeer his craft herself?

Both thoughts unsettled her. She tried to distract herself by paying more attention to their surroundings.

The fields and small villages were long gone. They emerged from the plains, and the chariot began winding around a rocky mountainside. As they ascended, she saw the lands of Hades' domain spread out before her. To the south was a marshland where the rivers met and the great gates which Cerberus guarded. To the east were the Asphodel Fields, with its tiny villages dotted upon the landscape like seeds sprinkled upon wheat cake. To the north, Hades' palace loomed, with its glittering walls of obsidian.

The higher they traveled, the colder it grew. The wind whipping her face chilled her to the bone. Her head felt as though it could drift away, but she was certain it was simply a result of her nervous state and dehydration.

"Take me back to the palace," Persephone said.

Xenia took one glance at her. At first she seemed poised to argue, but then she simply nodded. "Of course." She slowed the chariot and turned it around in a wide arc, backtracking part of the way to return to the road leading to the palace. Persephone massaged her temples and tried to focus on not vomiting as the landscape flew by, the greens and golds in the fields blurring into a long streak of muddy ochre.

The chariot pulled up near a side entrance and Persephone

leapt down, eager for her feet to touch solid ground once more. Xenia followed soon after.

"Perhaps you might like to visit the scribes this afternoon, or see the Hall of Judgment—"

"No. I don't want to see anything else. I'm not a tourist. I'm not a guest. I'm Hades' prisoner, and you might as well stop pretending otherwise," Persephone said as she strode down the cool and dark corridors, her sandals loud against the polished tiles.

"My lady—"

Persephone rounded on Xenia. "What? What is it?"

Xenia wrung her hands together. "Your room might not be ready. We have cleaning scheduled for this time and—"

"I don't care." Persephone turned right at the next corner, relieved that her sense of direction had proven correct as she recognized the door to her chambers. It would have been utterly embarrassing to learn that she'd been walking the wrong way.

She flung open the doors, expecting to see one or two girls scrubbing floors, but was met with an astonishing tableau. There was a whole troupe of servants in her room, who all turned as one and stared at her, eyes wide and mouths agape.

Spread out on the bed was the loveliest chiton Persephone had ever seen. It was the color of fig skins, a deep purple traced over with gold embroidery. Its hem dripped with tiny jewels and sparkling beads sewn in patterns of trailing vines and flowers. Three servants fussed over it, one with a needle and thread in her hand, affixing a loose gem to the shoulder.

Near the wash table, another two servants were busy polishing jewelry, including an elaborate stephane. A young girl sat on the floor, tying the laces on a pair of sandals, the straps inlaid with more glittering jewels.

"What is all of this?" Persephone asked.

The girl with the sandals stood up. "Begging your pardon, mistress, but it's for your nuptials—"

The other women all gasped in unison. The girl clasped her hands over her mouth, the sound of the sandals hitting the floor like a slap in the face.

"I beg your pardon?" Persephone grabbed the edge of the door frame, fighting a sudden burst of vertigo.

Xenia slid into the room beside her. "Out, you lot."

One by one, the servants trudged out, the young girl giving Xenia a terrified look before she too shuffled away.

When they were all gone, Persephone closed her eyes for a moment, counting petals in her head. The dizziness eased a little. She walked to the bed and poked at the chiton. The fabric dimpled, catching the light like the flash of a carp's belly.

Prior to that moment, Persephone had assumed that Hades wanted what all the other gods wanted from a young maiden— a fleeting pleasure to be taken and just as quickly forgotten. That would have been terrible enough, true, but as soon as Hades tired of her, she would have been able to return to the surface and see the sun once more.

This chiton, though? These jewels, the stephane?

A wedding would bind her for eternity, no matter if their marriage was happy or not. Zeus could not free himself of Hera, as powerful as he was. If they wed, how would Persephone ever be free of Hades?

She began to cry, shedding tears that she could not afford to lose. She could not stay here forever; she simply could not. Reign in the underworld and never see the sun again? Never dance barefoot over dew-kissed grass, never frolic in the streams of sweet water so crisp and clear that one could count every pebble in the riverbed?

Xenia walked up to her and placed a hand on her shoulder. "Please, don't be frightened. She may seem cruel, but she is a just ruler."

Persephone had forgotten about Xenia's presence. She shook herself free of the woman's touch and straightened to her full height, raising her arm and pointing at the door. "Get out."

After a moment's hesitation, Xenia hurried out. As soon as the door closed behind her, Persephone picked up an amphora and threw it, the jar shattering into thousands of pieces as it hit the wall. She fell to her knees, cradling her head in her hands.

"Demeter, Mother, Bringer of Plenty, Heart of the Harvest, can you hear me? Am I too far from your gaze?"

She'd not prayed to her mother before, having never been separated for any significant amount of time. Who else could she turn to? None of the other gods would be looking for her.

She shifted her weight, stretching her arms up before her, knees locked together in prostration. Her breath fogged the cold tile. "Forgive me, Mother. I should have listened to you. Should have been more wary of Hades. If only I'd kept your favor..."

She remained in that position for long minutes, until her fingers and toes grew numb and her joints protested. Demeter would not hear her. And even if she heard her, what could she do? Hades' rule in the underworld was absolute.

She picked herself up off the floor, walked through the rubble of the shattered amphora, and tried the door. It was locked. She banged on it with her fists, but no one answered.

The chiton on the bed seemed to mock her. She shoved it to

one side and fell into bed, curling up with her knees to her chest. Few options seemed to remain. A virtuous human woman in her position might have killed herself, but Persephone wasn't even sure how that could be done, and besides, a successful suicide would bind her to the underworld forever, putting her eternally under Hades' command.

She could mutilate herself, make herself so hideous that no one would want her, but most wounds of the gods could be healed.

Persephone wrapped her arms around her knees, holding on tight to make herself as small as possible. No matter what, if she were ever to see the surface again, she had to survive. If she couldn't escape, she had to live until someone came for her.

She had to believe that someone would come.

6

THE RIVER

A sound woke her in the middle of the night. She sat still in bed, thinking to cry out to Demeter before remembering that she wasn't at her mother's estate.

She wiped a tear from her eye and sat up. She had kicked off her sandals before falling asleep, but now she put them on again, remembering the floor was littered with shards.

The pale light of night time in the underworld streamed through her windows. She walked to her door, broken pieces of amphora crunching underfoot, and tested it.

The door swung open with an ominous creak. Persephone had been leaning her whole weight against the doorknob, and the unexpected lack of resistance meant she almost spilled out into the corridor.

Outside, all was silent. She could not see any servants or guards, nor any sign to indicate something out of the ordinary.

Had something happened?

As much as she longed to run and make her way out of the palace, she couldn't just leave. She quietly pulled the door shut once more, leaving a small gap in case it locked automatically, and grabbed a himation from her storage chest, wrapping it around her shoulders. She went to the dressing table and picked up a jeweled torc, placing it around her neck. There could be servants she might have to bribe, though she wasn't certain whether mortals still cared for riches in the underworld.

Something else caught her eye. On the dressing table was a dagger and a ceremonial belt with a sheath. She took both, strapping the belt around her waist and sheathing the dagger. The blade was useless for everyday wear, the hilt encrusted with jewels, but it still seemed sharp enough to cut or to threaten someone.

She had scarcely even raised her voice in anger at another person before now; what made her think that she could use a weapon?

Persephone tried to ignore the worm of doubt inside her and pushed open the door. It creaked upon opening, but once again, there was no one outside.

Something wasn't right. The door had been locked before. Someone must have opened it—but to what end? Had Xenia's conscience gotten the better of her? Persephone couldn't believe that.

Regardless of whether this was a trap, she had to take the opportunity. Persephone walked quickly through the empty corridors, heading to the kitchen. There was only one servant boy stoking the embers of the fireplace, so she pressed herself against the wall and waited until she heard him walking to the other side of the kitchen. When his back was turned, she ducked into the cold cellar and grabbed a link of sausages hanging from the ceiling. She draped them around her neck like a pungent scarf and headed back out past the kitchen when the servant was not looking.

To her growing unease, she saw no one else between the kitchens and the side entrance. Even the stables were empty, save for the horses greeting her with soft whickers.

"Hey, boy," she said, greeting a gelding she vaguely remembered Hades calling Alastor. She fitted him with a bridle and blanket and leapt onto his back.

Alastor obliged her by trotting out of the stables into the brisk night air. She wished she had brought a torch. Overhead, pale light akin to that of a full moon rained down upon them, but still she feared that Alastor might lose his footing and throw her. He seemed quite content to venture out in the near darkness, however, increasing speed as they hit the open road.

The nagging feeling that something was wrong never left her. Where were Hades' guards, her other servants?

Persephone could not let such doubts plague her. She rode Alastor as hard as she dared, only slowing when they approached the great gate. Cerberus was lying down with his heads resting on his paws, but he raised one of them as she drew near, cocking his ears toward the sound of Alastor's hoofbeats.

Persephone unwound the sausages from her neck and broke them into three equal segments. She tossed each one to Cerberus's heads, and the giant hound happily began to gnaw on them.

Persephone clucked her tongue at Alastor, and they slowly trotted away. She glanced over her shoulder to see that Cerberus was still eating, paying her no mind. Once she saw that the beast would not follow, she urged Alastor into a canter, leading them to the marshlands where the Styx and Acheron met.

At the sight of water she dismounted, leaving Alastor by the road. She ran down to the river bank, where there was a pier and a boat but no Charon. Even when she turned to the south, searching for a glimpse of him, there were no signs of any activity. The water was flat, a dark mirror reflecting her ghostly form clad all in white.

She untied the boat from its moorings and climbed into it, picking up the pole. It drifted a short distance from the pier, then stopped, as though stuck.

Persephone looked pensively into the water, using the pole to push against the pier. The boat resisted her again.

She had no desire to step into the water, but saw no other choice. She took off her sandals and tied them to her belt by their straps. She left the pole in the boat and hiked her chiton to knee length, tucking the excess into her belt, before jumping from the boat into the water.

She regretted this decision immediately. The water was colder than she'd anticipated, and the weight of her sodden chiton clung to her like a ballooning sack. Nevertheless, she took a breath and dived down, feeling around the sides of the boat for whatever it was caught upon.

After some groping around the hull, she thought she had found the problem. She surfaced for air, shivering as rivulets of water ran down her face. As she treaded water, she unsheathed her dagger, then dived down once more and began sawing through a fibrous cord that seemed to be holding the boat in place.

As she cut the last thread free, the boat began to drift to the side, no longer constrained. Persephone rose to the surface and gulped in a mouthful of air before grabbing the side of the boat. She sheathed her dagger, then clung to the boat with both hands, preparing herself to climb aboard.

She was still catching her breath when cold, spongy fingers grabbed her ankle, pulling her off balance. She swung her legs around wildly, trying to kick her attacker, but it was no use. With a mighty tug, they dragged Persephone beneath the water.

More hands grabbed at her, pulling at her hair, clawing at her arms. She flailed, kicking and scratching at the bodies surrounding her. The flesh of the dead was cold and clammy, their skin disturbingly soft as she fought off their advances.

Bubbles escaped from her nose as she fought to stay conscious whilst not accidentally ingesting the water. Beneath the surface, it was so dark that she couldn't tell which way lay the pier or the riverbank. Dead fingers trailed down the side of her face, and it took all her discipline not to open her mouth and invite water into her lungs.

One of the dead pressed their lipless mouth to her cheek in the parody of a kiss. Persephone flinched away, but there were more hands on her, tearing at her chiton, pulling free the jewels at her neck and shoulders. Cold, bony fingers ran over her newly exposed skin, and she had to grind her teeth together to stop herself from trying to scream.

She fumbled at her waist for her dagger, but even if it was there, she couldn't quite reach it due to the floating folds of fabric obscuring her belt. She thrashed, the water churning to white froth around her. Her lungs burned, and her struggles grew more faint. Above, vague lights glimmered, but reaching the surface now seemed like an impossible dream. Tiny bubbles escaped from her lips as her mind screamed at her. She had to breathe.

The dead ran their fingers through her hair, but she could hardly feel them. Persephone kicked weakly, but the surface seemed so far away. It was easier to sink deeper into the water and accept her fate. This marsh would be her grave.

NOT YET WED

S trong arms grabbed hold of Persephone and pulled her out of the river. As soon as her head broke the surface, she coughed up the mouthful of water she'd been trying so hard not to swallow. Her first breath of fresh air almost made her delirious.

Hades carried her to the shore and laid her down on the grass. Persephone clung to her, shivering, her teeth clicking as they chattered. Her sodden chiton hung precariously from her left shoulder, the right side torn loose by the hands of the dead.

Hades' arms remained around her, banishing the chill of the river. Persephone's teeth ceased their chattering, and she slowly relaxed to the point where she could close her eyes and not see the faces of the dead swimming before her.

Try as she might, she couldn't let go of Hades. She needed to feel something real, someone alive beside her. The trees here wouldn't speak to her, the grass wouldn't answer, and so there was nothing left but to seek comfort from the one person she should despise the most.

She rested her head against Hades' shoulder, listening to

the steady beat of her heart. She was alive. Hades was alive. The warmth radiating from her body was proof enough.

Tears ran down Persephone's face until she was weeping in a breathless fit and the circle of Hades' arms turned from a comfort to an unbearable cage. She pushed against Hades' shoulders, trying to wriggle free, but Hades only tightened her grip in response.

"Hush. You are safe," Hades said.

That was laughable. How could she ever be safe in the underworld?

Another, more disturbing thought occurred, and she stilled, examining it from every angle. There could be no mistake.

Hades, sensing her shift in mood, brushed a sodden lock of hair back from Persephone's face. "What is it?"

Persephone flicked her head to one side, as if to throw off the memory of Hades' touch. "You knew." She coughed and tried again. "You knew where I was going and what would find me."

The empty hallways. The unguarded stables. Hades must have planned for it, must have suspected what she would do before Persephone herself had thought of leaving.

"Of course," Hades said, as though she were insulted by the mere suggestion that something could happen in her realm without her knowledge.

Persephone took a deep breath. She wanted to cry. She wanted to scream. But most of all, she wanted the sun to soothe her frozen limbs. "I almost drowned!" she said, her waterlogged throat making her voice hoarse.

Hades gave her a pitying look. "I have seen more drowned souls than you could dream of. You were nowhere close to joining their ranks. I would know," she added with a touch of peevishness.

Persephone still wore her jeweled dagger, nestled at her hip and currently poking into her side. She shifted her weight, as though trying to get more comfortable, and drew the blade, thrusting up.

Hades moved, taking hold of Persephone's wrist, her grip tight enough to bruise. "What are you trying to do, Kore?"

The tip of the blade had grazed the underside of Hades' arm, and a bead of ichor welled up on her skin, the golden liquid almost black in the low light. Persephone's fingers shook at the sight of it.

Hades plucked the blade from her nerveless grasp and released Persephone's wrist. She wiped the blade clean on the grass, then offered it to Persephone hilt first. "Try again. Mayhaps your luck will find you."

Persephone looked down at the knife, then back at Hades. A small smile played upon Hades' lips, though her eyes were cold as the morning dew.

Persephone sprang to her feet, turned and fled. The hateful sandals had been lost during her struggle in the marsh, and so she ran barefoot, the muddy ground squelching under her toes. She had no idea where she was heading, only knowing that she could not stand Hades' presence a minute longer.

"Persephone," Hades called behind her, softly, her voice carried by the wind.

The eerie glow that passed as moonlight here was enough that she avoided tripping over her own feet. She reached Alastor, waiting patiently by the side of the road. He snorted in alarm as she drew near, as though startled by something in her bedraggled appearance.

"Whoa! What's wrong, boy?"

What little light there was glinted off his bridle, and Persephone reached for it. As her fingers closed around the reins, Alastor reared, throwing her off balance.

A dark shape slammed into her side, and she fell into a roll just as Alastor's front hooves came crashing to the ground where she'd been standing just moments ago. She righted herself and caught her breath.

After pushing Persephone out of danger, Hades had taken hold of Alastor's bridle and was soothing the horse with a touch. "Are you trying to get yourself killed? Should I be flattered?" Hades asked, her voice clipped.

Persephone's hip ached where she'd bruised herself in the fall, but nothing seemed broken. "I don't understand. He was so docile before."

Hades gave Alastor one last pat on the nose and then walked to Persephone, crouching beside her. "Where are you running to?"

Persephone shook her head. "I don't belong here."

Hades reached out to touch her face, and Persephone drew back. This time, Hades allowed her to maintain her distance. "You will learn to see its beauty, one day."

The taste of ichor was bright on Persephone's tongue. She must have bitten her cheek during the accident. "If you must, then... take me as your m-mistress, if that's what you desire. I will go to you every time you visit the surface. But please, don't condemn me to live here."

"Oh, Persephone. Is this world truly so awful that you would consign yourself to live such a life, without the protection of my claim, to suffer the predations of your father and others of his ilk?"

"I have been doing just fine without your protection!"

Hades gave her long look, then shook her head. "Your father had plans for you. Demeter would not have had the power to intervene."

Persephone wanted to deny it, to defend her mother's power, but she knew Hades was right. As for Zeus... It was unthinkable, but she would be a fool not to examine her father's history and be wary. Still, Hades' protection would only extend so far, unless the other gods recognized them as bound by marriage.

Persephone would never be her wife.

"We are not wed," Persephone said.

"We will be."

"You haven't even asked me!"

Hades' lips quirked in a lopsided smile. She swept the skirts of her chiton behind her and lowered herself gracefully to her knees, uncaring of the mud ruining her fine attire.

"Persephone, daughter of Demeter, would you do me the great honor of marrying me?"

If this were a comedy, not even the chorus would be laughing. "No!"

Hades moved before Persephone could scramble away and grabbed her hair, pulling it tight at the base of her neck. Persephone immediately reached up to free herself, and Hades captured her wrists with her other hand.

"It does not matter what you say, daughter of Demeter. We will be wed, and you will rule beside me, as you were born to do." Hades leaned forward and kissed the pulse in Persephone's neck.

Persephone screamed.

"A voice to rival the harpies, I see," Hades said, flipping her over until Persephone's cheek pressed into the grass. Hades tore her sodden chiton free of its remaining fibula and then ripped it along its side seams, using the wet material to bind Persephone's wrists behind her back. She grabbed Persephone's ankles and used the other side of the chiton to bind those, too.

Persephone struggled the whole time, her mind warring between hyper vigilance and longing to sink down into the deep, dark forgetting, where bulbs went after spring. She tried not to cry, knowing her tears would not move Hades, but it seemed a losing battle.

Hades tugged at the knot of Persephone's strophion, her breastband, until the material loosened. She pulled, and the strip of fabric came free, slithering over Persephone's skin and baring her breasts. It left Persephone nude save for her perizoma, the scrap of fabric covering her sex, secured to her body by ties at both hips.

"We are not wed," Persephone repeated as Hades rolled her over until she was looking up into Hades' eyes. A slight breeze ran over her naked skin, and she shivered, her nipples hardening.

"No," Hades said. "Do not despair. I only wish to look at you."

Persephone shifted uneasily in her bonds, testing their strength. The wet fabric would tighten as it dried, though Hades would have to release her before that happened. Wouldn't she?

Hades' ravenous gaze traveled over her body, as if devouring her. She ran a finger across Persephone's neck, and Persephone flinched.

"You took something of mine, did you not?" Hades asked. "You stole from me. Where is it?"

Persephone tried to shift a little to the side, to avoid the pressure of Hades' touch. "It fell... It will be somewhere in the marsh."

"Well, my little jewel thief, I will have to take something of equal value." A dagger appeared in Hades' hand, and she spun it between her fingertips while looking down at the taut arc of Persephone's body.

It was *her* dagger, Persephone realized, recognizing it from the design of the hilt. She made a small sound of disbelief as Hades used the edge of it to tickle her collarbone.

"At least you did not try to leave unarmed," Hades said. She traced the curve of one breast using the tip of the blade, although she did not press hard enough to break the skin.

Persephone couldn't bear to look, but she also didn't dare look away. There was something hypnotic about the play of light on metal, the way the tendons in Hades' hand stood out where she gripped the dagger.

The blade trailed down, over the plane of her stomach and across the rise of her hipbone. It dipped under the left tie holding Persephone's underwear together and moved away from her body, sawing through the fabric.

The last thread broke and the tie fell away. Hades repeated the movement on the right side and then used the tip of the blade to pull away the remaining cloth, removing the last scrap of Persephone's modesty.

Persephone was grateful for the obscuring gloom of the night. Her hands clenched and unclenched, the unpleasant lump of her bound wrists digging into the small of her back. When Hades set the dagger down and ran her hands over Persephone's hips, she exhaled in a hiss. "You said you would only look."

"I know."

Hades' hands trailed upward, briefly cupping her breasts. She pinched a nipple, and Persephone flinched, shoulders rising as she pulled at her bonds.

"We are not wed," she ground out between her teeth.

"I know. I am all the things the legends say I am."

"Merciful?" Persephone tried, as though Hades had a better nature that was vulnerable to flattery.

"Not today." Hades pressed her knee in between Persephone's legs, spreading them. With her ankles bound, this pushed her legs to either side, exposing her sex. Hades placed a hand on the inside of Persephone's thigh, her fingers cool against her flushed skin. Hades exhaled in a hiss. "So soft."

Persephone turned her head to one side and bit her tongue. The dreams of the earth called out to her, but her head was too clouded to sink down in their embrace.

Hades ran her fingertips from the inside of Persephone's knee along her thigh, pausing when she reached her sex. She crooked her fingers in a single, long swipe, and Persephone gritted her teeth together not to scream as Hades' calluses ran over her overly sensitive flesh.

Much to Persephone's shame, Hades brought her fingers up to inspect them, seeing how they glistened. She placed them between her lips and ran her tongue over them, her eyes dark with lust. "Which one of your nymphs has tasted you?" she asked.

In any other conversation, Persephone would not have understood the question, but in this context, its meaning seemed clear. If there was a right answer, one that would make Hades lose interest in her, she wasn't entirely certain what it could be, so she fell back upon the truth. "None of them."

Hades nibbled at her fingers and looked down at Persephone like a starving man faced with a chalice of ambrosia.

If Persephone had been able to sink down and become one with the earth, she would've done so. Better to disappear than to remain in this fleshy body and be subjected to Hades' all-seeing gaze.

Persephone's voice trembled. "We are—"

"Not yet wed. I know." Hades heaved a great sigh and rocked back on her heels, chewing on her bottom lip. Her breath fogged in the cool night air as she exhaled.

"Hades—"

"Be quiet, Persephone." Hades took the dagger, wrapped it in Persephone's ruined underwear and tucked it into her belt. She then picked up Persephone, still bound at wrists and ankles, and slung her over her shoulder.

The sudden movement made Persephone gag, and she might have thrown up if there had been anything left in her stomach. Every step Hades took made her head sway from side to side, the tip of her long braid trailing against the grass. She didn't dare believe that Hades was not going to assault her that night until she caught a glimpse of Alastor's head as he munched idly on some grass. They were leaving this place and returning to civilization. Relief swelled in her chest.

Hades swung Persephone sidesaddle over Alastor's back. Persephone gripped his mane with the tips of her fingers, unable to properly balance herself.

Hades climbed up behind her and wrapped her arms around Persephone's waist, her chin nestled above Persephone's head. It was a disturbingly intimate position, even accounting for what she'd almost just done, and had Persephone not been bound hand and foot, she would have found the proximity intolerable.

Hades took the reins and clicked her tongue. Alastor began to move, jolting his riders and forcing Persephone to lean against Hades in order to avoid falling off.

"You're taking us back? Like this?" Persephone asked.

"If you would prefer me to leave bite marks all over you first, there is still time for that."

Persephone swung her ankles and managed to kick Hades' shin, bruising her own heels in the process. "I'm naked!"

Hades rolled her eyes, but she released the reins for a moment to pull off her chlamys and place it over Persephone's shoulders. The cape was too short to be anywhere near decent, but Persephone shrugged her way into it so it at least covered her from shoulders to thighs.

They didn't speak the whole ride back, Persephone preoccupied with trying not to lean against Hades whilst not falling off as Alastor picked up speed. Despite their combined weight, he galloped faster than before when it had only been Persephone at the reins. She was dizzy and aching by the time he trotted to the stables, coming to a halt by the door.

The young groom came out to greet them, his face turning red as he averted his eyes from Persephone. "M-my queen," he stammered, the lump in his throat bobbing.

Hades gathered Persephone in her arms and leapt down. "The hour is late, Eustachys, but please find a treat for Alastor. He has endured much tonight."

"Of course, Queen Hades." The groom—Eustachys— reached out and took Alastor's reins, though he cast a single sideways look at Persephone before heading into the stables.

She couldn't believe that Hades would allow the servants to

gawk at her like that. "Are you going to untie me now? I can walk," she said in her frostiest voice.

"Why should I? You might run, and then I would have to chase you again. I cannot promise you restraint next time."

If that had been restraint, Persephone didn't want to know what Hades would do to her once they were married and her virtue became a distant memory.

It startled her to find herself imagining a life after marriage, as though she had already given up on the idea of an escape or rescue, not more than a day after her arrival. She blamed it on the underworld itself, which was dreary enough to make anyone lose hope.

Before Persephone could protest, Hades swung her over her shoulder again as though she were nothing more than a sack of grain and walked into the palace. Persephone couldn't even scream for fear of attracting more servants; instead, she hung miserably in Hades' grasp, the ichor in her veins rushing to her head, the ends of her wrist ties dragging on the floor.

To her relief, only Xenia was waiting for them in her chambers. Xenia's eyes widened briefly, then she lowered her gaze. "Queen Hades."

"Please do not permit her to run around for the rest of the night. I want her well-rested for tomorrow."

"Yes, my queen."

Hades set Persephone on her feet and then was gone.

Persephone flinched away, almost falling when Xenia tried to place a hand on her elbow to steady her. "Just untie me already!"

"Of course, mistress," Xenia said in the calm, measured tone of a servant who could pretend she had not seen her mistress's humiliation.

As soon as she was free, Persephone threw off the chlamys, unwilling to wear an article of Hades' clothing for a minute longer. She pulled on a tunic, and Xenia escorted her to the bathing chamber, which was empty and silent at this time of night.

The water was cold, chilling her as it sluiced over her back. She washed quickly, trying to scrub out the memory of Hades' hands and the hands of the dead wandering over her body, and then it was time to crawl into bed and pretend that this night had never happened.

"Good night, mistress," Xenia said from her seat at the other end of the bed.

Persephone rolled over until she was facing away from Xenia. "You don't need to sit here. Just lock me in and be done with it."

"Yes, mistress," Xenia said without moving.

Persephone wrapped a pillow around her head and closed her eyes. She could still hear Xenia's breathing. The sound sawed at the edge of her consciousness, despite her body's fatigue. She forced herself to try to relax, knowing she could not face the next day without sleep. In time, her mind floated down into the dreaming earth and her worries evaporated, at least for a while.

8

THE WEDDING

The next day, Xenia did not allow Persephone to be unattended. Her fingernails and toenails were scrubbed and trimmed, her hair neatened, and once dressed she was taken to a temple dedicated to Gaia, where she spent hours on her knees in prayer.

She could scarcely pray for her marriage to be blessed, as a bride should. Instead, she prayed for deliverance and compassion. Failing that, she prayed for Hades' ruination. If the goddess heard her, Persephone saw no sign.

The servants gently coaxed her out of the temple, where she would've remained forever, given the chance. The rest of the day saw her fitted in her wedding attire, the serving girls taking up the hem by a few fingers' widths.

Persephone had never felt so decorative and useless. She watched the needlework; the girls might as well have been sewing her shroud.

The day ended without a single glimpse of Hades, though she was never far from Persephone's mind.

The morning after that began with a bath. She had to be dragged out of the cold water, her fingertips wrinkled, and then was forced to sit in a chair for what felt like hours as her hair was coiled into an elaborate confection of braids interwoven with precious gems.

Persephone suffered through all of this in a haze of detachment. This could not possibly be happening to her, and therefore it was not.

Xenia brushed some powder over her cheeks and dabbed at her lips. She stood back to observe her work. Persephone's head was heavy with gems, and even the slightest movement of her neck was tiresome. Nonetheless she could not fail to be moved by Xenia's undisguised joy.

"You'll make a beautiful consort," Xenia said.

Persephone's kind mood vanished. She longed to run her fingers through her hair, rip out all the accoutrements, stamp her feet and insist on being taken back home. The only thing stopping her was the knowledge that such actions would be futile. Every denizen of the underworld obeyed Hades, and Hades, it seemed, had no intention of letting her go.

"I don't wish to marry her."

Xenia fussed around, placing a saffron-dyed veil over Persephone's hair, delicately draping the yellow fabric as not to snag on any of the jewels in her stephane. "It's normal for a bride to have jitters on her special day."

Had they not heard her? Persephone thought that all the screaming upon her arrival had provided sufficient indication, but it seemed everyone was conveniently ignoring the fact that she had been dragged here against her will.

"I never chose Hades," Persephone tried again.

Xenia glanced at her with sympathy, and she patted Persephone's shoulder. "Most brides don't choose, dear. Be glad your father permitted such a fine match."

Persephone needed to throw up, but there was nothing left inside of her. Terrified of accidentally binding herself to this place, she had neither eaten nor drunk since arrival. Gods and goddesses could survive much longer than mortals without sustenance, but the process was not pleasant.

"Are you almost done?" Persephone asked. Not that she wanted the day to go any faster. As soon as the rituals ended, she would be left alone with Hades, and she wished to delay that moment as long as possible. But listening to Xenia prattle on, as if Persephone were some kind of blushing bride, was almost just as unbearable.

"Not long, dear, not long."

Persephone's head ached. She needed fresh air and the touch of the sun against her skin. She was a wild violet, plucked and left to wither in some dark corner, far from her natural home. Could Hades not see that this would be the end of her?

Xenia set down her brush, and foolishly, Persephone thought this meant her ordeal was over. But Xenia only pursed her lips, looking at Persephone's face, as if she could see something not visible to the eye. She clapped her hands, and all the other servants looked up. Until that moment, Persephone had almost forgotten about their existence—her mother's servants were always gaily chattering, and so it was impossible to forget they were there—but the ladies serving her were either so well-trained or so terrified that they had uttered barely a sound as Xenia had worked.

Xenia gestured, and they all obediently made a single file

and left the room. She closed the door on the last of them and then leaned against the door as though warding off any stray maid who would dare try and interrupt.

When at last she and Persephone were alone, she plastered a smile on her face and brought her hands together. "Now, mistress, forgive me for being forward, but... did your honored mother explain to you each facet of a wife's duties?"

Persephone's mind went blank. Now? They were doing this now, and with a servant who would report directly back to her abductor, no less? "Yes," she said, jaw clenched. She turned aside, but Xenia would not be thwarted.

"It's only that... well, after the feast, there won't be much time for us to speak in private if you have questions—"

"Why is she doing this?"

Xenia had clearly braced herself for a different sort of question. She opened her mouth, closed it again, then spoke. "Every hard-working ruler needs a good wife by their side."

It was as though Persephone were yelling down a deep chasm and nothing was coming back save for the twisted echo of her own voice. "Not everyone takes that wife by deception."

Xenia smiled sadly, giving her a pitying glance. She wasn't so indecorous to mention Persephone's father, but they were both thinking it. Fine—the rest of the gods were no paragons of morality; everyone knew that. It didn't make it right.

Persephone placed both hands flat on the small table and rose, the folds of her chiton weighing heavily about her as the hem settled around her ankles. "Enough. Let's be done with this farce."

Outside, the other servant girls were already waiting for them, lining the corridors on both sides and dressed in identical gowns of pale green, like the calyx to her flower. They bowed their heads as Persephone approached, then turned to follow behind in rows of two.

Xenia led the way to the Great Hall. Already, Persephone's elaborate coiffure was beginning to weigh down on her skull. She wondered how she could dance in all this finery. Would she be expected to dance? The thought of having to feign any kind of joy at this travesty of a wedding was utterly repugnant.

They stopped at the doors to the Great Hall, where Xenia swept her gaze once more over Persephone. She fussed with the veil, arranging it to fall over Persephone's eyes, concealing her face and blurring the world in an amber-colored haze.

If this were a proper wedding, Demeter might have been the one to perform such an intimate function. Persephone pressed her lips together, resolving not to weep as the doors swung inward, revealing their wedding party to the crowd.

It seemed like the underworld had emptied itself to attend her wedding. There were not enough seats for all of them, and so people crowded in every nook and cranny of the room, some even watching from the rafters.

Most were formed in the image of gods and humans, but some were curious indeed, with wings like bats, or a crown of snakes instead of hair. Persephone recognized no one—none save her bride, whom she detested most in all the world.

Hades waited at the furthermost end of the Great Hall, standing beside an altar. She wore a chiton of pure white, held fast against her body by crisscrossing ties encrusted with sapphires. Her black hair was held back by a myrtle wreath made of gold, matching a single chain that adorned her throat.

Her eyes were fixed on Persephone, but Persephone could

not watch her as she approached. Instead, she looked past Hades. Standing beside her was a tall god, broad-shouldered, with a pair of great, feathery wings at his back.

Persephone walked slowly, as a mortal walking to her gallows, but soon enough she was at Hades' side. An unseen musician ceased strumming their lyre, though she had not noticed the music until it had stopped.

"Friends and family, we are gathered here today to witness my marriage to the beautiful Persephone, daughter of Zeus and Demeter," Hades said.

Persephone was astonished when the crowd cheered, as if they were attending a comedy and not a solemn act of matrimony. Someone even called out, "It's about time!" to which Hades only laughed, instead of striking down the person who'd dared speak, as Ares might have done.

"Yes, you have all been very patient, but the wait is over! Now, you shall have another queen truly worthy of your devotion."

The crowd roared with approval, and Persephone's stomach fell. Did no one see her for what she was—a captive and not a willing participant in all of this merrymaking? She looked at those around her, trying to meet their eyes, but no one seemed to see the despair she felt.

"As my wedding gift to the mortals, though they may not know it, while Thanatos is present with us here, no one born of woman will join our ranks tonight," Hades said. She gestured to the god standing behind her as she spoke, and Persephone recognized him now for what he was—the personification of death, though he looked hale as anyone. He had a pleasant though utterly forgettable face, but when he looked at Persephone, she thought perhaps he might understand her plight.

"Help me," she mouthed from beneath her veil, but his placid expression did not change. She would find no mercy there.

"May I have your hand?" Hades asked.

With all eyes upon her, Persephone did as she was bidden. Hades turned her palm upward, then released her, turning her own hand the same way. Before Persephone could cry out, Thanatos took a blade and sliced both their palms in a diagonal line, starting between the thumb and forefinger and angling down toward the wrist.

Hades grabbed her hand, locking their fingers together, and the golden ichor spilling from their veins dripped as one over the altar.

Thanatos sheathed his blade and wrapped a cord over and across their interlocked hands. Hades' grip did not lessen even as the cord ensured that Persephone could not have freed herself. Her palm stung, but that was nothing compared to the way that Hades' gaze seemed to pierce right through her, despite the veil.

"This is not how we do things on the surface," Persephone said.

"There will be time enough for you to learn all our customs," Hades said.

"Is it your custom to abduct brides without a blessing?" She had raised her voice, but she didn't care who heard her. Hades seemed immune to censure, in any case.

"This wedding was blessed," Hades said.

"By whom? Not Demeter!"

"By your father."

Persephone's breath caught in her throat. She wanted to

deny it, to call Hades a liar, but she could feel deep in her bones that she was telling the truth.

"What I have joined here today, let no god nor goddess tear apart," Thanatos said. He unbound the cord joining them, but Hades did not release her straight away.

"I assure you that you will be well loved here, by my subjects, and most of all, by me."

Persephone wrenched her hand away. Already, the gash was closing, but the cut stung worse than a superficial wound.

"I present to you my wife," Hades said and lifted Persephone's veil, draping it back so that it covered her stephane and the crown of her head. Stripped of her meager defense, Persephone flinched to feel the night air against her bare skin and glanced away as Hades studied her.

"Dearest," Hades said. "You are a vision, but something is missing." Hades unclasped the necklace she was wearing and placed it on Persephone. The metal was warm from Hades' skin, and it sat like a noose above her collarbone.

Hades' subjects crowded around them, offering their congratulations. Persephone was forced to stand beside Hades, blank-faced and unsmiling, as she went over things in her head. Had Demeter known of this? Surely not. But why had she counseled Persephone to stay away from Hades? Was it just a mother's instinct?

And if Zeus had blessed this union, would anyone come for her? Would they dare? To do so was to risk his wrath, and few gods were willing to chance that. Not for Persephone's sake, in any case.

Thanatos requested all guests to take their seats, many spilling out into the courtyards, then he departed with some final, private words to Hades. Persephone supposed this meant that mortals would begin dying again, their brief reprieve over.

She was seated beside Hades and not with her guests as she had hoped. Very soon servants trudged into the Great Hall, carrying great platters of food, steaming trays and baskets of loaves. The appealing scents mingled in the air, and Persephone's throat moistened itself in anticipation.

Her hunger became worse when the food was placed directly in front of her. She sat still as a statue, as if moving would invite weakness and give her leave to succumb to her appetite.

Hades glanced at her empty plate. "Is there something else you would prefer from the kitchens?"

Persephone shook her head.

"Xenia tells me you have fasted all day. Surely you must be hungry?"

Persephone's stomach rumbled as if on cue. Her cheeks colored, but she kept her lips firmly pressed together.

Hades frowned. "Speak to me, wife."

A muscle ticked in Persephone's cheek. "You have no right to call me that."

"Let us not fight over words on this blessed day. Persephone, then. Are you so determined to refuse my hospitality?"

"I don't wish to stay here. You know that!" Persephone said, trying not to watch all of the diners digging into their food with gusto.

"You have not eaten since your arrival?" Hades asked, her words clipped.

Persephone shook her head. She hadn't dared. One sip and it would bind her here forever.

Hades gestured at the spread before them. "Nothing at our

table has been grown here. You may partake of it freely." She beckoned a servant to her side. "Bring me that plate," she said, pointing at a platter laden with figs on another table.

The servant came back and set the plate down. Hades took a fig from the new plate and a fig from another plate already on their table. She hid them both behind her back for a moment and then held out her palms, each with a fig upon it.

"Which one is from the surface?" she asked.

Persephone shook her head. She would sit through this farce, but she needn't play these games.

"Humor me."

Biting back a sigh, Persephone touched both figs in turn. One of them roused nothing within her. But the other evoked clear skies, torrential rain, and the fragrance of freshly dug earth. She pressed her hands over her mouth, trying hard not to cry.

Hades took that fig and with her knife destemmed it and cut it into segments, placing them upon Persephone's plate. "Please, eat."

Persephone popped a slice into her mouth, and the juice exploded on her tongue. She chewed slowly and then devoured the rest of it.

She hadn't realized that fruit grown from the underworld's soil would feel different to her senses. But why wouldn't it? Never feeling the sun, not following the natural order of the seasons. Of course it was bound to be different.

She picked up another of the surface-grown fruits, and with her other hand she held the fig from the other table. They were both firm and rich in color. She could not tell the difference between them simply by looking at them.

Hades watched her. "Our marriage places you under my

protection and proves to the other gods that you are mine. It could not be delayed any longer. But binding yourself to the underworld is a choice you will make for me and only for me."

What kind of choice was that? "I'll never taste of your food, nor drink your wine," Persephone said.

A small smile played about Hades' lips. "We shall see."

Persephone could not believe her arrogance. She turned her attention away from Hades before she could lose her temper. She drank her fill of water next, easing her dry throat, then sampled each dish before her, forcing herself to chew slowly to avoid overwhelming her empty stomach. Hades slipped a few choice morsels onto her plate and the finest garnishes, and Persephone was not so proud that she would leave them uneaten.

Hades was a different goddess in the underworld, more relaxed than she'd even been above ground. She chatted to her guests, jested with them, her pale cheeks flushed with color and her lips curved into a smile more often than not.

Her pleasant countenance hid a dark heart. Persephone could not forget the way she'd been manhandled in the over-world, nor the way Hades had humiliated her the other night and enjoyed it, no less. Was she as bad as Zeus, with his endless philandering? Persephone ought to hope that was the case, as it would mean that Hades would pay her less mind. But she didn't think she would be so fortunate. Knowing how gods loved gossip, she would've heard rumors.

As the night wore on, a steady stream of well-wishers approached their table. Hades introduced each of them in turn, with their name, function, and a few words about their person.

Persephone stared at them in silence, her face expression-less before their ingratiating smiles and pithy words. She would form no ties here, cultivate no friendships. She wanted nothing of substance from the underworld, save for an exit.

During a lull in the flow of visitors, Persephone took the opportunity to have some of her nagging questions answered, though she misliked her chances of getting an answer she wanted.

"Why did you unlock my door the other night? Was it simply for sport?" she asked, unable to keep the bitterness from her voice.

Hades lowered a chalice from her lips and set it on the table before speaking. "I cannot deny it was an enjoyable side effect."

"You humiliated me! Is that how you want your consort to be remembered?"

Hades ran her finger along the rim of her chalice. "No. And no one of importance saw you." She raised her eyes, meeting Persephone's. "You needed to see how futile it was."

"I'll never stop trying to escape you," Persephone said.

"Then you are bound to be disappointed."

Hades' confidence, her conceit, was just as bad as any god's and not at all becoming on someone of the gentler sex. Persephone stabbed a morsel on her plate with her knife, imagining it to be Hades' face.

A bard began a series of songs praising her virtues and Hades', sensationalized in the way of lyric poets and highly inaccurate. Persephone stared longingly at her knife. If she were mortal, she would've had some semblance of choice over her own destiny. Now even that was denied to her.

"Would you care to dance?" Hades asked.

Persephone shook her head. She could think of nothing less suited to her mood.

Hades stood, joining the rest of the assembled dancers

midway through a song. They parted to admit her, their eyes shining with honor to have their queen beside them.

She danced well enough, a bright star in her white chiton amidst her guests' peacock-like finery. Persephone could not bear to watch. She left the table and slipped out of the hall into the adjoining courtyard.

Once she was outside, she found that the cavernous sky, bereft of stars, did nothing for her nerves. She lurched toward the nearest planter and vomited up half her dinner, clutching the sides of the planter with both hands to steady herself.

"Is there anything I can do to help you, mistress? More water?"

Persephone wiped her face with the back of her hand and turned to find Xenia shadowing her. "I'm fine," Persephone said.

"Of course," Xenia said. "Every bride is nervous."

"I'm not every bride!"

"And the Ruler of Many will not be any old boorish groom."

Persephone laughed. "How do you know that?"

"I would trust her with my own daughter."

It occurred to Persephone that she knew nothing of the woman's life before her death. "You have children?"

"Four who lived to maturity, praise the gods. And many descendants after them."

"You're not my mother," Persephone said.

"Of course not. I would never dream to put myself beside the generous Demeter. But if I may offer you some comfort whilst you are bereft a mother's counsel, then I will do whatever is in my power to guide you."

Persephone placed a hand over her throbbing forehead.

"You can't help me. No one here can, except the one who won't."

If she looked at Xenia now, she would cry, and so she stared instead at the nearest tree, an ornamental fig. Its leaves were smooth and soothed her fingers, though they did not respond to her touch as they ought to do.

A servant came to them. "Beg pardon, but Queen Hades has requested your presence."

A chill fell upon Persephone. She was certain that if she refused to go, someone would be forced to drag her, and she had no desire to cause such a scene.

She followed the servant back inside the hall. Hades looked slightly more disheveled than before, her color high, strands of her hair loosened from dancing. She turned as Persephone entered and smiled.

"Time for you to depart," Hades said. She held out her hand, and after a moment, Persephone took it, wincing as the movement caused the newly healed skin on her palm to stretch.

Hades cleared her throat, and a hush fell over the hall. "Friends, thank you for your company this evening. We must now depart"—she was forced to pause until the snickers died down—"but please, continue to enjoy yourselves as long as the night permits. Eat, drink, and celebrate the dawning of a new age!"

The crowd cheered, warm with inebriation.

Hades raised Persephone's hand to her lips and kissed her knuckles. "I will see you anon." She released her and turned to talk with a few last well-wishers eager to catch her on her way out of the hall.

Xenia took Persephone's arm in her stead. "Come with me," she said.

There was to be no procession, then, no ritual blessings. At least there would not be the scandal of someone else holding a torch in her mother's place. Persephone supposed she ought to be thankful for small mercies, but she could not find it within herself to feel gratitude. She walked with Xenia beside her, and her heart filled with dread.

9

THE MARRIAGE BED

Xenia and another two girls herded Persephone to her room, sitting her down at her dressing table and working to undo the monstrosity of her coiffure. Many hands disentangled the small pins from her hair, inevitably tugging a little too hard at the braids when they snagged. Her scalp tingled as the tension eased, and she sighed with relief.

Once all the ornaments were gone, a girl combed out her hair. The chiton was next to go, though she was somewhat more ambivalent about taking it off. It was a garment of such rare beauty, she missed admiring the shimmer of the weave, despite its weight and the discomfort it caused her. Nevertheless, she changed into a plain white chiton, smoothing her hands over the reddened marks where the wedding garment had cinched in.

"Is there anything else you need?" Xenia asked her.

Persephone shook her head, and Xenia and all the servants departed. She sat on the bed and swung her legs over the side, for once at a loss as to what to do with herself. She hadn't heard Xenia lock the door this time.

Tempting as it was to run, she had no place to go and no desire to repeat the events of the previous night. Hades wouldn't be satisfied with just a taste this time, and tonight with the wedding feast and resulting guests, the halls would not be so empty if she decided to humiliate Persephone for trying to escape.

Her stomach felt unsettled. It would be easy to blame it on the rich food, but it was more the thought of what was yet to come. If only she hadn't been so captivated by that narcissus! Would she now be safe in her mother's chambers and not preparing to surrender her maidenhead?

Whatever the answer, it couldn't help her. Persephone crawled into bed and pulled the covers up to her chin, trying not to think of all the could-have-beens. Avoiding the thought of something only made it worse, and so her mind stepped around in circles until she finally fell asleep.

She woke to find a weight pulling down the other side of the bed. She opened her eyes to find Hades sitting next to her, her face golden in the candlelight. She was still wearing her wedding chiton, though she had removed the ornate belt. As Persephone watched, Hades reached up and withdrew a single long pin from her bun. Her hair tumbled loose, falling down to frame her face.

"I would say you sleep like the dead, but the dead are frequently unable to rest. Is that a talent of yours?" Hades asked.

Persephone stiffened. Her mind was still foggy from waking as she shook off the last few remnants of her slumber. "I've always been a deep sleeper."

"I would not call that 'sleep.'"

Wasn't it the same for everyone? Persephone couldn't remember a time when there hadn't been the dreaming earth, calling her to its welcoming, protective embrace. She shrugged, glancing away. "From what people say of your schedule, you could use a little rest yourself."

Hades laughed and stepped away from the bed. "True. There is always something else to demand my attention. But not tonight." She stood by a side table and opened a carafe of wine, pouring a chalice. "Care for some?"

Persephone began to shake her head but thought better of it and nodded. Hades poured a second chalice and brought them both with her to bed.

Persephone sat up, pushing the sheets away and tucking her knees under her. She held the chalice in her lap for a minute, summoning the courage to drink. It was made from grapes from the surface, so there was no hesitancy on that end, but she wasn't entirely sure whether one chalice would be too much or simply not enough. She almost wished Hades had taken her in her sleep, so she didn't have to deal with the consequences of her marriage in her waking hours.

"May I help you?" Hades asked.

Persephone looked down to see that her hands were shaking so badly, a third of the wine had spilled across her lap, soaking into her chiton in pink splotches.

Hades took the chalice from her nervous grasp and held it to Persephone's lips. After a few sips, Persephone drew back, and Hades set the chalice down on a side table. She took hold of Persephone's chin, forcing her to meet her gaze. Hades' lips curved in a slight smile, her eyes deep as pools of still water.

Wife. She was her wife.

Persephone didn't know how to hold that word in her mind without her consciousness overflowing. She froze when Hades leaned in to kiss her, desperately reaching out to the earth to bring her back to the blissful unconsciousness of sleep, but there was no way she could find the peace of mind she needed, not with Hades' lips burning against her mouth and the warmth of Hades' hands enfolding her shoulders.

"You are as tense as Artemis's bowstring," Hades said.

"We don't have to... not tonight, please. We could pretend it happened. I wouldn't tell anyone."

Hades' sword hand fell upon Persephone's knee. "A marriage is not valid unless consummated." She pressed a kiss just below Persephone's ear, her breath tickling.

"But I didn't—"

"Hmm?" Hades drew back to look at her. It was the first time Persephone had seen her with her hair unbound; it softened her strong jawline, giving her a more delicate appearance. Her lips were darkened slightly from the wine.

"Hera hasn't blessed this marriage, so it's not—final."

Hades turned away for a moment, bending down to undo her sandals. "Zeus has approved this match. She has no reason to challenge him—or me—over this matter."

"And what of Demeter?"

"She will learn to accept our union. As will you, in time."

"Never. "

"We shall see about that." Hades ran a hand through her hair. "Enough of this. I wish to see my wife undressed." When Persephone made no move to comply, Hades sighed. "Would you prefer if I stripped you myself?"

Persephone shook her head. Anything to keep Hades' hands off of her a little longer. She reached for the fibula on her shoulder, fumbling with the clasp until it came free. Her chiton peeled away, revealing the shape of her strophion. She moved to the other shoulder and repeated the gesture, placing the brooches down on the table.

Hades had already seen her naked, but this time felt different. They were married. As one of the elder six, Hades outranked her. It was clear she expected Persephone to fulfill all her wifely duties, and if she did not perform as required, Hades would be well within her marital rights to exact punishment. The thought of what Hades might require her to do made her cheeks burn.

"And the rest, my lady wife."

Persephone longed for the enfolding shroud of darkness, but the candlelight, though weak, illuminated all too clearly Hades' ravenous expression. She reached up behind her and fumbled with the tight knot of her strophion. It was difficult enough to undo at the best of times, but now, in this moment, her clumsy fingers worked as though they were made out of lead. Hades made no move to help her, reclining on the pillows, still fully dressed.

She worked the fabric free at last, and the band fell to her hips, revealing her breasts. A shiver ran over her skin, the cool air giving her gooseflesh.

With the strophion off, Persephone waited, clad only in her perizoma, which covered her sex. She knelt on the bed, her hands folded in her lap. She imagined herself to be a sapling, settling her roots into the ground. There was no shame in bending under the force of the wind. Any sacrifice was worth it, if it meant survival.

She watched from the corner of her eye as Hades brought her chalice to her lips, took a sip and replaced the chalice on the side table. When Hades next kissed her, Persephone tasted the tart acidity of the wine, its sour notes warming her throat.

She was drifting off into the fragrant haze of a summer vineyard when Hades pinched her arm, hard.

"Your gifts are very interesting, dear wife, and I look forward to learning more about them. But now is not the time."

Persephone blinked, her vision momentarily blurred by tears. The scent of grapes ripening on the vine faded, replaced by burning tallow and the faint fragrance of asphodels. She grabbed the bed frame for support, waiting for the dizziness to pass.

"Let me be clear. In my presence, you will not do any of that"—Hades waved her hand in the air—"what do you call it?"

It didn't really have a name, it just was. But Hades was waiting for her, none too patiently. "I think of it as... embracing the dreaming earth."

"Yes. That."

"But..."

"What is it?"

Persephone gnawed on the inside of her mouth. "I've never... I'm not sure if I can. Stop, that is."

From the way Hades' eyebrows raised, it was clear this was not the answer she'd expected. "What has Demeter been doing with you? No. You will have to learn to control it."

Persephone's eyes welled with tears. "But I—"

"It comes easily when you wish to avoid something, does it not? But life is filled with pain, dear Persephone, and to pretend otherwise will not help. You want to disappear now, is that so?"

Persephone nodded mutely.

"Well, stop. Hold back. I need you to feel me when I touch you." Hades placed her hand on the side of Persephone's cheek and brushed her lower lip with her thumb.

Persephone closed her eyes, then gasped as Hades' nails dug into her skin.

"No. Look at me."

Hades' usually stern features were softened by the candle-light, her sleeveless chiton leaving her well-muscled arms on display. Her body could have been carved by Praxiteles, from her small, high breasts to the slight curve of her waist. Her long, slender fingers resumed caressing Persephone's cheek, and with her other hand, she pushed on Persephone's shoulder until she lay flat on the bed, with Hades leaning over her. Persephone's hair spilled over the pillow, and she froze, all too aware of how Hades' chiton brushed against her bared breasts. It was not the fault of the fabric—the linen was soft and finely woven. It had been grown on the surface, but so long ago that the fiber scarcely remembered the touch of the sun upon its stalks.

Hades pinched one of her nipples, and Persephone squeaked in protest.

"It comes upon you quickly, it seems," Hades said. "Every time you do that, I will hurt you."

Persephone stared up at her in silent resentment, but Hades wasn't paying attention to her face. She ran her hands over Persephone's body, her calloused fingertips warm and sure. Persephone gritted her teeth and tried her best to endure it, but as the pressure of Hades' knee against her thigh disappeared from her consciousness, it was like falling into a warm and tranquil pool—

Hades grabbed both of Persephone's hands, pulling them above her head. She transferred her grip so that she was holding onto Persephone's wrists with only one hand, squeezing tightly enough that her bones felt like they were grinding together.

Persephone cried out as all her prior sensations of comfort and warmth evaporated. She squirmed in Hades' grasp, her senses assaulted all at once by the horrific rasp of Hades' chiton, the way each fold of fabric pressed against her, and the warm weight of Hades' body pinning her to the bed. If there was nowhere to go, then she had to feel—but she had dulled her senses for so long that opening herself to awareness was like waking up to find herself in Tartarus.

"Breathe, Persephone."

She inhaled, struggling to draw enough breath with Hades crushing her. The ceiling almost looked like it was spinning, so she focused on her breath, forcing herself to relax until it stopped. Hades still hadn't released her hands.

"Let me go."

"Wait."

Hades leaned in and kissed the salt on her cheeks. She released Persephone at last and her hands moved down over Persephone's body, stopping at her hips. She untied the cords holding Persephone's underwear together and pulled the garment free.

Persephone reached down to cover herself, and Hades shook her head. "No. Hands back where they were."

When Persephone didn't move, Hades sighed, her lips pursed. She raised her hand and struck Persephone across her face. "When I give an order, I expect to be obeyed. Even by you. Especially by you."

"You have no right!" Persephone said, clutching her cheek. She tasted copper on her tongue.

"I have a god-given right," Hades said, her mouth twisted on one side, as though she resented having to be grateful to Zeus for anything. "Do not make me tell you again."

Persephone slowly moved her hands above her head, palms up. Hades grabbed her wrists again, straightening her arms, then took her perizoma and used it to tie her wrists together before securing them to the bed frame.

Persephone's cheek stung. She cautiously probed the inside of her mouth, tasting more copper. She must have bitten herself in shock.

Hades kissed her cheek, which made it throb, and scooped up Persephone's legs behind the knee, pushing them up and to either side.

If there was ever a time she needed the dreaming earth, it was now, now, now. But she didn't dare turn to it as Hades kissed a line across the inside of her thighs, not pausing until she reached Persephone's core.

Persephone's fingers curled into fists as Hades found her sex. The movement of Hades' tongue made Persephone arch her back, prevented from rising off the bed by the pressure of Hades' hands upon her thighs.

Hades paused and lifted her head, her lips glistening in the candlelight. "You are still here. Good." She stroked Persephone's hip as if to underscore her approval, then lowered her head once more.

It felt softer and less urgent than the times when she'd touched herself. Persephone tried to move her hands, and the cords cut into her wrists, too narrow for comfort. The strings not only anchored her to the bed but to her body, the gnawing sting keeping her in the present moment.

The soft sounds of Hades' tongue upon her flesh were obscene. Persephone shifted, placing her foot on Hades' shoulder and trying to push her away, but it was as though the goddess were made of stone. She pulled at her bonds once more, but it seemed her skin would break before either the bed frame or the knotted cords.

Hades did not stop. If the sensations had been unpleasant, or merely distracting, Persephone might not have minded so much. But she could not deny Hades' skill. How many lovers had she taken, over the ages? Had any of them lain in this very same bed?

From the knowledge of her own body, Persephone knew she was close to release. She shifted, trying to angle her hips to provide less contact with Hades' tongue, but the way Hades was pinning her to the bed made it impossible to move far. The slight rocking of her hips only served to inflame the sensations until at last she could not hold herself back. Persephone dug her nails into her palms and turned her face into the pillow, willing herself not to scream as Hades pushed her into unbidden spasms of pleasure.

When it was over, she lay there, spent and boneless, listening to the thudding beat of her own heart. Her skin felt unpleasantly warm, relieved slightly by the cool chill to the air. The candles had guttered out, leaving only the gray twilight streaming through the window. Hades shifted and sat up, her weight leaving the bed. Persephone rolled onto her side, brought her knees together and raised them to her chest, wishing her arms were free so that she could wrap them around herself.

She heard Hades pouring more wine and the scrape of objects being moved. Hades returned to the bed and offered Persephone a chalice, holding it up to her lips.

She sipped from it. It was well-watered, the way she preferred to serve herself. Its cool, acidic tang helped to ease her dry throat.

Hades set the chalice down and untied her wrists. Persephone whimpered as the feeling came back to her fingertips and massaged the red marks the cords had cut into her skin.

Hades moved the hair back from Persephone's face, and she flinched. Had she been so foolish to think this nightmare might be over?

"You remained present," Hades said. "It pleased me."

"Not from lack of wanting."

"Even better. To desire something and resist the urge is the type of discipline that civilizations are built upon."

"Why don't you resist your urges?"

Hades stilled, and she wondered if she'd gone too far. But then, Hades smiled. "Why should I? I have been waiting a long time for you, Persephone, Demeter's daughter. I will not be denied a moment longer." She placed two fingers beneath Persephone's chin and kissed her. Persephone tasted the salt of her own arousal, its edge bitter on her tongue.

Persephone drew back and swung at her. Hades allowed the blow to connect, receiving the flat of Persephone's palm across her face. When Persephone drew back her hand for another strike, Hades grabbed her.

"One was enough, I think."

Persephone tugged at her arm, but Hades' grip was firm. "Let me go."

"No." Hades turned her attention to Persephone's neck, her teeth closing around the soft spot just above the gold chain encircling her throat.

Persephone forced down a scream, her free palm braced against Hades' shoulder trying to push her away.

Hades drew back and looked at her work. She hooked a finger beneath the necklace and rubbed the metal with her thumb. "My chain suits you. As do bruises."

"You are a degenerate."

"If I were a god, would you say such a thing? One man's sin is another man's pleasure."

Persephone remained silent. If Hades had been a god, Persephone would not have been compelled to eavesdrop upon her at Zeus's party, all those years ago, and perhaps she would not have aroused Hades' interest. Surely that would've been the better outcome for both of them.

"I have caught you, Persephone, and I intend to keep you. It will be easier for you to accept that." Hades smiled, her eyes dark as the depths of Tartarus. "But your struggle is just as sweet as your eventual surrender will be."

Persephone grabbed the sheet and pulled it over her breasts. She moved back until the bed frame dug into her shoulder blades, as far away from Hades as she could manage.

The bed was made from olive wood and the joints from oak dowel. They all sang to her, discordantly, but she was too mindful of Hades' command to let herself fall prey to the enticement.

Instead of pursuing, Hades rose and walked to the window. She pulled down the shutters until only the tiniest sliver of light fell upon the floor. Persephone had not realized how much she'd grown used to the light until she was plunged into darkness. She heard the small clicks of fibulae being unclasped and a rustle of fabric. Hades' footsteps came next, slow and deliberate.

The bed creaked as Hades sat down beside her. Even though Persephone was aware of her presence, she still jumped when Hades' hand fell upon her shoulder.

"No need for this," Hades said, tugging the sheet from Persephone's fingers. She pressed her nose into the curve of Persephone's neck and inhaled.

A goddess wiser than Persephone might have been able to imagine that Hades was someone else: not her abductor, but a secret lover, one she could only meet in darkness. Such fantasies might have brought her comfort, but Persephone could not rely upon pretense. The scent of asphodels clung around Hades, distinguishing her even without the benefit of sight.

The rustle of fabric must have been Hades disrobing, for when Persephone moved her hand she accidentally grazed Hades' naked thigh. She drew back as if burned and squeezed her hands in her lap, uncomfortably aware of the heat that radiated from Hades' skin.

Hades buried her hand in Persephone's hair, tilted her face up and kissed her. In contrast with the angular, muscular frame of her body, her lips were uncommonly soft. After a moment, Persephone found herself returning the kiss.

She stopped as soon as she realized what she'd done, but Hades did not mock her for it. Instead, she picked up Persephone and laid her flat on the bed, crouching with her knee in between Persephone's thighs, pushing them apart.

She must have made some sound of distress, for Hades

paused. "Can you keep your hands by your sides?" Hades asked. "Even when it hurts?"

Persephone didn't know how to answer that, so she said nothing. It seemed to be answer enough. Hades reached over the side of the bed to pick up a loop of fabric, probably a discarded strophion. She rolled Persephone onto her side and bound her lower arms together behind her back, from elbows to wrists. The wide fabric was at least more comfortable than the strings of her perizoma had been, but it pulled her shoulders back in a way that made her feel more exposed despite the darkness.

Hades returned Persephone to her original position, though now her bound arms were digging into her spine. She shifted, trying to draw away from the pressure of Hades' knee, until the top of her head bumped against the bed frame.

Hades lowered herself over Persephone. She bent her head, and her lips closed around one of Persephone's nipples. The novel sensation sent a jolt through her, and she heard herself gasp. Hades' mouth was warm and soft and unexpectedly gentle. She lathed her tongue around the hard peak, then released it and blew cool air over it. She repeated her attentions on its twin, providing such distraction that Persephone did not realize that Hades' hand had crept down to her sex until it was too late.

"No," she said as Hades thrust her fingers inside, taking her maidenhead. Persephone screamed and then froze, tears in her eyes, too terrified to move for fear of doing herself more damage. The stretch of Hades inside her was a new and entirely unwelcome sensation, one that she could not simply wish away.

Hades moved her fingers, drawing out and then back in.

Persephone had never known such distress, not even when she had tripped and tumbled to the bottom of a ravine around the cliffs of Mykenos. She whimpered, biting her lip so hard she tasted ichor.

"Shh, dear one." Hades' thumb rubbed distracting little circles at the apex of Persephone's sex, though they were not quite distracting enough to cancel out the pain.

Persephone lay with her cheek resting on the pillow, which was quite damp with her tears. But goddesses healed quickly, and she was no exception. With the next thrust, the pain was already easing as her tortured flesh healed itself, though it did not restore her maidenhead.

Hades seemed aware of this, as she increased her pace, settling into a comfortable rhythm. In the dark, Persephone could just make out the vague outline of her face and the reflective gleam of her eyes.

Persephone did not think she could peak again so soon, not like this, but Hades showed no signs of stopping. The constant friction turned the vague ache into an unpleasant burn. Persephone whimpered, trying to angle her hips in a way that would ease the ache.

With her free hand, Hades brushed her fingertips over Persephone's cheek. She leaned in and briefly grazed Persephone's lower lip with her teeth, drawing it into her mouth before releasing it. "Do not cry, dear one," she said, her voice a throaty whisper. "Your body was made by the gods to receive pleasure."

That was true of even the lowest slave, but it didn't make pleasurable the touch of the whip. Still, Persephone could not deny that she felt... something.

Hades withdrew suddenly, leaving an empty void that

yearned to be filled. She rolled Persephone onto her side and slipped behind her, one arm snaking around Persephone's waist and holding her tightly as the fingers of her other hand resumed their duty, three fingers thrusting inside and her thumb stroking her on the outside.

The press of Hades' naked body against her own made her skin crawl. It was disturbing how closely they fit together, as though she'd been destined for this marriage bed. To peak again would be a betrayal by her own body, as though it were tacitly accepting Hades' sovereignty. She couldn't give her the satisfaction.

"No. I'm sore," she said, kicking her heels against Hades' shins. "You have to stop."

Hades pressed her lips against Persephone's ear. "Just for that, I shall continue after you finish."

Persephone turned her head and blindly lunged. She caught Hades' earlobe with her teeth and bit down, then recoiled in shock when ichor spilled into her mouth.

Hades only laughed and rolled Persephone onto her back once more. "Is that enough, or should I muzzle you?"

"Go to—" Persephone paused. All the usual curses didn't quite work in the underworld.

"Oh, my dear one. I have something for you."

Hades withdrew from the bed, leaving her aching and hollow. She returned, not with a muzzle, as Persephone had feared, but with something far more sinister.

In the dark, she did not know the shape of it until its head bumped into the inside of her thigh as Hades settled back down on the bed. She shrieked in horror, trying to press her knees together, but Hades roughly spread them, drawing them up and apart.

"Shh. The servants might think I have turned murderous and burst in with the hopes of rescuing you."

"That's not funny!" Persephone said. Her voice broke into a strangled whimper as Hades entered her again, not with her fingers this time, but with a leather phallus that she'd belted on like a loincloth. The stretch was worse than before, as her recently virginal body struggled to accommodate such girth.

"Good girl," Hades murmured. She ran her hands over Persephone's breasts and stomach, feeling through her palms every time Persephone flinched at a particularly violent thrust.

This wasn't right, not even for a degenerate. Women were only meant to use these when their husbands were at war, or during the Dionysia. Any other usage was... decadent.

She had no idea how Hades could derive pleasure from such an act, but it was clear that she was pleased, nonetheless. She spoke softly, with filthy words of encouragement that Persephone had never heard, not even at the bustling ports of Attica.

Against the onslaught of all this sensation, her body was helpless to resist. She tried to stifle her cries as she peaked, pressing her face into the pillow, but it seemed a hopeless endeavor.

Hades' hands wandered possessively over her hips as Persephone shuddered beneath her. She thrust a few more times, lazily, as Persephone shivered in the aftermath, but then mercifully pulled out. She loosened a buckle and discarded the toy, then crawled behind Persephone and unwrapped the bindings pinning her arms. She pressed her naked body against Persephone's back and wrapped an arm around her, beneath Persephone's breasts.

Persephone hiccupped and bile filled her throat. She swallowed it down before it could overwhelm her. Her heartbeat was still too rapid, her breath coming in wet sobs. She lay on her side with her knees clamped shut and her thighs slick but cooling unpleasantly, longing for the cocooning embrace of Gaia's earth.

"Hush, my little jewel," Hades said. "All is well."

All was certainly not well, but she didn't feel like arguing. She pushed back at Hades, trying to disentangle herself.

"Are you cold?" Hades found the sheet and swept it over them both.

Persephone wasn't cold, but she wrapped the sheet around herself to form a barrier against Hades' skin. She reached above and pressed her palm flat against the carved scrolls of the bed head, imagining the dark whorls of olive wood shifting beneath her fingers. Surely now...

Hades clucked her tongue and gently took Persephone's hand, replacing it by her side on top of the sheet. "Now, now. You are still in my company, after all."

Persephone didn't know how she was to sleep without sinking down into the dark spaces where bulbs went to winter, but she tried nonetheless, knowing that any kind of sedation would be better than having to sleep with Hades and be aware of it at the same time. She buried her cheek into the pillow, trying to block out all outside noise, and concentrated on the sound of her heartbeat.

"Have you forgotten something, little one?"

Persephone froze, rigid with terror. What was it now? What could Hades possibly do to her, after all that she'd taken?

Hades kissed the back of her neck. "Good night, sweet Persephone."

"Good night," Persephone croaked, her voice hoarse.

Hades seemed satisfied enough with that, although she continued to lie too close, one arm draped across Persephone's hips. Persephone tried to ignore it. Even though she wanted to, she never let her hands wander back to the headboard to find the dreaming earth, and eventually, she drifted to sleep of her own accord, though it was not as restful as she'd imagined.

10

NOT DREAMING

In the middle of the night, Persephone woke to find herself feverish and shivering, with the covers fallen off and one of Hades' legs lying akimbo over her own. Her head pounded and her throat was dry. She carefully slipped out from under Hades and crept out of bed. At some point Hades must have opened the shutters once more, for cool air streamed into the room along with the gray evening light. Persephone looked back and saw Hades sleeping with one arm over her face. She had re-dressed in a man's tunic, so short it only came to the tops of her thighs. Her legs were lean and powerful, her toes delicately pointed like a dancer's in sleep.

Persephone shuddered and went to the side table. She poured herself a watered chalice of wine and drank it quickly, washing away the fibrous taste in her mouth.

Her thighs were unpleasantly sticky. She glanced down at herself, seeing dark flecks on her skin. Her head pounded as she stumbled to the washstand at the other end of the room. She longed for a bath, but there was no way of getting to the bathhouse without running into a servant, and she had no desire to speak to anyone this night.

Persephone filled the wash basin from its matching jug, took a cloth and began to wash herself. She wet the cloth and squeezed it over her forehead, relishing the cool trickles running down her face, though she was careful not to open her mouth, as the wash water hadn't been brought from the surface. She ran the cloth over her arms and then across her body, scrubbing away the sticky residue and the ichor on her thighs until her skin was raw and irritated.

She was wringing out the washcloth and laying it to dry when she became aware she was no longer alone. She froze as Hades came up behind her and wrapped her arms around her waist.

"I thought Hypnos had blessed me, but then I saw I was not dreaming," Hades said, burying her face in Persephone's hair.

Persephone remained as still and straight as a column. "I thought you were asleep."

Hades kissed a line from her elbow to her neck. "How could I sleep when my bride has need of me?" She took the washcloth from Persephone's nerveless fingers and began to trace over each line of her body, from her wrists to her neck, across her back, then turning Persephone to face her so that she could wash her torso, kissing each nipple as she bathed her breasts.

Persephone grabbed the washcloth from her and tossed it aside. "Thank you. I have already washed," she said, willing her voice not to tremble.

"Really? I think you may have missed a spot," Hades said, reaching between Persephone's legs.

She slapped at Hades' wrist, pressing her thighs together, her face flushed with heat.

Hades laughed and brought her fingers to her lips. Her eyes glittered with delight as she licked Persephone's arousal from her hand.

Could there be anything more humiliating? Persephone longed to disappear into the earth, to scour the events of this night from her memory. "Let me go," she said, flinching as Hades leaned against her, one hand placed on the small of Persephone's back, holding her as she kissed the pulse point in her neck.

"Never," Hades whispered.

Persephone placed both palms on Hades' chest and pushed as hard as she could manage. She had wielded scythes and cut grain with those hands, shoveled earth and built levees. She had always thought of them as strong, hard-working hands.

But Hades only laughed, immovable, plucking them from her chest and kissing each palm in turn.

Persephone tore one hand free and grabbed the pitcher of water, swinging at Hades' head. Hades ducked, and the pitcher went sailing, landing somewhere in the room with a crash.

"Are you trying to seduce me?" Hades asked.

"You're disgusting."

Hades kicked Persephone's knees apart, then her fingers were inside her, sliding in without any resistance. "You might say so, but your body tells me otherwise."

"Don't. Don't! I'm still sore," Persephone said, shuddering when Hades flicked her thumb across her clit.

"Are you sure?" Hades asked, a third finger joining the first two already inside.

"Yes. Yes!" Persephone whimpered, tears stinging her eyes. "I'll do anything else."

"Anything," Hades echoed, going still. Her pupils were enormous in the low light. "That is no way to make a bargain."

Persephone almost cried with relief when Hades withdrew, leaving her aching but strangely empty.

"On your knees," Hades said, gently pushing down on her shoulders.

Persephone obeyed, welcoming the chill of the floor over the heat of Hades' touch. She pressed her knees together, lip curling in revulsion at the dampness between her thighs.

Hades touched her hair. "Persephone. Look at me."

Persephone raised her eyes. Hades' tunic barely covered what it needed to cover. Her face beyond that was a bit of a blur in the darkness, aside from the way the light caught her eyes.

"Have you ever kissed a woman?" Hades asked. "Intimately?"

It took Persephone a moment to understand. She shook her head.

"Then let me explain." Hades raised her tunic, exposing the curve of her mons. It was hidden by a frosting of tight curls, as black as the hair on her crown.

With a hand on the back of Persephone's head, Hades guided her forward. She smelled of musk and oiled leather, salt and freshly tilled soil. Hesitantly, Persephone pressed a kiss upon Hades' sex and was rewarded with a shudder.

Hades told her what she wanted. Persephone listened in silence, then angled her head, using her tongue to part Hades' labia. Within her folds was a valley of wetness; Persephone obediently lapped it up, then almost jumped when Hades' fist tightened in her hair.

"Keep going."

She quickly learned how to move her tongue in a way that made Hades moan. She glanced up, seeing Hades' eyes half-lidded, her breathing uneven.

Hades continued to direct her in clipped, one-word statements: slower, faster, harder. She obeyed as best as she could, wincing as Hades pulled at her hair, pressing her face forward so much it was hard to breathe. She clung to Hades' thighs to keep her balance, feeling their rigid muscles beneath her fingertips.

She didn't know how long she stayed on her knees, toes grown numb and tongue aching, before Hades froze up for a moment, her fist dragging so tightly on Persephone's hair that tears leaked from her eyes. Hades trembled against her mouth as she licked the last few spent shudders out of her.

It was a blessed relief when Hades let go of her hair. Hades leaned back against the wall, breathing hard, her eyes closed. Her tunic dropped down, covering her once more. Perhaps it was Persephone's imagination, but there seemed to be a slight tremor in Hades' hands.

It was oddly gratifying to know that, unschooled though she was, she could have this effect upon the Lady of the Damned. Persephone wanted to tell herself that she had done as she was told, nothing more, but then why did she feel conflicted about seeing Hades so vulnerable?

"Come here," Hades said.

Persephone stood, and Hades kissed her, long and deep and hard.

After that, they tumbled back into bed, like before. Hades

wrapped her arms around her waist, holding her tight, and Persephone tried to ignore the ache between her legs that begged to be soothed by another's touch.

She didn't want this. She couldn't want this.

She pressed her knees together and tried to sleep.

11

TARTARUS

Persephone woke to find the room bathed in gray morning light. Hades was already awake, donning the last pieces of her jewelry as she stood before a plate of polished bronze.

Persephone closed her eyes, feigning sleep. She tensed as she felt Hades' presence hovering over her, but Hades merely placed a kiss on her forehead and tucked a stray curl of hair behind her ear.

The door opened and closed, but she waited a few more moments before opening her eyes.

She was alone for the first time since their consummation. She tossed back the covers and ran across the room, grabbing the dressing table and dragging it over to bar the door. It would not stop a determined person from entering, but it would buy her some time.

The smashed pottery from the night before had been removed, and a new jug stood in its place. Persephone washed herself again before dressing in a pale green chiton with crocuses embroidered around the hem. She looked at herself in the mirror and touched the dark bruise on her neck, her lip curling in distaste. All her other bruises had healed, but that one remained stubbornly defiant.

The legs of the dressing table squeaked and Persephone jumped. The door swung ajar, hitting the edge of the table.

"Good morning," Xenia said, peeping through the crack. "May I come in? I brought breakfast."

"Is it just you?"

"Yes, mistress."

Persephone hesitated for a moment, but then her stomach rumbled. She moved the table.

Xenia brought in a tray of food and set it down near the window. Persephone touched each item in turn, determining their safety before eating.

She saved the seeds from a cut tomato, then opened the window and scattered them outside. The ghost of a raven watched her from the branches of an elm.

Persephone closed her eyes and stretched her hand through the window, hovering over the seeds. She felt them moving, splitting, but no more.

"Stupid," she muttered, her hand clenching into a fist. The raven squawked and flew away.

Xenia cleared her throat. She'd been so quiet Persephone had thought she'd left.

Persephone pulled herself back from the window and wiped the tomato juice from her fingers with a cloth. "What is it?"

"I have your directives for the day, mistress."

Directives. As in... chores? "Has the underworld never heard of a honeymoon?" Persephone asked, her eyes narrowed.

Not that she ought to be surprised. It was a farce of a marriage; how could she expect the day after to be anything more?

Xenia fumbled uncomfortably with her braid. "Queen Hades simply wants you to become more familiar with your new subjects and to receive their wedding gifts—"

"If Hades wants me to do something, she can tell me herself," Persephone said. She stood up so quickly that her seat toppled over. "And no one here is my subject, for this is not my home."

Xenia winced, stepping aside in a hurry as Persephone flounced past her. "Mistress... where are you going?"

"For a walk," Persephone said.

As she strode toward the gates, groups of servants stopped whatever work they were doing to greet her. She had grown so sick of hearing her own name by the time she reached the outer courtyard, she would've been glad not to hear it for another century.

She passed the gleaming walls of obsidian, seeing her face reflected in the stone, then noticed something else besides her reflection.

Xenia trailed behind her with another two serving girls she had managed to pick up along the way. Part of Persephone admired her tenacity.

"I said I'm going for a walk. I don't need an escort," she snapped.

"Yes, mistress," Xenia said, eyes demurely downcast, but still she did not leave.

"Oh, by Zeus!" Persephone threw her hands up in the air. "I do not need an escort. Surely no ills could befall me, for are these not all Hades' lands?"

Xenia and the other servants glanced at each other. "We've been ordered—"

"I don't care what you've been ordered! I am ordering you to leave me alone!"

"Begging your pardon, but you do not have that authority," Xenia said.

The woman had courage, she would grant her that. "Fine." Persephone stalked away, heading to the stables. Inside, she took down her own tack and picked out one of the mares, a dappled gray. There was one place in the underworld where Hades' mortal servants were unlikely to tread.

"Keep up, if you can," she said to Xenia and her unrelenting helpers, then mounted, sitting astride. She nudged her mare forward without looking back and soon urged her into a canter, then a gallop. She bent down low over her mane, reveling in the wind rushing past her face. They crossed the lowlands of the Plain of Judgment together, not pausing even when the dead called out her name. They'd find no mercy from her this day.

When the lowlands became desolate and barren, her mare slowed, as though reluctant to venture further. Persephone had to nudge her into continuing, each step more hesitant than the last.

Persephone felt it, too—the sense of impending dread. She passed through a valley, rocky cliffs looming tall around her. She glanced from side to side, noticing how even the hardiest of weeds refused to grow here.

Xenia drew up beside her, mounted on a soot-colored gelding. "We should not be here," she said, her kind face creased with worry. "Please, let's turn back."

"I want to see."

The air seemed even cooler here, making her shiver. Her mare whinnied piteously and would not be calmed. Persephone was forced to dismount and proceed on foot, followed by Xenia. The other servants appeared not to have made it this far.

Waiting for them at the end of the valley was a monstrous giant with dozens of arms jutting out from all over his torso. From his shoulders sprang a multitude of heads. Each one of his eyes watched Persephone and Xenia as they drew closer.

"Good day to you," Persephone said, craning her neck to look up at the giant's many faces. "What are you called?"

"Cottus," the giant said, a few of his mouths moving at the same time, so that it sounded like a chorus. "You are not dead. You should not be here." He looked at Xenia. "Your judgment does not lie here. You should not be here."

"I hold Hades' favor," Persephone said, hooking a finger under her necklace and holding it away from her skin so that Cottus could see it more clearly. "I wish to pass."

Cottus leaned down and squinted at her. He made a grumbling noise like rocks being crushed. "You may pass," he said, clearly unhappy. "Not you," he added when Xenia tried to follow.

"Please, don't be long," Xenia said with tears in her eyes. "It isn't safe."

Persephone's gaze softened. "Don't worry. Nothing can hurt me here."

Xenia looked stricken, but she bit her lip and said nothing.

Persephone turned from her and walked past Cottus. Behind him was a large wooden platform, attached to a trolley system with a winch. Below the platform was darkness as far as the eye could see, a color so deep it seemed to suck the light into it.

Truth be told, Persephone had no desire to see the heart of Tartarus for herself, but now that she was here, pride demanded that she not falter.

"Do you have a torch?" Persephone asked.

"There are lights beneath," Cottus said. He pulled on a cord, and far below, she heard the faint ring of a bell.

Persephone stepped onto the platform and tried to smile reassuringly at Xenia. The poor woman was as pale as new milk.

"Hold on," Cottus said.

There was nothing to hold on to. Persephone opened her mouth to ask what he meant, but then Cottus unhooked a rope, and the platform went plunging into the darkness.

Persephone screamed for the first few feet and then had to conserve the rest of her breath as the platform hurtled downwards at a breakneck pace. She had made a terrible mistake, but there was no way to turn back and no one to hear her cry for help. The air was cold and brutal, blowing the hem of her chiton back into her face. At least there was also no one to see her disheveled state.

When she thought she could bear it no longer, lights appeared from below, and the platform ground to a shuddering halt. Persephone was amazed to find herself still in one piece, although the coiffure that Xenia had created was completely ruined.

Muffled noises filled the air—screams and pained groans, crying, the same pleas and prayers repeated over and over again.

Xenia was right. She should not have come.

Persephone stepped off the platform. She was in a huge cavern, carved laboriously from the bedrock of the earth. Lit torches glowed orange in the dark, illuminating paths that extended out from the cavern. Below her hung a multitude of wooden walkways, providing transit over a deep abyss.

On her level, she saw another monstrous giant speaking to a number of men wearing Hades' colors. She took one glance at them, then turned and walked the opposite way, moving quickly, as if she knew what she was doing. Awful as this place was, she had no intention of being brought back before Hades quite so soon.

She found herself naturally taking walkways that led her further downwards, until it felt like forever since she'd last walked on level ground. As she walked, she passed cells carved into the rock and sealed by bars of iron; cells sealed by spider silk, by glyphs and incantations carved into the walls and floors.

Hands reached out to her from the dark.

"Mistress... save us..."

"Mistress, I've been here some hundred years. I've never harmed a living soul. Please—"

Persephone hurried past them all, not daring to look too closely at any wretched soul. Her stomach was turning from the noise and the smell of cold iron and dried ichor. She didn't know where she was going, only that she was in too deep to admit her mistake and turn back.

"Daughter."

The word was whispered, so faint she scarcely heard it. She froze, rigid with terror, then forced herself to relax. Zeus was not here, would never deign to bring himself here, and Demeter's voice had never been that deep.

Nevertheless, she took a torch from a wall sconce and walked toward the voice. She found herself in front of a cell set apart from the others in its own row. Inside, there was a body chained to a rack, so still and gaunt that at first she doubted whether it had the strength for speech at all. Each limb was overly long and ill-proportioned, as though he was a Titan made small by sorcery.

The creature opened his eyes—eye. One of them was in the process of growing back, covered in ichor and slowly reforming itself from the inside out as she watched, unable to look away.

"Daughter," he said, his voice a dry croak, so disused she could scarcely make out the word. "No. Granddaughter? Come closer, that I might see you."

Slowly, as if drawn by invisible thread, Persephone approached the cell.

Its inhabitant ran his tongue over cracked and ichor-stained lips, staring at her like a starving man might stare at a feast. He lunged forward, straining so hard on his chains that there was a cracking noise, perhaps one of his bones snapping.

Persephone screamed and dropped the torch. She quickly snatched it up again before it could roll through the bars into the cell, afraid of what any disruption to the cell boundary might do to the fragile powers that kept this place functioning.

The creature—Titan—laughed, his bony chest shuddering with each exhalation. He was clad only in a loincloth, dirt, and ichor, though his dark beard reached almost to his waist.

"Which one are you then, girl? And speak up. My ears aren't what they used to be."

"I'm called Persephone," she said, grateful that her voice did not quaver. "Born of Demeter and Zeus."

"Zeus... I should've torn his head off before swallowing. Crunched his bones to dust."

Persephone shuddered. This thing, this creature, was her grandfather, Kronos?

"Ah... don't look at me like that, girl. I was once a handsome brute, revered among men. Tell me, what do they say of me, up in the overworld?"

She could not help but pity him, tortured and reduced as he was. "They say you ruled over a golden age of mankind."

He grinned with a mouth full of broken teeth. "Golden... yes. When the air was sweet and the world new and honey dripped from the trees." He moved his jaw, as though recalling the taste of it. "Do you have any?"

"Honey?" Persephone's brow creased. "No. I'm sorry."

"Wine? Water?" When she shook her head, Kronos scowled. "What good are you, then? You reek of Hades. All the attar in Aigyptos could not mask her stench on you. Mayhap you could tell her to make my stay here a little more comfortable. It's been long enough."

Persephone fought the urge to sniff at her garments, though her cheeks flushed. "I'll ask."

"Ask!" Kronos screeched, loud enough that Persephone winced. "Ask, she says, like a lapdog and not the proud scion of Kronos that she ought to be." He stared down at her, his eyes half-lidded. "Did Zeus tire of you and throw you like a bone to poor venereous Hades?"

Persephone stiffened. "He would never! Zeus had nothing to do with this," she said, though she wondered if that were the case. Hades had been adamant she'd secured his approval, at least.

Kronos shifted a little on the rack, his chains clanking. "But you are a prisoner here. The same as me," he said, his mouth opening in a wide grin.

Persephone grasped the bars of his cell and pressed her face against them. "We are nothing alike," she said. "When Hades grows weary of me, I'll be free."

Kronos stared at her, the whites of his eyes large and luminous in the dim light. Then he broke into a raucous, braying laugh, so loud Persephone took a step back and looked nervously to check for anyone approaching.

"Stop that," she said. "You'll summon a guardsperson."

Kronos's laughter died down, though a tear of mirth remained in the corner of his eye. "Oh, girl. How young you must be. How fortunate, to be so naive. You wear Hades' favor and yet you know her so little?"

Persephone's hand went briefly to her neck. "I'd had no chance to know her. I wasn't exactly courted."

"In my days, the chase was the courtship. You saw a girl you wanted, you kept her in your bed until she was round with child and no longer had the strength to flee."

That practice was alive and well. It was a hard tradition to break, seeing as the gods were unwilling to change their ways. But she'd thought—hoped—that Hades could be different.

It was stupid. She ought to have run whilst she still could.

"Nothing has changed," Persephone said.

"Sometimes the old ways are the best ways."

"That's not true!"

"Oh?" Kronos leered at her. "And who would you be without Hades' favor, Demeter's daughter? Nobody. All you have to offer is what lies between your legs."

Persephone bit her tongue, grateful for the bars and for the distance between them. She would not ever have dreamed of striking an unarmed old man before today.

"Hades will never let you go, not after what she did to have you. But don't despair, girl. If it's freedom you want, then you shall have it," Kronos said.

"What did she do?" Persephone asked.

"Help me and I'll tell you."

"How?"

Kronos dropped his voice to a conspiratorial whisper. "Free me and free yourself. We shall crush this prison and its jailers along with it."

Persephone paused as though considering his offer. He really thought she was so selfish, so naive as to betray all of Olympus just to fulfill her wish? Nothing justified treason, not even her freedom. "I must go," she said. "Goodbye, Grandfather."

He strained to raise himself partially off the rack. "Foolish girl! Without me, you are nothing! Hades will never let you leave. Never!"

Persephone turned her back on him and kept moving, her heart racing as she ascended via the long walkways. It wasn't true. Hades would tire of her, in time. Poseidon spent his seed as though it were endless as sea foam; Zeus had bastards in all the lands surrounding the Aegean. A century from now, maybe two, Hades would find some nymph or other to divert her attention.

Persephone wasn't sure she could wait that long.

12

INTERROGATION

The ascension from Kronos's cell level was hard on Persephone's muscles, and her thighs ached by the time she'd reached the platform. The giant guarding this area was not amused to see her.

"You are not authorized to access the depths of Tartarus," he said whilst tapping the fingers of half his hands in irritation. "Hades will be displeased."

"I won't tell her if you won't."

He sniffed but nodded to the guards to prepare the platform.

Persephone stepped upon it, holding her hands by her sides to flatten down her chiton.

The ascent was much slower and gave her time to think. It was not long before she lost sight of the guards and the giant below, and even the glow of their lights faded from view, leaving her in darkness.

She made a promise to herself never to commit any crimes so heinous as to merit punishment in this place. She would never be condemned to live forever in the darkness, tortured eternally, slowly going mad, with only her own thoughts for company.

Xenia almost cried to see her emerge safely at the top of the pit, which made Persephone glance aside, unable to look her in the eye. They found their horses, which had obediently stayed nearby, and set off together toward the palace.

"Did you find what you were seeking?" Xenia asked.

Tartarus held only questions, not answers. "I'm glad I went," Persephone said. It was not a lie—seeing Kronos and the other prisoners had only strengthened her resolve to escape this place.

When they arrived at the palace, a flock of serving girls descended upon Persephone and prevented her from making her way back to her room. The girls washed her feet and brushed her hair, tying it in a loose braid, and served her food, which she ate alone. When she was done, Xenia guided her not to her own room but to Hades' chambers, which adjoined hers.

Hades' rooms were at least twice as large as her own. They had an austere air about them, with the walls carved from black marble, softened with tapestries in abstract geometric patterns. There was a partition for dressing, with clothing stacked in neat shelves, and the most enormous collection of shoes, boots, and sandals that Persephone had ever seen. She supposed something had to break the monotony of Hades' clothing—most pieces being various shades of black, save for the white chiton she'd worn on their wedding day and a few others in deep, jewel-toned hues.

A bathing chamber adjoined the room, but there was no vessel for a servant to fill with water. Instead, Persephone turned a lever, and water flowed freely from a faucet, disappearing down a grate placed below. There was even a separate tap for heated water, which she used to wash the chill from her hands.

"We gained much when Daedalus joined the ranks of the dead. I had thought to expand the plumbing more extensively, but alas, he finds such projects rather menial."

Persephone jumped, clutching a hand to her chest as she turned around. "I didn't hear you come in."

Hades wore black today, the color almost as dark as the center of Tartarus. Perhaps Daedalus had also crafted the dye, for Persephone had seen nothing of its ilk on the surface.

"Turn that off, please."

Persephone's cheeks flushed as she turned the lever once more so that the water stopped flowing. "Mother could use something like this for her crops."

"Mm hmm." Hades sat down at her writing desk and moved a stack of scrolls to one side. She had turned the chair so that she could sit and face Persephone at the same time. "Come here and tell me about your day."

Persephone walked back into the main sleeping area. Her palms were sweating, and she wiped them over her hips. She had done nothing wrong. Why did Hades have such an effect on her?

It was awkward standing when Hades was not, so she sat on the end of the bed, for there were no other chairs to be had. "I visited Tartarus today."

"I see. Did Xenia not instruct you about your duties as my bride, to receive your wedding gifts?"

She tried to read Hades' face. She seemed calm, but her gaze had such an intensity that Persephone felt the need to look away. "She may have mentioned something."

"And yet it was not done. What did you do within Tartarus?"

Persephone stood. She walked to the window and opened the shutters, closing her eyes as the cool night air wafted over her. "You already know, don't you? Why are you asking me this?"

"I wish to hear you tell me. Please do not walk away when I am talking to you."

"Is this an interrogation? I've committed no crime."

"Come back here and sit down, Persephone."

"No."

"Do not force my hand."

Oh! The gall of her! "You do as you please, and you don't care what I think!" Persephone said, raising her voice at last. "You took me here against my will—you took my maidenhead— you took my freedom! Don't pretend I have a say in this!"

There were not enough loose objects nearby for Persephone's needs, but she made do, grabbing an ornamental vase and throwing it at Hades, followed by a small hand mirror, then a bust of what looked to be Athena but might have been one of her acolytes, and finally, when she ran out of hard implements, every single cushion on the bed.

Tears blinded her eyes, but she was not surprised when Hades strode up to her and grabbed her wrists, crushing them in her grasp.

"If you wish to behave like a child, then I will treat you as one," Hades said, her voice low and soft and dangerous. She advanced, forcing Persephone to retreat until the wall was at her back. Hades' eyes softened, and she dropped one of Persephone's hands, reaching up to trace the bruise on her neck.

Persephone turned her head and bit Hades' thumb.

"Oh!" Hades said, recoiling.

And then Hades pushed her, and she landed on the bed, the frame squeaking with the impact.

Hades climbed in after her and grabbed her by her braid. She positioned Persephone over her knee and pulled Persephone's chiton up to her waist, exposing her legs.

"Let go of me. You're hurting!" Persephone said, reaching behind herself to swat at Hades' hands.

Hades tightened her grip on the braid and used her other hand to pull down Persephone's perizoma, down and off over her legs. She ran her hand over Persephone's bare bottom and caressed her thighs.

"Don't touch me," Persephone said.

Hades adjusted her grip on Persephone's hair, rolling her over for a moment so that she could look at her face. "You should know that I am not angry with you. And while I am disappointed in your choice of actions, this is not a punishment. I am only doing this because you need it."

Persephone's eyes burned with tears. "What do I—"

Hades rolled her over again so that she was lying face down over her lap. Hades released her braid and adjusted her chiton once more. The air was cold on Persephone's bare skin, and she shivered.

She wasn't prepared for the first slap, and so she yelped, arching her back. "How dare you!"

"This is for your own good." Hades' hand descended again onto her bare ass, harder this time. Persephone screamed, choking on her tears.

"Let me go!"

Hades continued to smack her as she talked, settling into a steady rhythm. "You should realize by now that I have no intention of doing any such thing. The sooner you accept that, the sooner you can begin to enjoy your new life."

Persephone couldn't remember the last time she'd been beaten. When she'd been a young child, perhaps, centuries ago.

"Stop, please. You're hurting me."

At first, each slap left an initial sting which soon faded away. But over time, as Hades continued to hit the same areas, Persephone's flesh grew warm, and it felt like each strike was igniting a fire under her skin.

"There are many beautiful, wondrous things you have yet to discover here. I would not have condemned you to such a life if I had thought it would make you miserable forever. But you will have to find meaning for yourself."

Persephone gave up on pleading. She pressed a fist to her mouth, trying not to scream, her tears dampening the blankets below her head. At some point, Hades repositioned her so that she could start smacking Persephone with her other hand.

Persephone clung to the bed frame, but the olive wood it was made from had been sourced from the underworld and therefore was useless to her. She tried to concentrate on her breathing, but every time Hades created a new burst of pain, it broke her concentration.

"Stop," Persephone said. "Stop. Stop. Stop."

"What did Kronos want from you?" Hades asked. She gave Persephone another bone-jarring smack, then paused.

Persephone rushed to fill the void of silence. "Nothing!" She screamed as Hades hit her again. "Freedom! Of course he wants—he wants to be free."

Hades rolled her over. Persephone whimpered as the movement caused friction between her skin and Hades' chiton.

"What did he offer you?"

"Nothing. Wait!" she said as Hades tensed her hand. "He said—he said he could help me. But I refused him." Her eyes were wide and tear-filled, pleading with Hades to believe her. "I swear, by Athena's virtue."

"What else did he want?"

Persephone ran through the conversation in her mind. "For his conditions to be improved."

Hades scoffed. "When one is a tyrannical despot, one must suffer the consequences."

"He has suffered for many a year."

"More than your lifetime."

"When I close my eyes," Persephone said, "I can still see the pit, the darkness that swallows the light. I can feel the cold. I—"

Hades gathered her in her arms, and Persephone buried her head against Hades' chest, tears running down her cheeks.

"It was too soon for you to see that place. My tasks for you are not randomly constructed; they are designed to introduce you to your new domain in the correct order." Hades took a breath. "Do you not understand how precious you are? How fragile? We may be immortal, but we can still suffer."

Suffer, like Hades was forcing her to suffer?

Hades' heartbeat was steady and even. She wasn't even breathing hard. She wasn't angry, just as she'd said, so why did she have to hurt Persephone so much?

"I want to go home," Persephone said. She shifted, pulling back. Hades wasn't looking at her. She reached out and placed her hand on Hades' cheek, turning Hades to face her. "I want to go home."

Hades covered Persephone's hand with her own and kissed the tips of Persephone's fingers. "You are trying my patience."

Persephone snatched her hand away. Hades pressed her down to the bed and bit at the hollow of her neck, re-marking the bruise that had started to fade.

Persephone made a choked sound at the back of her throat.

Hades abruptly released her and left the bed. She closed the shutters, then snapped her fingers. As one, the candles winked out, plunging the room into darkness. The burnt-out scent of wax filled the air.

When Hades returned, every inch of her skin was uncovered. She kissed Persephone's tear-stained face and pressed herself against her, pinning her to the bed.

Persephone could hear her own heartbeat like a pounding drum within her temples. Her breath came quick and short as Hades' hands roamed over her body, raising Persephone's chiton as high as it would go to expose her breasts. It was easier to be with her when she didn't have to look at her face, didn't have to remember who was doing this to her.

Persephone's first thought had been wrong. Hades wasn't completely nude. She was wearing that awful thing again, the degenerate thing Persephone could not bear to name, this time strapped to her thigh instead of being worn like an undergarment. It pressed against Persephone's hip, cold and dead, and she shrieked.

"No need to be frightened," Hades murmured. She shifted so her back was against the bed head and pulled Persephone on top of her, facing her. She reached around and loosened the tie that held Persephone's braid, then ran her fingers through her hair.

In the dark, her hands were warm and gentle, but Persephone couldn't forget how they had felt before—hard and merciless. "I want to go—" Persephone began.

Hades pressed her fingers against Persephone's lips. "No more of that tonight." She reached down between Persephone's legs, making her flinch. "Did you enjoy being over my knee?" Hades asked.

"No!"

"Liar."

Hades grabbed her by the hips, lifted her up and placed her back down, impaling Persephone on her phallus.

Persephone whimpered and bit back a curse. She had cried so much already that night, but new tears rolled down her cheeks.

"Shh. You can accept this."

No, she couldn't. She would never stop fighting, never stop seeking her freedom.

"Shh, Persephone. Do not cry, dearest." Hades kissed her cheeks, twice on each side. Her fingers traced down Persephone's spine, her hand resting on the small of Persephone's back to keep her in place.

This was still new, this sensation of being split open, of her inner walls stretching to accommodate a foreign invader. Persephone froze, her mouth open in a silent cry, and then Hades moved, and the phallus moved with her.

Persephone gasped, placing her palms on Hades' chest to brace herself. She clamped her eyes shut, pressing her lips together. She wouldn't make another sound. She wouldn't give her the satisfaction—

"Move with me," Hades said, her voice husky with desire.

The air seemed to leave the room, for she couldn't breathe, much less move. There had to be a magic key, some secret incantation she could say to unlock Hades' heart and make her stop, but whatever it was, Persephone lacked the wiles to know.

Hades flexed her thigh impatiently, and Persephone whimpered.

The sooner she did as Hades requested, the sooner this would be over.

Locking her arms around Hades' neck for balance, she moved, only a little at first, rising up from her knees and settling back down again. She heard Hades sigh in the darkness.

"Here," Hades said. She took one of Persephone's hands and guided it in between her splayed legs.

Persephone knew the mechanics of how this worked by now, but she had never touched anyone like this before. Hades was wet and warm; so very warm. And when Persephone's fingertips slid over her clit, Hades groaned, the sound filled with need.

"Is this—should I—"

"Yes," Hades said and shifted, grinding against Persephone's hand.

Persephone pressed two fingers inside of Hades, surprised by how it felt. She was so warm and tight and yet so open for her. When she moved her fingers, rubbing her thumb over Hades' clit, she heard the hitch in Hades' breath, felt her muscles squeezing. She wanted to see her face. What did she look like when Persephone was inside her?

Hades kissed her neck and moved her thigh, one hand pulling on Persephone's hip to guide her movement. "Don't stop." She grabbed Persephone's free hand, entangling it with her own, and kissed her on the mouth. She tasted of grapes from Thera. The room smelled of sex. Hades no longer had to encourage Persephone to ride her; Persephone's body had settled into its own rhythm, without her being quite conscious of it happening.

"This is—" Persephone gasped. "I—"

"Don't you dare stop."

She wasn't sure who came first in the end. Hades bore down on Persephone's fingers, her thighs crushing Persephone's hand in place. Hades kissed her, again and again, as Persephone rode out the last dregs of her climax.

The silence afterward seemed deafening. Persephone's heart fluttered in her chest, and she was breathing hard, a bead of sweat rolling down her spine. By Artemis, she needed this thing out of her. She climbed off of Hades, rolling to the other side of the bed in a daze.

She felt Hades stand up and heard the sound of running water. Hades returned with a damp washcloth. She wiped Persephone's hand and then between her legs.

"I can do that myself," Persephone said.

"Really? You seem exanimate right now."

She supposed it was true. All the fight had left her, at least for the moment.

Hades climbed into bed and kissed the back of her neck. Her arms encircled Persephone's waist, pulling her close.

"I wish you wouldn't hold me so tightly."

"Is that so?" Hades didn't loosen her grip. Her fingers traced circles on Persephone's skin.

"Hades?"

"Yes?"

"You didn't do anything to Xenia, did you? She counseled me not to go, but I ignored her."

Hades' hand stilled. "Do you care for her?"

Was that a note of jealousy? "I've only just met her. But she has been kind to me."

"As you say; I have no quarrel with her."

Persephone closed her eyes in relief. Her limbs felt heavy, but her head felt effervescent, her thoughts impossible to hold. Was this what marriage meant? She had been wed for just two nights, but already she felt like she was becoming someone else when Hades was around her.

"Good night, my lady wife," Hades said.

"Good night, m—Hades."

She heard Hades' breathing deepen and slow. She lay awake for some time, her thoughts churning in endless circles.

13

LESSONS

I n the days that followed, Persephone held a salon to properly receive her wedding gifts. Though she lacked the exuberance expected of a new bride, she took pains to banish the sullen creature she'd been at her wedding feast. She had no wish to offend potential allies any more than she already had. Hades had made it clear she answered to no one; Persephone would not hold Hades' subjects accountable for their queen's behavior.

Persephone grew, if not fond, then at least accustomed to Hades' attentions, though she told herself she misliked them.

Everything about Hades was a contradiction: her cold gaze and warm hands; her hardened heart and tender words. So perhaps it was no surprise that Persephone learned to both dread and hunger for the night, when Hades' touch would set her body aflame.

Mornings were easier, as she usually woke alone with the other side of the bed grown cold. But a few weeks into her captivity, she was startled to find Hades sitting at her writing desk, dressed with her hair braided and coiffed, scribbling furiously.

Persephone clutched the covers to her chest as she watched the light playing on the muscles in Hades' neck. Before she could lie back down and pretend to be asleep, Hades turned.

"You're awake. Good." Hades tapped the end of her stylus against her lips as she watched Persephone. A stray curl had escaped her braid and lay across her cheek, framing her face. "Did you sleep well?"

Persephone nodded. She shifted uncomfortably under the covers, aware of her nudity.

"I left you a list of things to work through today. There will be time left in the afternoon for you to do as you please, but only on the condition that you have finished your assigned tasks." Hades tossed a small wax-covered tablet to Persephone.

She caught it, careful to hold the edges as not to smear the imprint. She knew that much, at least.

"I know it sounds tedious," Hades said, walking to her dressing area. She flung a chlamys over her shoulders, fastening it at the side. "But you will have to learn this sooner or later, and I would prefer sooner."

Ought she to say something? Persephone felt as though an invisible fist were squeezing her heart. "Hades..."

"What is it, my dove? I am aware the hour is later than ideal. I think I can be forgiven, given the circumstances."

"Hades, I... I can't read."

Hades paused in the motion of adjusting her hair and turned to stare at Persephone. Her expression of shock might have been comical in other circumstances. "Why not?" she asked.

What sort of question was that? "I guess I... just never learned."

"But then how could you help Demeter forecast the harvest and track the planting of each field?"

"I know my sums," Persephone shot back, blushing. Her ignorance was not blasphemous, unlike her lack of filial piety. When was the last time she'd even thought about Demeter? Surely she had to be regretting her harsh words and harsher sentence by now. Had she even noticed that Persephone was missing? Would she be searching for her?

"Be that as it may, your mother has done you a great disservice." Hades glanced at the tablet lying atop the coverlet. "No, this simply will not do." She gnawed at her bottom lip. "I had hoped—never mind. I shall find you a tutor to assess your scholastic development, or lack thereof, and we will progress from there."

It could be an opportune thing, Persephone supposed. A tutor might be easier to elude, as opposed to Xenia, who smothered her, or Hades, who... "I'll do my best."

"I know you will." Hades placed a hand on Persephone's cheek and kissed her. "Now, I really must go."

Once Hades left, Persephone crawled out of bed and used Hades' bathing chamber before dressing herself.

As if on cue, a serving girl knocked on the door, bringing in Persephone's breakfast. After she'd eaten, the same girl helped her dress her hair, adorning it with a curved metal band.

"Where is Xenia?" Persephone asked.

"It's her day off for the month, mistress," the girl said.

Persephone bit her lip to hide a smile. Xenia was gone, and Hades was preoccupied. Perhaps fortune was finally turning in her favor.

"Are you ready to go to the library?" the girl asked. "Your teacher will be waiting."

Hades had found her a tutor so quickly? Some of her mirth evaporated. "Yes, I suppose."

When the girl had said 'library,' Persephone had pictured a room no bigger than a courtyard. But what they called the library could have housed as many as twenty families. Every wall was filled with scroll racks, and more racks stood in straight lines, as far as the eye could see. In between were writing tables, lounges, and seating areas for reading. There was little natural light to be had, the area lit artificially—not by torches or candles but by something that glowed like fireflies caught behind glass. The rooms smelled of papyrus and carbon ink.

"You shelved me beside Straton? That hack! I demand you move my work to somewhere more accessible."

A short, somewhat rotund man was harassing a spotty-faced boy. The boy had several scrolls under his arm and strained to balance his cargo while surreptitiously backing away.

If the boy was to be her tutor, Persephone thought it would be a simple thing to intimidate him into doing her bidding. But she was not to be so fortunate.

The man turned and saw her. He had a thick black beard and deep-set eyes framed by brows so lush they reminded her of the caterpillars she'd find on stinging nettles. "Ah, the lady of the hour," he said, rather sourly. "Sit! I haven't got all day."

The boy fled with his scrolls in hand. Persephone's maid also turned to go, but the man waved her over.

"Wine and food, girl. And hurry! Teaching is thirsty business." The man plopped down in the chair opposite Persephone with a table separating them. "Now, it's been a long time since I've had to teach anyone. Might be a bit rusty." He fished out a wax tablet from a drawer inside the table and scratched at it with his stylus. He showed it to Persephone. "Do you know your alphabet at all then, girl?"

Persephone went still.

The man seemed to recognize his mistake, for he chuckled in a self-deprecating way. "Please, pardon my manners. I mean nothing by it, mistress. I've been down here too long, is all."

"And what should I call you?" Persephone asked.

"You don't recognize me?" She wasn't sure whether he was acting hurt or was genuinely disappointed by her ignorance. "Mayhap you'll know the name. Stephanus, playwright, poet. Three-time winner of the Lenaia."

"Sorry," Persephone said. "I don't go to festivals." Not from lack of wanting; Demeter hadn't allowed it.

"You've never been? Well, if it were up to me, we would start with some theater. There's nothing more restorative than a well-earned laugh. But Queen Hades sets the score, and"—he looked down at his tablet—"she was very prescriptive."

The food and wine arrived. Stephanus talked as he ate, which Persephone found repulsive, but she did not wish to antagonize him by pointing it out. In truth, to find a mortal who wasn't in awe of her was somewhat refreshing. Though she hoped for his sake that he improved his manners if and when he spoke to Hades.

She spent the next several hours working through the alphabet and its associated sounds, dividing the vowels and consonants. She copied letters onto the wax tablet until her hand was sore.

After some time, the food was gone and the wine had run

dry. The servant girl sat quietly in the corner, her head nodding almost to her chest.

"Here," Persephone said, picking up the empty tray of food and the wine jug. "Allow me to find more refreshments." She kept her eyes lowered, not wanting to seem too eager, but Stephanus merely grunted in response, not glancing up from the scroll he was perusing.

She made her way to the closest kitchen, holding the wine jug at her side with the tray balanced against her hip. She was rounding a corner of the corridor when someone grabbed her, covering her mouth with one hand.

"I'm a friend," a man said. "Don't be alarmed."

Persephone's hands shook, but she managed to maintain her grip on the tray and jug. She felt the solid plane of the man's muscles as a warmth against her back. A living man, in the underworld? Oh, Hades would not be pleased.

She blinked slowly, and he released her.

"You're not dead," she said, taking two steps back, clutching the serving tray and the wine jug to her chest.

"My name is Ismaros," the man said. "I've come to rescue you."

"Did my mother send you?"

Ismaros's brow crinkled. "She is sorely missing you."

He must have done well to evade detection thus far, but how long could it last? He was dressed in a servant's garb, though it ill-suited him. Ismaros had the musculature of a blacksmith but the bearing of a king. If anyone looked at him too closely, surely they would suspect something was wrong.

Still, what other choice did she have?

"Did she send you?" Persephone repeated. She glanced

aside to check if anyone was nearby, but the corridors were empty.

"Yes, of course she sent me," Ismaros said, sounding impatient. "Will you meet me at dawn tomorrow? That's when the next wagon is due to the overworld, to retrieve more supplies for your table."

It made sense that they had some way of regularly replenishing their pantry with stores meant only for Persephone. She was even more grateful for Hades' decree that she need not eat food from the underworld.

"I'll be ready," she said. "Where?"

"By the stables. We will journey some way by wagon. It... will not be pleasant."

"I'll survive."

"We'll need a way past Cerberus," he said.

"I've eluded him once before."

"That might be a problem. Whatever you did, the same trick will not work a second time."

Persephone frowned. "I'll think of something."

He nodded. "Until we meet, do nothing to attract suspicion."

What did he think she was, a simpleton? "I could say the same for you. You don't look like a servant."

Ismaros grimaced. "I'll be careful."

They had already spoken for far too long. Persephone continued on her way to the kitchen. Finding it devoid of people, she helped herself to more wine and food before returning to Stephanus.

She would not be taken back to Demeter. Once she reached the surface, she would find a way to dodge this Ismaros and instead seek out her father. Zeus could annul her marriage and grant her the true freedom she desired. And if he wanted something she could not give him in return, then... she would deal with it, later.

She hastened back to the library, where she found Stephanus sound asleep, a scroll held loosely in his lap.

Well, it was past noon already, and Hades did say she would have the afternoon to herself. Just as she was planning to creep away, Stephanus sat up with a start.

"Oh!" he exclaimed. "It's you. Where's the wine?"

She refilled his cup for him. "I believe lessons are over for the day, for it is past lunch," she said.

Stephanus hemmed and hawed at this, rubbing his beard. "Another tablet's worth of lines and you may go."

Persephone groaned, but she sat down and set to work erasing her previous letters with the end of her stylus before rewriting the same material all over again, carving laboriously whilst imagining she was stabbing the old man in the gut with each stroke.

"I'm done," she said, showing her tablet to Stephanus.

He looked at it. "Your slope is off. Let's fix that tomorrow."

"I thought you were teaching me how to read; what does it matter how my slope lies?"

Stephanus took a stylus and rapped her knuckles with it. "Do I lecture you when spring comes three weeks too late? Or question why we are cursed with more suicides in your season than at harvest time? No? Then we will proceed with this in my way."

Persephone cradled her hand to her chest, rubbing her knuckles. Any prior charitable thought she might have held for this man had evaporated. Luckily for his sake, she did not intend there to be a second lesson. "I see. May I go?"

At his curt nod, she stood up and all but ran from the library. It was wonderful to be in the courtyard again, inhaling the fresh air after spending the whole morning indoors.

There wasn't much time left in the day. She needed some way to dissuade Hades from spending the night with her, so that she would be free to leave in the morning. A feigned sickness, perhaps, or...

Hades wouldn't be tricked by a claimed headache, but Persephone had no wish to damage herself in order to seem convincing. She needed something else. Something foolproof. And on top of that, a way to bypass Cerberus.

It came to her as she was walking. She abruptly turned on her heel and headed toward the stables, counting her steps so that she would know them in the dark. Eustachys greeted her at the doorway.

"Good day to you, Lady Persephone."

She looked at him. The man had seen her almost naked. What had mortified her only a few weeks ago seemed rather comical now. He glanced away, blushing. "Would you be needing a chariot, or...?"

She walked around the stable, looking at the horses. "Let's see them."

"Of course."

He led her to a nearby cart house, which stored an array of chariots and wagons both large and small, plus tack. The loft of the cart house seemed to serve as his living quarters, containing a bed roll and a small shelf for personal belongings.

She dithered over chariots. Hades' gold one was nowhere to be seen; she must have taken it for the day. Some of the wagons did not look spacious enough to hide her. What would she do if she could not stow away in the morning? What if

Ismaros was caught and their plan ruined? Would she get another chance?

"Mistress?"

She was overthinking this. No need to make it more complicated than necessary. "I've changed my mind. I'd prefer to go for a ride." She glanced at the storage area for the tack and other cleaning supplies. "And I need some oil."

Eustachys blushed and stammered.

"What?" Persephone snapped, more harshly than she'd intended.

"O—of course."

A few moments later and she was trotting out of the stables on the dappled gray mare that Eustachys had called Nereia. She soon urged Nereia into a canter, then a gallop. They crossed the wide plains of the Elysian Fields together, only slowing when they reached the river Lethe.

The path descended, ending at the foot of the river. The air blew cool and wet, rising as mist from the ground. Persephone dismounted and walked down to the river, slipping off her sandals to feel the damp grass beneath her feet.

Nearby grew clumps of poppies, crimson and swaying in the breeze. She picked one and placed it in her hair, then gathered more in her arms. Nereia snorted but stayed still and patient as Persephone braided flowers into her mane.

She ought to be careful. She remembered what had happened at the junction of the Styx and Acheron. But here she could see no ghostly faces in the river and heard only the gentle babble of the water as it polished its pebbly shallows.

She sat on the grass and dipped in her toes. The mud was cool and soft beneath her heels. Tiny fish darted around her and nibbled at her feet.

She had never thought the underworld to be beautiful, but this corner of it seemed like it might well be. Her reflection stared back at her. She looked calm. She looked almost... happy.

Could she be happy here?

She glanced behind her. Nereia contentedly munched at a patch of herbs. Persephone smiled to see it, and then she yawned, stretching her body like a cat. Her eyes seemed too heavy; she struggled to keep them open.

The vial. She took out the small bottle of olive oil Eustachys had given her, his mind clearly leaping to vulgar things. She poured it out on the grass and went to the river, dipping the vial in the current until it was full. She capped it and tucked it in her cleavage, held in place by the pressure of her strophion. She fluffed the neckline of her chiton over the top, arranging the folds to hide any lumps.

She glanced above her. The light would soon fade; perhaps she ought to have left a message before she'd ventured out. But Hades claimed to know all that transpired in her realm; Persephone was counting on it. Better to have said nothing—let her think this was a spur-of-the-moment decision.

Persephone could not keep herself upright. Her bed of grass was so inviting, her limbs so heavy, that she could not help but close her eyes.

The river Lethe sang to her its lullaby.

Movement jostled Persephone awake. She opened her eyes to find the day had grown dark. She was seated on Alastor with Hades behind her, her arm wrapped around Persephone to keep her upright. Nereia followed in their wake, her mane devoid of poppies.

Hades held a lantern in her other hand, but Alastor seemed to know the way. Around them, the shadows loomed tall and leering, the weathered branches of trees creeping out like hands along the path.

"Where are we?" Persephone asked.

"Almost home." Hades' body pressed against Persephone's back, their skin separated only by thin layers of fabric. As always, Hades felt warmer than she'd remembered.

"Was I... asleep?" Persephone's hand drifted up and plucked a poppy from her hair. In the dark, its petals seemed the color of dried blood.

"So deeply I could not wake you. There are safe ways to approach the river Lethe. I suggest you stay away from it until you master them."

Persephone shifted slightly and then exhaled as she felt the vial press against her skin beneath her strophion. She'd managed to accomplish what Ismaros had asked of her. "Of course," she said. "I'm sorry for the trouble."

They traveled in silence for a time. It felt... comfortable. Alastor's gait was gentle, and she relaxed against Hades' shoulder.

Would she miss Persephone, when she was gone?

She needn't think so highly of herself. After all, she couldn't even read. Hades would be better suited by a clever wife, one who could assist her to rule.

"How were your lessons?" Hades asked.

Persephone jolted awake, her head cradled in the crook of Hades' arm. She pinched herself. It would not do to miss her morning appointment with Ismaros. "He hit me," she said, picturing Stephanus's caterpillar-like eyebrows.

"Did you do something to deserve it?"

"No! Well, I don't think so."

Hades shifted behind her. "Once you are done learning, you could have him tortured for eternity, if you would like."

She wasn't serious. Was she? "He didn't hit me that hard," Persephone said. *Not like you.*

"Jests aside, you will need to extract as much knowledge from him as you can. I have a stack of reading material for you three cubits high."

"That sounds tedious."

"It is. But if you are to be my consort in more than name, it will be one of your duties."

All the more reason for her to escape to the surface as quickly as she could. "Hades," she began.

"Yes?"

"Is it true that there are more suicides in spring than at harvest time?"

Hades was silent for a moment. "You will have to compare the records in the repository. Why?"

"Something Stephanus said. About my season."

"Are you certain you do not wish to have him tortured?"

"Hades!" Persephone lightly slapped Hades' thigh. Hades might be jaded and cold enough to jest about something as cruel as an eternity of torment, but Persephone could never be that cynical. If she left now, she would never have to be.

"We are here," Hades said, making Persephone jump. Had she fallen asleep again?

They were just outside the stables, and Eustachys awaited them. Hades helped her to dismount. She leaned heavily against Hades, her feet unsteady beneath her. She looked down and saw that Hades must have strapped her sandals on before taking her back home. Before taking her back to the palace.

Persephone's weakness was not feigned. She could scarcely keep her eyes open as Hades escorted her to her room.

"Supper has been left for you. Are you feeling unwell?" Hades asked. She pressed the back of her hand against Persephone's forehead.

Persephone shook her head. "No, I'm just tired." She smiled tremulously at Hades through her lashes. "Would you excuse me for tonight?" she asked, her heart in her throat.

"I could send someone to watch over you—"

"No!" Persephone silently cursed herself. "No," she said again, more quietly. "Please. I'm tired, is all."

"Very well," Hades said and kissed her. "Good night."

"Good night, Hades."

Persephone fled into her room and closed the door, pressing her back against it as she heard it slide into place. She was alone. Hades had left her alone for the first night since their marriage.

14

ABOVE YOUR STATION

She couldn't believe her luck. She wanted to giggle at the thought of it, but she pressed her lips together, swallowing her growing elation.

What to pack? She didn't want to take anything from here, save for the clothes on her back. Ismaros had promised to help her.

Persephone sat down at the end of the bed. She reached up to her neck to find she was still wearing Hades' gold chain. She ran it through her fingers, trying to find the clasp. She fumbled with it for some time but could not find the secret to unlock it. This was ridiculous. Hades had bestowed it upon her, which meant it could be opened. Eventually, she was forced to give up. She promised herself she would return it by messenger after her escape. She would not provide Hades the opportunity to call her a thief once more.

Persephone ate the supper that had been left for her, then tugged on the pull cord by the bed. A knock came at her door some time later.

"Come in," Persephone said.

A girl opened the door and stood nervously under the threshold. Persephone handed her the empty plates. "I'd like some broth," she said.

"Of course," the girl said and promptly disappeared.

She came back eventually with a steaming bowl, which Persephone directed her to leave on a table. Once she was gone, Persephone fanned the broth, impatiently waiting for it to cool. When the bowl was only warm to the touch, she emptied Lethe's water into it, then stirred it before pouring the mixture into a waterskin.

With her preparations complete, she doused all the lights in the room so that someone passing by would not see anything amiss. She sat back down on the bed and waited, pinching herself every so often to stop her eyelids from drifting shut. She didn't dare sleep again, not after the river. Sleep could wait until she was safely above ground.

A sliver of light shone from beneath the door connecting her room to Hades'. She pressed her ear against the door and thought she could hear the faint scratching of a reed pen.

Did Hades ever stop working? Any other goddess would still be on her honeymoon.

Persephone crept away from the door and paced the room in the dark. She passed the time by running through place names and flower names in her mind, imagining the sights and smells of the overworld until she could almost taste the crisp salt air from over the sea.

The dawn could not come quickly enough, but at last, pale bands of light crept across the floor. She opened the window shutters and tossed her sandals outside. She swung herself over the ledge, landing softly on her feet, her waterskin and the empty bowl tucked under one arm. Turning, she shut the window once more so nothing would look suspicious from the outside.

There were a few servants around but none close by. She put on her sandals, draped her epiblema over her hair, and kept her eyes lowered, walking quickly toward the stables.

The horses turned their heads as she entered, their eyes deep and liquid in the gray morning light. A hand touched her shoulder, and she almost screamed.

Ismaros wrapped his hand around her mouth. Persephone stiffened but forced herself to relax when she saw it was him.

"Begging your pardon," he whispered, releasing her.

Her heartbeat seemed like it ought to give them away, it was so loud. "You startled me."

"The wagon is ready." Ismaros led her to the side of the stables, where he had hitched up a pair of horses to a wagon. "How do you mean to distract Cerberus?"

Persephone showed him her waterskin and bowl. "This skin contains broth along with Lethe's water," she said. "Offer this to him, and he will forget his purpose."

Ismaros gravely took the items from her. "A wise choice," he said. Next, he drew back a cloth, revealing a large storage chest nestled next to several amphora.

"In there?" Persephone asked. Small spaces did not suit her.

"It won't be for long." Ismaros unclasped the lid of the chest and opened it.

Persephone climbed onto the wagon and lowered herself into the box. She had to lie sideways in it, her knees folded next to her shoulders. Stray bits of hay lined the bottom of the chest, perhaps used as packing material for whatever had been transported previously. The tough fibers tickled her neck, and she longed for her soft and comfortable bed lined with furs in Hades' palace.

"Not a word from now on, Lady Persephone," Ismaros whispered and lowered the lid, plunging her into darkness.

Her breathing sounded too loud in the box. She heard Ismaros climbing onto the wagon and taking the driver's seat, then flicking the reins. The horses began to move, and Persephone was jostled as the wheels ran over a bumpy patch of ground.

She gritted her teeth, taking a deep breath. This was temporary. She hugged her knees to her chest, wincing as every bump rattled the amphora in the wagon.

Ismaros drove for some time, quietly whistling to himself. Persephone wondered where she'd seen his face before. What had her mother promised him in exchange for her safe return?

Ismaros rapped on the chest. "We near Cerberus," he said.

The wagon slowed to a halt, and she felt it shift as Ismaros hopped out. Cerberus growled, low in his throats.

Ismaros muttered something indistinctly. Persephone strained to hear, distracted by the sound of her own breathing.

Cerberus howled in triplicate, a tortured, lonely sound. The wagon rocked again as Ismaros leapt aboard, and he snapped the reins, the horses hurtling into a gallop.

Persephone rapped on the inside of the lid. "What happened?"

"He drank," Ismaros said, sounding breathless. "But that noise! He could have woken half the palace."

Their wild pace did nothing for Persephone's stomach, as she was jostled from every side in her tiny prison. She bit her lip and reminded herself it would all be worth it; they had to maintain their lead. A part of her could not fail to pity

Cerberus and rue her hand in the betrayal. With luck, the hound had not suffered.

They maintained a frantic pace for some time, but eventually the wagon began to slow and then ground to a stop. Persephone hugged herself tighter. There was no need to panic.

She heard Ismaros talking, though she could not make out the words, and another man answering. Charon? But no, they would not be using that crossing.

Persephone pushed up on the lid of the chest, raising it by a finger's width. Ismaros had covered it again with a cloth, and through the fabric she could see only vague shadows.

"You promised to wait by the dock," Ismaros said.

"What can I say, Theseus? I could not allow you to assume all the danger. And the glory," said the other man.

What glory? And why had he used that other name —Theseus?

She heard the wagon boards creak. It had to be the other man, stepping aboard. Ismaros—Theseus—had not told her of an accomplice. She did not much like being surprised.

"Pirithous, don't," Theseus said.

The cloth was drawn from the chest, and the lid swung open. Persephone shielded her eyes from the morning light, covering her face with her hands.

"I apologize for the indignity, but you should be safe to rise now. I saw none on my journey here." A man hovered over her, clean-shaven with bright brown eyes set in a weathered face. Pirithous, she assumed. Behind him was the gray-brown, cavernous sky of the underworld, glowing with its approximation of daylight. Its emptiness seemed to mock her, being both of Gaia's earth and something completely other. She'd hoped, however foolishly, that she'd be met with pale blue vistas the next she raised her eyes to the aether.

She took Pirithous's offered hand and climbed out of the box, glancing around herself. She felt rather than saw the dark blight of Tartarus in the near distance. "We are not safe here."

Theseus snapped the reins, and the wagon began to move once more. "We must keep our pace."

"You lied about your name," Persephone said. She sat on the box that had once housed her, epiblema pulled tight around her shoulders, looking behind them for signs of pursuit. "What else have you lied about?"

Theseus glanced briefly at her over his shoulder. "I apologize for the small deception. It was necessary to secure your cooperation."

A shiver ran down Persephone's spine, and her fingers tightened in the wool of her epiblema. She opened her mouth to speak, but Pirithous interrupted her.

"You have your mother's eyes," Pirithous said.

"Excuse me?" Persephone turned and found Pirithous sitting closer to her than decency would allow. He was staring at her, not as a mortal might revere a god but with the same hunger she'd so often seen in Hades' eyes.

Persephone slid across the seat until the neck of an amphora jabbed into her side. "Who are you?"

"A child of Zeus, like yourself. King of the Lapiths of Thessaly," said Pirithous.

She looked between him and Theseus, seated on the driver's bench. "My mother sent you to fetch me," she said, as if by her speech she would make it true.

Theseus glanced back at his friend, eyes narrowed. A warning.

"In a sense," Pirithous said. He was a very poor liar.

Persephone leaned forward and grabbed the back of Theseus's chiton. "Stop the wagon."

Instead of obeying her, Theseus used a crop on the horses and the wagon lurched forward, hurling her off-balance. Pirithous tossed the blanket over her, throwing her into darkness as he grabbed her. He wrangled Persephone back into the storage box, pushing her to the bottom before slamming it shut.

Persephone tore at the blanket, bruising her elbows and knees as she struggled to uncover her head. When that was done, she pounded at the lid. "Let me out!" she screamed, but it would not budge. He had to be sitting on it.

Persephone screamed again in wordless fury. There was no one around to hear her, and even if they did, they would most likely think her cries were those of the unquiet dead.

"Please, don't be aggrieved," Pirithous said. "When we are wed—"

What?

"—I will lavish upon you the finest of silks, jewels, whatever you desire."

"What I desire is to choose for myself!"

He said something, inaudibly. She hammered at the lid once more, splinters lodging in her fingers for her efforts.

It was not a particularly hard wood—spruce, grown in the underworld. Persephone lay back in her box, forcing herself to breathe slowly. Her throat was raw. Too late, she remembered where she'd seen Theseus's face. Athenians held his image in high regard. Hadn't he killed some monster or other? He was one of Poseidon's.

So. Both of them were demigods. Heroes. Who else would be foolish enough to venture into the underworld alive?

The wagon surged forward, tossing Persephone against the side of the box. They were heading downhill, quickly. How close were they to the great river Oceanus? She banged on the lid, and this time she heard Pirithous speak, so softly she had to strain to make out his words over the sound of the horses and wagon wheels.

"...My wife died, so long ago now. Theseus and I pledged we would remarry only the most beautiful of Zeus's daughters. We have traveled far to find you."

"The underworld is not meant for mortals," Persephone said.

"No. That is why we will not overstay our welcome."

It had only been a few minutes, but already she hated his voice, as greasy as an oiled pankratiast. She would kill him before she had to listen to that for more than a day.

Persephone leaned her forehead against her arm, closing her eyes to stave off a rising tide of nausea. "Hades will not let you go."

At that, Pirithous laughed, sending a chill down Persephone's spine at the blasphemy. "Hades is the weakest of the ruling gods. She is no match for her brothers, nor her brother's sons."

"Because she is a goddess and not a god?"

"Of course," Pirithous said. The lid of the box creaked, as if he was shifting his weight. "Kronos should have had three sons, not two. Hades defies her feminine nature by insisting to rule without a king by her side. The underworld will always be the weakest domain because of it."

Persephone touched the chain around her neck, which she had tried so hard to remove. The warm metal cut into her fingertips. "Hades did not choose a king. She chose me."

Pirithous laughed again. She hated him more and more with each passing moment. "She chose well, I'll grant her that. But a female could never hold you, sweet Persephone. You were destined for greater things."

A depression in the road made the wagon dip for an instant, and Persephone banged her head on the side of the box. She groaned, reaching up and finding her forehead wet. "You consider yourself greater than Hades?"

"As a husband, yes. At least I meet the minimum requirements."

"You reach above your station."

"I am a king."

"I will grind your bones to dust!" Persephone yelled, slamming her fists against the lid.

Pirithous laughed.

She had never asked a plant to kill for her before, but when they reached the overworld, her powers would return in full. Pirithous had no hope of holding her; this entire venture had been doomed before its beginning.

Her leg started to cramp, sending shooting pains up her spine. She flexed her foot as best she could.

She had been so stupid to assume they were Demeter's, simply because they had offered her freedom. She was too quick to jump for the nearest branch, not seeing the dangers beneath, waiting for her to fall.

Persephone heard shouting. The wagon moved from left to right, as if Theseus were driving it in a zigzag pattern. The movement flung Persephone around, and she cried out.

For a dizzying moment, she felt herself tossed in free fall, but then the box struck solid ground, and she was thrown against one side. She heard amphora shattering around her.

Her ears rang, and she tasted ichor. She must have bitten her tongue. At least everything had stopped moving, though she had lost track of which part of the box was up or down.

The box moved again, and Persephone yelped, falling once more to one side. The lid swung open, letting in a sliver of daylight.

Persephone reached for it, and her fingers touched grass. With renewed strength, she crawled toward the light.

Once she was free of the box, she climbed to her feet, blinking in the light. Something rolled toward her, and she glanced down to see a severed head, stopping just shy of her foot.

Persephone screamed at the sight of Pirithous's glassy eyes, almost falling as she staggered back against the box in her haste to get away.

"A wedding gift, for my lady wife."

Persephone tore her gaze away from Pirithous to see Hades standing before her, wearing a black chiton soaked through with blood all down the front, clinging wetly against her body. More blood coated the side of her face. She looked as vengeful as any of the Erinyes, her gaze haunting. She must have left the palace in a hurry, without donning any armor.

Hades beckoned her with a crimson hand. "Come here."

Persephone looked down at Pirithous again. There was so much blood, soaking into the grass around them. The soil of a battlefield was always enriched by the life spilled upon it.

She went to Hades' side, although her steps were halting. She could not bear to look at her.

"Did they hurt you?" Hades asked.

Persephone shook her head, then winced as the movement reminded her of how much she ached after having been trapped for so long. "I'm fine. You're the one who's injured," she said, glancing at a cut on Hades' arm.

"The ichor has spilled from your veins," Hades said. She touched Persephone's forehead, where it had matted her hair.

Persephone flinched. "I can't feel it."

Hades' voice grew cooler. "I see. We had best return. Can you walk?"

Persephone nodded.

Around them lay the wreckage of the wagon. The horses must have become loose at some point. The wagon was over-turned, its contents spilled around in an arc, pieces of broken pottery scattered everywhere.

Hades held her sword by her side. Mortal blood ran down its length, dripping onto the grass. Persephone felt each drop striking the earth as if they were falling upon her own skin. Hades pulled out a cloth and dried her sword before sheathing it at her hip.

They were not alone. Other members of Hades' retinue had arrived with her, helping to lead the horses away or to salvage what had fallen from the wagon.

Two women spread a clean sheet over a pair of bodies, blood spreading quickly through the fabric like strange flowers blossoming.

Persephone stepped a little closer to Hades. "Is Theseus dead?" she asked.

Hades looked at the bodies. "Of course. Their lives were forfeit the moment they entered my realm." She led Perse-phone to her chariot, and they set off immediately without waiting for the servants to be done with their grisly task.

Persephone looked over her shoulder, at the light glinting off the blue water of Oceanus. They had not been too far from the boundaries of the underworld. A little more time and she could have reached the surface.

But at what cost?

She glanced at the goddess beside her. Hades stared straight ahead, the reins held loosely in her hands. She barely needed to steer; the horses knew the way. Her face was grim, a muscle in her cheek twitching occasionally.

"Hades? Thank you... for saving me."

Hades glanced at Persephone, her gaze dark. "Your gratitude is noted."

They traveled the rest of the way in silence.

15

NAME ME

I t took a great deal of warm water and scrubbing to remove all of the ichor from Persephone's face and hair. Afterward, she lay on her (admittedly comfortable) bed, staring at the painted swans on the ceiling.

This was not where she had expected to be.

Her morning had been so full of hope and anticipation. Now, there was only an eternity of the underworld before her; that and the memory of Pirithous's sightless eyes boring into her soul.

Persephone curled up in her sheets and cried herself to sleep.

Xenia woke her some time later. "Begging your pardon, mistress, but Queen Hades desires your presence."

Persephone was tempted to disappear under the covers, but she knew no good would come of it. Still, she protested. "Now?" The window was dark, so it had to be night.

"Yes, mistress."

Persephone emerged from her nest of blankets and pulled a fresh chiton over her head. "Where is she?"

"In her rooms."

Persephone's pulse quickened. She turned her head to hide her blush. "Thank you."

Xenia nodded and left her.

Persephone had slept in her wet braid; there was really nothing to be done about her hair. She caught sight of her own reflection and winced. Bruises blossomed on her arms and shoulders, with more on her legs and hips, courtesy of her misadventures in the storage chest. She tossed a himation over her shoulders, wrapping it closely around her neck.

She opened the door between their rooms. Hades was sitting at her writing desk, as usual, her reed pen scratching away. The desk faced away from Persephone, such that Hades' back was slightly turned to her.

Persephone stood in the doorway for some time. Hades had also changed out of her bloodstained clothes and was wearing once more a chiton that seemed to be made of pure shadow.

After what felt like a candle mark had passed, Hades set down her pen, turned and looked at her. "That will not do. You must knock." She gestured. "Try again."

Persephone looked at the door, then back at Hades. "You asked for my presence."

"I insist."

Throwing her hands up, Persephone stepped back into her own room and closed the door. She hesitated, feeling foolish, then rapped upon the door with her fist.

"Enter."

Persephone did so, closing the door behind her this time.

"Do you know why I asked you to do that?" Hades asked, still seated.

The only boundaries you care about are the ones you set. "Your rooms are your own, and I'm here upon your sufferance."

"Yes, and?"

Persephone's face grew hot. Were they really doing this? She was a goddess grown, not an errant child needing a lesson! "And you want to remind me that you feel the need to control everything."

Hades paused for a moment. "Not everything."

"Me, then. You feel the need to control me."

"The gardener tends his plants to grow in a manner that is pleasing to the eye, does he not?"

"I can't fit the shape you're training me for."

"We shall see." Hades folded her hands in her lap. The index finger of her sword arm was black with carbon ink. "People look to you, Persephone. They notice how I treat you. You cannot be above the law."

"Your law."

"My laws, and the ancient laws inherited from those who came before us."

"Before us? You mean Gaia?" Persephone asked.

"I mean the gods that humans worshiped before Gaia. Before Chaos, before Nyx."

Persephone pressed her hand to her mouth. That was a form of blasphemy, to say that Chaos was not at the beginning of the universe. But she could not stop the question that slipped from her lips. "What gods?"

Hades shook her head. "Deities beyond counting, long forgotten. One day our time will come, and we too will be forgotten. No more worshipers; no more sacrifices."

For once, Persephone was grateful they were in the under-world. If anyone else had heard such treacherous words pass Hades' lips... she did not wish to think of what might have befallen her. "But... we are their gods."

"For a time, yes. And for that time to continue, we must fulfill our sacred duties, lest we be forgotten."

"What about my duty?" Persephone asked. "How can I usher in spring from beneath the earth?"

Hades smiled. "There was a time before you. Your mother will have to bear that burden once more."

Her mother... She had scarcely thought of Demeter in the last few days. "She will be greatly displeased," she whispered.

Hades sighed. "Enough. On your knees and tell me, from the beginning, what happened this morning."

Persephone trembled, her hands forming fists by her sides.

Hades pursed her lips. "In the overworld, you had no issue with proskynesis."

"That was before I knew what you were."

"And what am I?"

Persephone looked away. She could not say it. She was too weak of will.

Hades pushed her chair back and stood, walking over to her. She took Persephone's chin in her hand, redirecting her gaze. "Name me, Persephone."

She made herself look into Hades' eyes, which were as black as Erebus. "Hades, Queen of the Underworld, daughter of Kronos and Rhea."

"And?"

"And my wife," Persephone said in a whisper.

"And?"

"My abductor, and my defiler!"

Hades released her.

Persephone fell to her knees, her arms outstretched before her. "Please, my queen, I beg of you, don't keep me here. Don't confine me in this sunless land, this starless night. I will be your wife in name—your courtesan—your slave—but please, please! I can't bear it here. I can't," she sobbed, her voice choking up with tears.

Hades was silent for some time. When at last she spoke, her voice held all the sorrow of the Vale of Mourning. "Then you must learn to suffer well, my sweet Persephone."

Persephone pressed her forehead against the floor and cried, wondering if she would ever feel the earth beneath her feet once more. Her soul ached for the touch of overworld soil, for the heat of the sun across her back.

"I cannot say that I regret my actions," Hades said, far above her. "But I have done you harm. I could not wait for you to love me. It is not the way of the gods."

Persephone rocked back on her heels and wiped a hand across her face. "You're not a god."

"No," Hades said bitterly. "I fall under greater scrutiny. People expect more and are less forgiving." Her voice softened. "I cannot show mercy, not even to you. They would consume me if they knew."

"Knew what?"

Hades knelt beside her and covered Persephone's hand with her own. "How precious you are to me."

Persephone drew her hand back and wrapped her arms around herself.

Hades stood, the dark folds of her chiton sighing around her. "I will not ask for your forgiveness, nor your understanding. Believe what you may, but I never wished for you to suffer."

As an apology, it wasn't much, but it was more than what another god might have offered her. She hadn't been taught to expect any more.

"You hurt me," Persephone whispered.

"I know."

Was it always to be like this, her on her knees, Hades above her, somewhere in the periphery of her vision? Would she always feel this hollow inside?

Hades sat on the end of the bed, the frame creaking under her weight. She steepled her fingers, pressing her lips to them before glancing up. "I will grant you a favor, as my penance. I relinquish my marital rights; I will not force you into our marriage bed. If you wish to join with me, it will be of your own choosing."

Persephone turned her head so that she could see Hades through her tears. "And if that time never comes?"

"Then we shall both be poorer for it."

She didn't believe her. It had to be some kind of trick.

Hades stood, walking toward her. Persephone stiffened, but Hades merely leaned over and unwrapped her himation, sliding it off her shoulders. She tossed it aside. "Tell me what happened today. You might as well start with how you acquired those bruises."

Persephone glanced aside, shivering a little, the fine hairs on her arms standing up. Still on her knees, she told Hades it was merely the result of being trapped in the storage chest on the wagon. Then she backtracked and started with seeing Theseus near the library, working down all the way to when she climbed out of the box to find Pirithous's head rolling at her feet.

One thing bothered her. "How did you find me so quickly?" Persephone asked.

Hades was facing away from her at this point, staring out of the window with her hands clasped behind her back. Brooding, Persephone supposed. The view certainly didn't warrant such close inspection.

Hades turned and gestured toward her neck. "That chain. I had it enspelled by one of our sorceresses. All the best and brightest of humankind make their way to my domain, sooner or later."

A charm? Persephone's hand went to her necklace, the necklace for which there seemed to be no clasp. "It won't come off."

"As intended."

Even if she reached the surface, she would never be free. Not until she could find someone talented enough to remove it.

"You poisoned my hound," Hades said. "My houndmaster tells me it may take years to recover his training."

"I'm sorry."

"Are you?"

Perhaps Lethe's water would make it easier for her to bypass Cerberus a third time, if she ever had the chance to try. She could not truly be sorry for that. "I had to," Persephone said.

Hades nodded, apparently satisfied with her honesty. "Zeus and Poseidon will be unhappy to hear of their children's misdeeds, but considering the circumstances I am well within my rights to punish them. However, these kinds of incidents must be handled delicately." Hades leaned her back against the window frame, her arms crossed over her chest, one of them bandaged at the bicep. "As for your punishment—"

"My punishment?"

"Yes, your punishment. I haven't decided—"

"But why?" Persephone asked, her eyes filling again with tears. Hadn't she been punished enough?

Hades was clearly not accustomed to being interrupted, but after a moment's pause she went on. "You are not above the law, my dear. No one is permitted to leave the underworld without permission."

"Not even you?"

"I cannot move as freely as my brothers." Hades stepped away from the window, pacing across the floor. "It was the only way they would allow a goddess to rule," she said with venom in her voice. "Did you think I chose this fate? To be feared by gods and mortals alike, to be loathed for the judgments I am duty-bound to make?"

Persephone shrank back from Hades' anger, even though she knew she was not its target.

Hades took a breath and continued, more quietly. "I expose myself beneath Zeus's sky for only three reasons: when performing my duties, by invitation, or by negotiation."

"But when you took me—the cave—"

"That place was liminal, in neutral territory. There are many such spaces, some beneath the depths of the ocean, others scattered high and low." Hades looked at her sideways. "It was fate that brought you there to me."

Fate? No, no; it was a coincidence. Wasn't it? First Demeter's fields rejecting her, then the narcissus. She should've known it wasn't right; should've felt... something.

Hades glanced at the burning stumps of the candles. "The

evening grows late, and you must rest." She waved her hand in a clear dismissal.

She was leaving her alone? Truly? Persephone gaped, but it seemed Hades had no more use for her that night. Hades turned her back on her, sitting down at her writing desk and dipping her pen into ink.

Persephone rose from her knees and fled.

16

JUDGMENT

S he planted herself above Hades, her hair unbound, the ends trailing over Hades' collarbone. Hades' face was free from sorrow; her lips curved into a smile, her eyes soft and heavy-lidded.

Persephone traced the outline of Hades' lips with her fingertips. Hades kissed her fingers, then drew them into her warm, wet mouth.

Persephone giggled.

A knocking at the door made her draw back. She pulled a sheet over her naked chest and turned towards the interloper.

"Mistress! You must rise, else you'll be late!"

Persephone opened her eyes with a sharp intake of breath. She looked up to find Xenia throwing back the shutters, welcoming in the weak morning light.

It was too early to be woken like this. She looked down to see she was still partially dressed from the previous night. Her skin was clammy, and an unpleasant warmth lingered between her thighs. Was she so depraved as to desire Hades' touch after two nights without it?

"Queen Hades has asked you to join her in the throne room," Xenia said. She reached into a storage chest and pulled out a chiton, belt, and sandals. "You must hurry!"

There was no time for elaborate hairstyles. Persephone undid the loose braid she'd slept in, finger-combed her hair and re-braided it whilst Xenia slipped the sandals on her feet. She changed quickly and then was ushered out the door, still fumbling with the fibula that was meant to fasten her chiton's left shoulder.

She was so engrossed with her task she almost ran into Hades straight on.

"Allow me." Hades fixed the clasp for her, the tips of her fingers brushing Persephone's skin as she did so.

Persephone blushed and glanced away, the echoes of her dream still vivid in her mind. A dream... or a vision, yet to pass. Would there ever be a time during her long immortality where she could bring herself to forgive Hades?

The goddess in question wore black again, as if it were some kind of uniform, the color bringing out the unnatural paleness of her skin. The fabric was so diaphanous it billowed out behind her as she walked, like smoke floating in the air.

"Come," Hades said. "We should not keep our shades waiting." She proceeded, not glancing back to see whether Persephone was following. Her strides were long, so that Persephone had to hurry to catch up.

"Our shades?"

"The dead." Hades had seemed so talkative the night before, but this morning her words were clipped, the expression on her face neither tender nor kind.

Persephone tried to maintain the silence but failed. "Did

you sleep well?" she asked, then bit her tongue, silently cursing herself.

"Well enough. And you?"

Persephone blushed again, grateful that Hades was not looking at her. "Yes, thank you."

They reached the back of the throne room. A raised dais held two thrones, one black and tall, the other slightly smaller and finished with its natural grain. They were both carved from olive wood, with anthemia ornamenting their backs. Above them was a large cupola with arched windows inset, pouring natural light into the room.

Past the dais were statues of some of the other gods and goddesses of the underworld: Thanatos, Hypnos, and the Moirai, larger than life and lining the walkway that stretched down for many lengths.

Hades took her place on the black throne and gestured to Persephone to sit beside her.

Already assembled were several members of Hades' court. Persephone crossed the dais and sat down, uncomfortably aware of all the eyes upon her. She should have fixed her hair, after all.

"I thank you all for your attendance," Hades said, her voice pitched to carry through the chamber. Black drapes hanging along the walls dampened any echo. "We have a long list of judgments to administer today, so let us begin."

A herald standing to one side of the dais glanced down at a scroll and announced the first mortals. "The hero Theseus, of Athens, and King Pirithous, of Thessaly."

Persephone gripped the arms of her throne, watching as the two men came into view and began the long walk down toward the dais. She was somewhat relieved to see neither of them showed the wounds of their death, no ragged scar encircling Pirithous's neck and no stab wounds soaking Theseus's tunic. They both looked alive enough, though somewhat grayer of face.

"Theseus. Please explain in brief the circumstances of your death," Hades said.

The man had courage, Persephone could grant him that. He stood tall and proud, unperturbed by the weight of the eyes upon him. He explained the pact he'd made with Pirithous, how they each had chosen a daughter of Zeus to wed, and how Pirithous had chosen Persephone. How he had journeyed here, as Pirithous's friend, just as Pirithous had helped him to claim his own bride.

"King Pirithous, do you concur?" Hades asked when Theseus had finished speaking.

Pirithous gave his own version of the events, which differed little in substance. He, too, was unbowed by the scrutiny cast upon him, though his hand did drift to his neck at times, as if he was checking that his head and body were still attached.

"Wife, do you have anything to add?" Hades asked, turning in her seat to look at Persephone.

Persephone placed her clammy palms on her knees. "What Theseus said is true, to my knowledge."

"And did you leave with him, believing you'd be escorted to the surface, to your mother?" Hades asked.

A murmur went up around the crowd. Hades hushed it with a slight gesture of her hand.

Persephone looked at the two men before her, then back at Hades. "Yes, it's true," she said curtly. Hades knew what her answer would be—could not fail to remember the substance of her interrogation the night before. Persephone hadn't expected this theater, to have her sins examined so publicly like any commoner.

She supposed that was the point. Hades had told her that no one was above the law, and now she was making good on her word.

Hades turned from her and gestured to Theseus. "Level eight." She then pointed to Pirithous. "Level ten." She waved her hand, and a pair of guards took hold of the men, leading them away.

Persephone had no idea what that meant, but it seemed to be a severe kind of punishment, judging from the murmur that rippled through the crowd.

"Great queen!" Pirithous said, breaking free. He scrambled toward the dais. "Queen Hades, please. Have mercy." He fell to his knees, crying out when the guard came once more to drag him away.

Hades watched, impassive and silent, as the two men were withdrawn. Then she turned to Persephone. "As for my lady wife..." She looked down at the crowd, addressing them. "This is her first offense, and she does not yet know our ways. Therefore, a hundred lashes and a period of exposure, the length of which is to be determined by myself."

Persephone dug her nails into her thighs to stop herself from saying anything. She stared at Hades in mute shock.

Hades leaned toward her, although she still faced her audience, and spoke under her breath. "Thank me for my mercy."

Persephone's mouth moved, but no sound came out. She tried again. "What mercy?"

"Would you rather the alternative?"

"If this is mercy, then perhaps I should take my chances," Persephone hissed.

"Continue to try me, and you may see for yourself."

Persephone picked at a loose thread on her chiton. "Thank you," she mumbled, her eyes downcast.

Hades sat back in her chair and gestured to the herald to continue.

More names were read out, and the rest of the session passed in a similar manner, with Hades hearing the deeds of mortals and then pronouncing judgment upon them. Persephone barely heard a word that was spoken. Hades had said she would be punished, yes, but she'd naturally imagined something nominal—not a flogging! And exposure? For how long? And would it be public, her humiliation laid bare for all to see?

She glanced at Hades from time to time, to try to gain some insight into what she might have been thinking, but Hades studiously ignored her, focusing instead upon whichever mortal stood before her. Persephone might as well have not existed at all.

When at last it came time for a recess, she walked with Hades from the dais and cornered her beside a refreshment table.

"What was that? Are you mad? I am your wife!" Persephone said, her hands in fists.

"Your actions belie your words," Hades said and popped a grape into her mouth, chewing slowly and swallowing before speaking. "Have you listened to any of the other cases? That last one now, the farmer. What was his misdeed?"

"I don't know! What does it matter?"

Hades turned and looked at her. "Then this exercise is pointless, given your current frame of mind. You might as well go and work on your reading with Stephanus, instead of attending this afternoon's session."

"I—what? Him? But we haven't discussed—"

"There is nothing to discuss." Hades jerked her head toward the exit.

"I—oh!" Persephone threw her hands in the air and all but ran out, wishing for a door to slam behind her, to show her displeasure, and having to satisfy herself instead with the sharp sound of her footsteps echoing down the hallway as an unsatisfactory proxy.

17

WHERE PRAISE IS DUE

Hades did not request her presence again for a week, or maybe two. Each morning, Persephone would look to Xenia to read her the day's tasks as she got dressed, dreading her punishment and yet longing for something to break up the monotony.

But it never came. Instead, she continued her lessons with Stephanus, walked among the fields, even met some of the dead. Her hand was getting better, Stephanus told her grudgingly.

Each day, she wondered whether it was raining or sunny upon the earth, whether the acanthus she'd planted last season were still blossoming. She thought of her mother, too, but less and less. Thinking of Demeter was painful, but like a bruise, it would smart when prodded and did not trouble her otherwise.

It could not last forever.

One gray morning, like so many other mornings before it, she was guided not to the library but to the back of the palace. Xenia joined her in a chariot, her eyes sad and her expression grim, giving Persephone forewarning of what was to come.

As the horses pulled away from the palace, Persephone's stomach dropped. The long wait had been intolerable, yes, but now that the day was finally here, this imminent anticipation was even worse.

The horses led them up a winding path encircling a large hill. From the top, she could see the great elm of false dreams to the east, the ever-burning fires of the river Phlegethon to the north, and Oceanus to the west. The view around them was charming—insomuch as the underworld could be charming—marred only by the knowledge of why she'd been brought here.

At the crest of the hill stood a magnificent willow, easily the height of eight men and just as broad. Its silvery leaves rustled in the wind as though it were sighing, and in its shadow the air seemed sweeter. Its foliage was trimmed so there was ample room to stand beneath it.

From this lofty height she saw Hades' golden chariot from some distance away as it approached. The lay of the land was such that at the top of the hill one could easily distinguish people in the distance, but from below they would be quite obscured.

She didn't have to wait long before Hades' chariot arrived. Its rider wore a peplos as her gown today, of linen or some other sturdy material. Black, again.

Hades dismounted. Persephone's gaze instantly went to the whip attached to her belt. It was made of braided leather, with multiple tails, each tipped with a small knot. Persephone pressed her palms against her thighs to stop them trembling.

"Xenia," Hades said by way of greeting. "Wife." She walked to Persephone and cupped her cheek, tilting her face up.

This close to Hades, Persephone's lips tingled. She almost thought—she wanted—

Hades' finger traced a line down her cheek, but then she released her and stepped away. "Persephone, daughter of Zeus and Demeter, you have been convicted of attempting to leave the underworld without my express permission. On this day, I, Hades, will carry out your punishment, being one hundred lashes and a period of exposure, the length of which is to be contingent upon your actions."

Listening to Hades recite her sentence brought back the memories of that day in the throne room, hearing it for the first time. Persephone clasped her hands together, her nails digging into her palms. She would not beg. She would not.

"Strip to the waist," Hades said.

Persephone waved Xenia off and proceeded to do it herself. She unfastened her fibulae, and the top of her chiton fell to her hips. She then unwound her strophion and handed it and her fibulae to Xenia for safekeeping. Her belt held her chiton in place like a layered skirt.

"Stand facing the tree," Hades said.

Persephone walked to the willow. Its bark was gray and brown, striated with moss. A beetle climbed its trunk, taking no notice of her.

Xenia took her left wrist and bound it to a branch, tugging on the restraints to make sure they were secure. She did the same with Persephone's right wrist.

Arms outstretched, Persephone felt as though she were poised to take wing. The air was cool against her naked back, and she shivered.

"Xenia, please count for me," Hades said.

"Of course, my queen."

This would never have happened on the surface. Demeter would not have allowed it, and besides, Persephone could not be punished this way whilst standing upon Gaia's earth—she would simply sink her toes into the dirt and let her mind drift, as stoic and patient as the willow before her. But this soil was not her soil, and this tree did not know her name. So she waited, her muscles trembling with the effort of holding still.

The first blow struck between her shoulder blades, leaving thin lines of fire on her back. She jolted and pressed her forehead against the tree, willing it to lend her support.

"One," Xenia said.

She could not survive this a hundred times; she would go mad. What was Hades thinking? She was her consort, not some common thief or vandal! She did not deserve—

The whip whistled through the air again, its tails leaving their mark on Persephone's back. She cried out, grateful for the emptiness around them and the knowledge that no one else would hear her.

"Two."

Her skin screamed to her. She had only been flogged once before, and it had not hurt half as much as this. She had carelessly left her lantern in the fields, and it had burnt half the crop. Then, her punishment had been justified, the lesson clear.

This?

This just felt petty.

She willed herself to relax, for her muscles to soften against the force of the blow, but she could not. Just hearing the soft whisper of the whip made her tense.

"Three."

Tears rolled freely down her face. The willow bore all her

weight now, as she could not hold herself upright without assistance. Every nerve sang out to her, and it felt like the heat on her back would set her aflame.

She should've taken Kronos's bargain, consequences be damned. He had true power; he would've been able to help her where Theseus and Pirithous had failed. If he had kept his word. If she could have trusted him. If, if, if...

"Four."

Persephone screamed. She hated Hades with all her might, loathed her with all the passion that Kronos felt toward Zeus. Anyone would have run, in her position. What right did Hades have to take her from her home, deny her the earth and then punish her for trying to leave? It wasn't fair!

"Five."

She shouldn't have run. Hades had warned her, and she'd not listened. She hadn't listened to Demeter, either. If she'd been good, if she'd been quiet, she would still be home, and all of this would be a bad dream. Her mother would still love her—

"Six."

"Please stop," Persephone cried, her speech filled with tears, her voice a broken thing. "I can't. Please."

She was still crying when Hades went to her and placed her palm on her cheek, turning Persephone to face her. Through her tears, Hades' outline shimmered. She blinked them away.

"You will survive, dear one," Hades said. "You are stronger than this." Hades placed a kiss in the middle of her forehead. The pressure of her lips burned rather than soothed.

Persephone rested her cheek against the willow tree. The beetle had long gone, having reached greater heights than her eyes could follow. Never before had she felt so alone.

"Seven."

Persephone continued to cry, not making any effort to stop her tears, or her screams. She was becoming less a person and more a mass of throbbing, burning pain, a flame consuming itself. A bead of liquid slid down the hollow of her spine; sweat, or ichor. She wasn't sure.

"Eight."

"Please," she sobbed in a chant. "Please, please, please..."

"Nine."

Theseus and Pirithous had to be hurting much worse than this by now. How was that fair? How was any of this fair? Death was no release from suffering. Was that the rule the gods had to uphold? Was that justice?

"Ten."

Ninety more to go. She couldn't. She would faint, surely. If she were mortal, it could have killed her.

Through her tears and congestion, it was getting harder to breathe. She gulped down mouthfuls of air, her nails digging into the bark of the tree. Sap ran over her fingers, pale and sticky.

"Eleven."

She stopped listening to Xenia. She didn't want to know. There was no beginning and no end anymore, only this vast sea of pain, burning and relentless. She could not swim.

The ache in her arms was nothing compared to the fire on her back, but her shoulders still tingled with the strain of it. Her wrists chafed against their bonds, and her head throbbed. She wanted to throw up.

At some point, Hades paused. Xenia came forward with a cool cloth, pressing it against Persephone's forehead.

"It's all right, dear," Xenia said. "You're doing fine."

She was not fine. She might never be fine again.

Persephone glanced sideways to see Hades had clipped the whip to her belt and was stretching out her arms, rolling her shoulders to ease the tension in them. Persephone hoped her muscles burned. She hoped the whip would wrap around and strike its mistress in the face.

When Xenia stepped away from her, she knew Hades was preparing to begin again.

"No," she said, her fingers outstretched. "Don't go—"

"Fifty one."

Persephone howled to the treetops, to anyone who would hear her. Her skin must have parted; droplets of ichor fell off the tails of Hades' whip, dripping onto the grass below. This wasn't fair. This wasn't fair!

She let go of any thought of revenge, any fantasies of what she might do to Hades. Her vision went red, then black. There was only the pain, coming in waves, and the itch of her skin trying to heal between blows; the damp, sticky heat of ichor soaking into her chiton, and the sound of her voice, hoarse and despairing.

She was no longer Persephone, goddess of the springtime; she was only pain sculpted in the shape of a woman.

When Hades finally stopped, for good this time, Persephone was a sobbing, shivering mess. Her wrists were rubbed raw from straining against their bonds, and her cheek held the imprint of bark.

Hades walked up to her. "The first part of your sentence is complete," she said.

Persephone stared in her general direction, sweat and tears blurring her sight. Even thought hurt too much; she could barely summon the strength to breathe. Had she been able to see, she would have beheld Hades' ravenous gaze, as if she yearned for something more.

"For the second part of your sentence," Hades said, "you will remain exposed to the elements until such time as you escape from your bonds or I choose to end your punishment."

Persephone's head lolled to the side. Her mind was dull and useless, her back still a throbbing mass of agony, the specter of pain feeling larger than her body itself. "Are you giving me the tools to escape?" she muddled out at last.

"You already have them," Hades said. She placed two fingers beneath Persephone's chin and kissed her forehead, her lips feeling like a brand. Her hand lingered against Persephone's hair, fingertips tracing across her shoulder and brushing down her back.

Persephone whimpered, flinching away from her touch. Hades brought her hand to her mouth and tasted Persephone's suffering, her eyes half-lidded.

There was a threat there, more dangerous than the weight of Hades' authority in the Hall of Judgment. Persephone caught Hades' gaze, held it.

Hades' eyes softened. She brushed a stray tendril of hair back from Persephone's face, tucking it behind her ear. Persephone pressed her cheek against Hades' palm.

"You look—" Hades whispered. She took a breath, swallowed. "You are perfection."

"If you had any tender thoughts in your heart you would spare me this torment," Persephone said, squeezing her eyes closed.

"If I thought you powerless, I would do so. But you have the will to see this through." Hades' hand fell away, leaving Persephone with only the memory of the warmth of her skin. "Xenia will stay with you for some time," she said. "Suffer well, dear Persephone." She turned from them and went to her chariot. The vehicle jolted forward, the horses breaking into a gallop that soon carried Hades far, far away.

Persephone breathed out a sigh. Her heartbeat felt too rapid, her hands trembling.

With Hades gone, Xenia came forward, holding a jug of water and clean rags. Persephone had almost forgotten about her presence.

"This may sting," Xenia said.

She began to bathe Persephone's wounds. It did sting, but it was nothing compared to what she'd endured before. Persephone closed her eyes and clenched her teeth together. After her back had been gently patted dry, Xenia smeared a paste over her wounds and bound them before slipping off Persephone's damp and ichor-stained chiton and dressing her in a fresh one, draping it loosely over her bandages.

Xenia dipped a cloth in ambrosia and held it to Persephone's mouth. Persephone sucked on it greedily as the warming liquid soothed her wounds. Even now, she could feel her flesh itching and knitting together under the bandages. With such prompt attention, it was unlikely to scar.

As her back started to heal, she catalogued the rest of her body's complaints. Her arms and shoulders ached, and she longed to lie down, or even to sit. There was a spot on the side of her nose that needed scratching, and she could not quite reach it by rubbing her face against the willow's trunk.

"May I?" Xenia asked.

Persephone nodded, her cheeks flushing. Xenia gently rubbed at the spot until Persephone turned her head away. The woman had seen her bathe before, but somehow this felt more personal.

"How long will you stay?" Persephone asked.

Xenia began packing up the rest of the bandages. "Until nightfall, at least."

Persephone glanced up, unable to see much of the sky through the willow's leaves. They had left the palace in the early morning, and it couldn't be more than an hour later.

"How long does she mean to leave me like this?" she demanded.

"I really can't say, mistress. This is not a punishment I've witnessed before."

Persephone pulled uselessly at the cloth that bound her wrists to the tree. It did nothing but irritate the already inflamed skin on her arms.

She looked at Xenia as the woman poured water over her own hands, washing them. "You could release me," Persephone said. "Hades is gone. No one need ever know."

Xenia flicked the water from her hands. "You and I would know, and then our queen would know. I'm sorry, mistress. I cannot."

Persephone slumped against the tree and blew a stray hair from across her face. "Fine, then. If I'm to suffer, I don't wish to be bored. Tell me a story."

"What would you like to hear?"

"Something true. Tell me about your children. You did have children, didn't you?"

Xenia's face broke into a smile. "Oh, yes. Four children and twenty-one grandchildren. I stopped counting after that."

"How many more generations?" Persephone asked.

Xenia blushed. "I've been dead for almost two centuries."

Persephone blinked. She supposed the afterlife was a kind of immortality in its own way, where time held less meaning. "Do you still see them?"

Xenia nodded. "I visit from time to time, on my day of leave."

Even death could not save one from familial duties. "You must miss them the rest of the time, then? What did you do to deserve the punishment of serving me?"

"Punishment?" Xenia stood a little straighter. "I had to compete with hundreds of other women, some of far nobler birth than I, for this position."

"Why?"

Xenia allowed the silence to stretch on for so long that Persephone thought perhaps she'd misheard. But eventually, Xenia said in a low voice, "Forgive me for saying so, but you cannot afford to be this naive. The underworld has never been and never will be a democracy. The Host of Many is its mistress, and you have her confidence."

Persephone wasn't sure if she would forgive Xenia. "I've never changed her mind."

"Perhaps not yet. But in time, she will listen to you."

Persephone could not imagine that ever happening, but then again, Hades had seemed moved by her plight—and though she'd lingered over Persephone's suffering that morning, she'd also walked away, despite whatever else she might have desired. "In time? Do you mean a year, or a century?"

"Change can come faster than that. She may seem harsh, but it is only her duty. Perhaps you could help her see another way."

And perhaps Zeus would become celibate.

They turned to lighter topics after that, stories of Xenia's youth, of her experience as a young mother. Persephone realized she'd never spent this long in conversation with a mortal before. Their lives were as full as the gods', fleeting though they might be.

Xenia fed her more ambrosia from time to time and smeared ointment over Persephone's cracked lips. But no matter how hard Persephone pleaded, she would not free her.

"The night grows upon us. I must leave you," Xenia said.

Persephone had become accustomed to hearing her voice during the intervening hours. "Will someone else come?"

"I've not been informed. I'm sorry."

"What should I do?"

Xenia hesitated. In the gathering twilight, her shadow loomed long across the ground. "Queen Hades does not lie," she said. "If she believes you can free herself, you should do everything in your power to make the attempt."

"Hades doesn't mean for me to succeed."

"She must," Xenia said.

Persephone glanced at her and scoffed. How would she know?

Xenia chewed on her lip, looking as if she wished to say more. "I'm sorry, mistress. I wish you good fortune."

She stepped into the chariot, then she, too, was gone.

Persephone was left alone with her thoughts, and she did not much like them. "I don't know what you want me to do," she said to herself. She desperately needed to scratch her nose again, and now there was no one to ask.

She wished Xenia had left her a light. With the night came the dark, awakening her ancestral fears. The winds raised the hem of her chiton, and she shivered.

She could not sleep like this. Her body ached too much, her

arms screaming at her for release, the balls of her feet throbbing as if she were standing on a bed of needles. There was no comfort here, no softness. Too late, she wished for her warm bed in Hades' palace, the caress of her furs, the clean rasp of the sheets.

Something scuttled near her feet, unseen in the dark. She rose up on the tips of her toes and screamed, kicking out blindly.

Nothing was there. Her heart thudded in her chest. She rested her forehead against the tree and moaned, wishing herself to be anywhere but here.

If she could free herself, this would end. She could not rely on Hades' mercy. But what could she do?

She ran her fingers along the branches of the tree, as far as she could manage without moving her wrists. The willow had been planted here long ago and no longer remembered the touch of the sun. Its signature was alien, its being impenetrable.

Persephone banged her forehead against its trunk in frustration. The rough bark cut her skin, and a trickle of golden ichor slid down her face. She grimaced at the pain lancing through her head.

She wriggled her feet, kicking off the sandals that Xenia had so thoughtfully picked out for her earlier that day. With her soles bare, she buried her toes in the ground.

It was loamy here, with a low level of phosphorus. Perhaps the tree was too much to start with. She closed her eyes and searched for any sign of activity in the ground. Grass grew nearby. She struggled for long minutes to find its signature as the night sky seemed to grow even darker. Her pain interrupted her concentration; she had to bring herself back to the dirt more than once, corralling her thoughts until she could focus.

Grass. Grass should've been easy and plentiful; her frustration made her thoughts blur and snap like thread breaking.

Persephone leaned her head against the willow and sobbed, her breath coming sharp and dry in her throat. Her failure in some ways was more painful than the whipping had been.

Still, with no other end in sight, she persevered. Her extremities had gone numb by the time she caught it—something—a whisper that might have been everything, or nothing at all.

She strained to hear it. Gradually, the whispers of the grasses filled her awareness—she listened to their manifold complaints, their sleepy chatter. The horses had been unexpected; none had grazed here for quite some time.

She smiled as she listened. She was not alone, then; could never be alone, not when she could touch the living ground. Was it living? Or were these the ghosts of grass?

The plants did not know the difference, in any case. She withdrew from them and reached out for the next largest thing.

Ox-eye daisies spread through the grass, their flower heads dried-out husks. It would soon be harvest time, on the surface, and perhaps here as well, if the underworld followed the same seasons.

She could not move her hands, but she imagined herself with palms outstretched, summoning the spirit of spring into the ground. She was not sure that anything had happened until a plant brushed the side of her foot with a white halo of petals.

Oh! She would've leaned down to pick the flower if she'd been able. Giddy with elation, she longed to touch more: all the living things that grow here, cypresses and ferns, poppies and figs.

All this time, she'd been trying to make the land bend to her will, and all she'd had to do was *listen?*

She leaned her forehead against the willow's trunk. It had been a seedling before she'd been born, a young sapling when she'd been learning to walk. Its thoughts were slow to change, and it did not know her.

"Please," Persephone said, her fingers spread against its branches. "Please help me."

Its leaves rustled in the breeze. It did not understand her plight, only knowing she was in its shade, beneath its canopy.

For long years, it had stood above the black palace on the horizon. Through the earth, it had felt the footsteps of the dead marching by, two by two, the restless making the pilgrimage to Lethe, to drink of its waters.

She felt the network of its roots stretching into the void beneath her, its bone-white capillaries seeking moisture. Its hold upon the ground was absolute. It could not be moved.

There was something else growing there, near the base of the tree. Persephone went very still, opening her eyes in shock. "No. I cannot," she said to herself.

She could feel the wind shivering its leaves, the moisture feeding its roots. It was beautiful and old, and she had no right.

Then again, she'd received no instruction, only been told she could leave on her own merits. That was permission enough. And yet...

Persephone closed her eyes again and concentrated. Not on the tree this time but on the spores living in its bark and around the base of its trunk.

Could she really do this? No. Yes. Hades had forced her hand. It was time for her punishment to be over.

For a long time, nothing seemed to be happening. The

tree's branches creaked in the wind. And then rust spots appeared on the leaves, rapidly spreading and turning fresh green growth dry and brittle. The leaves started falling like rain around her, creating a thick layer of black and diseased litter.

Under the dim night sky, she could see dark bumps emerging from the tree's trunk, like tiny stepping stones for insects. The tree shuddered, and Persephone wept for it.

She did not break her connection with the willow. It seemed the least she could do for it, to witness its final hour. Its heartwood filled with decay, spreading rapidly from the trunk to its extremities. New fungus burst from its bark like scabs on a leper, consuming the tree from within.

It took a long time for the fungus to hollow out the tree entirely. She felt its last breath like a keening wail, long and drawn out, and she came to herself with a start, her face wet with tears.

She tugged at her bonds. The branches were now brittle, hollow from within, but they did not easily break. It took several attempts, straining until it felt like her wrists would break first, before she tore her first branch down from the tree.

The weight of it dragged at her hand. She wrapped her fingers around it, as best she could, her wrist still bound, and swung the branch against the trunk of the tree until it splintered and cracked. Once demolished, it was a simple thing to drag her cloth manacle over the broken ends of the branch until her hand was free.

She repeated this on her left side, now with her right hand to assist, and soon she was completely free. She slipped the last cloth band over her fingers and threw the hateful thing aside, dropping to her knees in complete exhaustion.

She landed in a thick pile of leaf litter that coated the

ground. Persephone had never thought herself vicious, and she knew this death—destruction, whatever it was—would haunt her for a long time.

She did not know how long she stayed there, head bowed in mourning. When she looked up, it was to find dawn breaking, bathing the world in its pale gray light.

The leaf litter was gone, consumed by the earth. All around her sprouted a riotous slew of flowers: crocuses and violets, roses, larkspur, irises, narcissus, all blooming out of season in a frenzy of color.

Persephone climbed to her feet, unsteady as a new colt. She took a step forward. Where her bare feet touched the ground, more flowers blossomed, erupting from the soil.

"Stop," she said. "Enough."

She took another step, but still they followed her: orchids and hellebore, aconite and asphodel. She broke into a run, delicate flower heads unfolding in her shadow.

There was an open-sided pavilion at the bottom of the hill, overlooking a stream. She felt Hades' presence before she saw her, the shape of her distorting the landscape like a bubble floating in glass.

She had not forgotten the list of ills she'd suffered at Hades' behest, but she could not stand on her pride. Power leaked from her every pore; she needed aid, even if it came from Hades. As a conduit, she was not fit to contain the glut of energy that threatened to burst from her. Persephone's skin felt incandescent, hot and tight and ready to fracture.

She barely slowed as she entered the pavilion, a ground cover of violets trailing in after her. Persephone grabbed the nearest column for balance, clinging to it as vines curled around her ankles and twined up along the column, seeking to be closer to her.

"Persephone," Hades began, reaching toward her.

A surge of energy sparked through Persephone, and she stumbled, holding out both hands to brace herself. She fell upon her knees, fingers digging into the dirt and then recoiling as a line of hyacinths sprang up beneath her palms.

Hades crouched before her and took Persephone's hands in her own. "You must breathe."

"Make them stop, please, make it stop. I can hear them, in my mind," Persephone said, her fingernails digging into Hades' palms.

"What can you hear?"

"All of them," Persephone whispered. Every tree, every bush, every riverside grass. It was as though the entirety of the underworld's vegetation had awakened to her presence and were making themselves known to her. She felt as though their voices had set her ablaze, their song too enormous for her to hold.

Hades gently took back her hands, placing them on Persephone's shoulders. "Breathe with me," she said. "In," she chanted, and paused. "Out."

Persephone closed her eyes and did as she was told, focusing on the sound of Hades' voice to drown out the others. She wept with the strain, her nails digging into her thighs deep enough to leave crescent-shaped marks.

"I can't," she gasped. "I—"

"Steady." Hades counted out loud the moments between her breaths, her pauses growing longer so that Persephone grew quite dizzy from lack of air.

Something brushed her cheek, and Persephone opened her

eyes, letting out a strangled cry. It was only a vine, moving toward the far columns of the pavilion.

"There," Hades said. "Have they stopped?"

Persephone turned her mind inward, then nodded, too worn for speech.

"I am proud of you," Hades said.

Persephone stood up too fast and swayed on her feet. Hades caught her, setting her down on a bench and then sitting beside her. Persephone was too tired to mind the proximity, their hips almost touching.

Hades was her lodestone, both attracting and repelling. When Persephone had left the hilltop, her head filled with ghosts, her first impulse had been to run to her. But now that she was here, Persephone could not stand the thought of breathing the same air.

They sat in silence for some time, broken by the gentle babble of the stream as it passed them by. Something else tugged at her thoughts. She turned to look at Hades. "You've not said that before."

Hades met her gaze. "Praise where praise is due."

Persephone glanced away. Words so lightly given meant nothing. But still, her cheeks flushed. "You have a strange way of showing it."

"Our ways are not kind. But life and death are not kind."

Hades was not kind. "Did you know what would happen when you tied me up there?" Persephone asked.

"Not exactly. I had my suspicions."

Persephone had gathered that much. "What if I hadn't managed to break free? What then?"

"Xenia would have come to help you, eventually."

"Eventually?" Persephone's voice shook. "How long did you plan to leave me there?"

Hades pressed her lips together. "I trusted you to find your own way."

"I could've been there for *days*!"

"No," Hades said firmly. "No matter what you think, no matter what Demeter might have said, you are destined for great things. Your gifts are unique and can be wielded like a sword—for good or ill. You need only learn to control them."

Persephone wanted to believe her but couldn't. The way Hades spoke about her, like she was some kind of—like she was a goddess, not a fool getting in everyone's way. That description suited Athena, Artemis... not her.

She pressed a hand to her chest. Her wrists still bore marks, but they were already fading. "I touched—I killed—" Her throat closed over with tears. She had thought she'd cried them all out, and yet here they were, still more to fall.

Hades looked toward the rise of the hill. "Not exactly. A shade cannot die twice."

"But then I—what—destroyed its soul?" Persephone asked, horrified.

"Do trees have souls?"

"Don't you know?"

Hades narrowed her eyes. "What would you have me say? You broke something, yes. But what you found was worth the price."

Persephone glanced up at the wooden roof of the pavilion. Vines continued to crawl over the structure, filling every corner with greenery. She reached out her hand. "Stop," she said.

The plant stopped climbing, but continued to mature, revealing greenish-yellow umbels.

"Beautiful," Hades breathed.

Persephone glanced over to find Hades staring at her, not at the foliage. Another time, she might have looked away, but now she held her gaze.

Hades' lips were as red as a pomegranate seed. It seemed like it had been so long since she'd felt those lips upon hers.

"Please take me back to the palace," Persephone said. "I must rest after my ordeal."

Hades was the first to look away. "Of course," she said and stood, holding out her hand as a courtesy.

Persephone took it, her fingers briefly entwining with Hades' before she let go.

In the chariot, she leaned against the side railing, placing as much distance between herself and Hades as possible. Hades said nothing, but her shoulders seemed stiff, her grip on the reins excessively tight.

Persephone flexed her fingers, squeezing them into fists then releasing them. She would give Hades no cause to punish her a second time; she was done with being humiliated, frightened, tormented.

Hades would never touch her again.

18

THE BATHHOUSE

The days passed swiftly after that. Her lessons with Stephanus progressed to the point where she no longer needed him and was reading on her own— texts on logic and history she left scattered around her room for Xenia to clean up, scrolls piling in untidy mounds until they spilled over onto the floor. Erato she took to her bed and read by candlelight, her lips moving to sound out the unfamiliar words, her cheeks flushing even though there was no one to observe her. She would bury those scrolls under old comedies and dry philosophical treatises, only bringing them out when she was certain of being undisturbed.

Persephone slogged through a history of the underworld and read summaries of the major judgments from the last ten years. Most had been performed by the judges of the dead: Minos, Rhadamanthus, and Aeacus, but for special cases, like Pirithous and Theseus, Hades intervened.

Hades bade her to sit and pass judgment from time to time, even allowing Persephone's voice to sway her mind on a number of occasions. Persephone worked hard to persuade Hades to lessen the punishment of several long-serving residents of Tartarus, even going so far as to move a few repentant individuals to the Asphodel Fields. This change did not endear her to the judges of the dead, but Persephone could not be touched, so long as she held Hades' favor.

The wounds on her back healed. Her memory of the whip's caress seemed to diminish in her mind, though she could not bring herself to forgive Hades for the insult. True to her word, Hades did not seek her bed. Persephone sometimes dreamed of what might have transpired if Hades had succumbed to her monstrous impulses that morning by the willow tree. Those dreams would leave her waking in a sweat, her mouth dry, her body racked with longing.

Hades granted her dominion over a patch of land that encompassed the site of her punishment and the pavilion below it. Persephone had the remains of the willow tree cut down to the stump, and she planted around it—fruit trees, poplars, and a pair of new willows to either side of the pavilion.

She spent as much time in her grove as she could but never tasted the sweet fruits of her work. Any food or drink that passed her lips continued to be imported from the overworld.

Persephone never lost hope that she would one day leave this place, though her stay was not entirely unpleasant. She renewed her acquaintance with her grandfather, Kronos, and though he remained in Tartarus, Hades permitted his living standards to be much improved. Whether that was from compassion or belief in his professed change of heart, Persephone could not tell.

※

Persephone threw down her knucklebones in disgust. "Again! Come now, surely you cannot be playing fair."

Kronos chuckled and wrapped his arm around her pile of drachmae, sweeping it to his side. "The bones never lie, my dear."

He looked much healthier these days, with his frame filled out and his musculature back to fighting order. His beard and hair had been trimmed, and he could almost be considered handsome once more. He sat with her at an actual table, no longer tormented, though a thick manacle encircled one of his ankles, binding him to his cell.

"Another round?" he asked.

Persephone shook her head. "Perdix said the new baths ought to be fit for use today. I intend to pay them a visit."

Kronos scowled. "Too much heat causes deficiencies of phlegm," he said. "Why go to all the trouble when it ruins the constitution?"

"What can I say? It's much too cold here, Grandfather; I need my little luxuries." Persephone stood up and leaned over, kissing him on the cheeks, once on either side. "And seeing as you've robbed me blind again, I could do with a soak to drown my sorrows."

Kronos scoffed. Coins clinked as he tucked them away in a pouch. "Do send my regards. Tell her to visit some time."

"Yes, Grandfather," Persephone said, though they both knew Hades would do no such thing.

She'd been telling Kronos the truth about the bath, however. The palace had needed its plumbing extended anyway, and what better time to install a new bathhouse? Persephone was almost giddy with excitement. Hot springs might have been nicer, but considering the environment, an indoor facility with a hypocaust heating system was the only practical option. As their fuel source, Perdix had used ever-burning stones from the river Phlegethon. The mortal had all the talent and half the ego of his more notorious uncle, Daedalus. Hades had been right about one thing—the underworld counted the best of humanity amongst its ranks.

She rapped on the bars of Kronos's cell, waiting for a guard to unlock it so that she could leave. Kronos's cage was still literal, unlike Persephone's, but neither of them could ever forget they were here on Hades' whim. Perhaps that was why they had developed a connection, unlikely though it might have been.

When she arrived back at the palace, she took a moment to admire the new wing. Scaffolding still remained against one of the walls, which gleamed in the daylight—obsidian, to match the rest of the palace, glowing with newness and smooth as a well-polished blade.

Inside, the black gave way to graceful white columns. Persephone turned to the women's side of the baths, her critical eye running over the interior but finding nothing to fault. The space was far roomier and more inviting than the old facility had been, gleaming in white marble.

In the changing room she slipped off her sandals and undressed, then picked up a towel, wrapping it around herself. As she approached the bathing chamber, the air grew pregnant with warmth and humidity, the tiles losing their chill against her bare feet.

When she turned the corner and beheld it for the first time, she sighed at the beauty of it. The skylights, sparkling with precious glass, flooded the chamber with light. The ceiling was high and airy, arched trusses supporting it. The walls were inset with enspelled light fixtures and lined with a glittering mosaic border of flowers and fruit.

It was perfect, except—

"Perdix outdid himself. Pass him my congratulations, would you?"

Persephone almost dropped her towel when she saw Hades reclining at one end of the bathing pool, the waterline only reaching to below her breasts, the light brown of her nipples contrasting with her pale skin. Her hair hung loose as a wet pelt across her back, gleaming like a raven's feather.

"What are you doing here?" Persephone asked before thinking twice.

Hades raised one hand out of the bath water to gesture carelessly, droplets scattering from her fingertips like diamonds. "What does it look like?"

"You have your own bathing chamber."

"True, but this one is ever so nice." Hades shifted on her seat, sinking down until the water reached her collarbone, her eyes half-lidded.

"Your fingertips have turned to prunes. It's not healthy to soak that long," Persephone said, her hand on the tucked-in fold of her towel, ensuring it was secure. She hated herself for sounding like her grandfather, but she would've said anything to make Hades leave.

Hades shrugged. "Have I spoiled your dream of deflowering your bathhouse? I apologize."

"What? That's not—I—"

"Perdix and his crew might have taken a dip besides, we would never know."

Persephone huffed. "That's not the point!"

Hades closed her eyes, leaning her head back against the rounded edge of the bath. "Do not be cross, Persephone. I have had a very, very long day."

Persephone was not about to let this one little thing ruin her enjoyment after months of hard work. There was room enough for thirty people, with space aplenty. She could just ignore Hades and pretend she wasn't there.

She had bathed nude with her nymphs many a time and thought nothing of it, but still she blushed to set aside her towel, keeping her back to Hades all the while. She walked to the open showers, standing under the cold spray to rinse herself, shivering as her skin turned to gooseflesh.

Once she was clean, she squeezed out the excess water from her hair, delaying the moment when she had to turn around and cross the steps between the showers and the bath. It took a few deep breaths to relax the muscles in her forehead. Deflower a building? She had never heard anything so ridiculous. Hades just had to sweep every innocent thought into the gutter.

When she turned around at last, Hades wasn't even looking at her, preoccupied with weaving her hair into a braid. Persephone stepped into the bath, flinching as the warm water enveloped her. She lowered herself on a seat until she was covered up to her chin. "You shouldn't do that when it's wet," she said. "The strands will break."

Hades finished her braid and tossed it over her shoulder. "You seem unusually concerned for my well-being today."

Persephone crossed her arms over her chest and glared, then forced herself to look away and relax her posture. Her well-meant intention to ignore Hades seemed impossible, like the gesture of an opium addict throwing away their pipe. She would always come back to her.

Wait. Always?

Persephone stewed in silence, trying to draw comfort from her warm and lush surroundings and failing miserably. The staccato drip of a water clock wore away at her consciousness, her thoughts spiraling in ever-decreasing circles.

She hated Hades. She *hated* her.

She didn't know how long she sat there, mute and miserable in her own personal level of Tartarus, when Hades waded to the steps and climbed out, water sluicing down her back in rivulets, leaving beads on her bare skin as it dripped down from the end of her braid. Persephone caught a glimpse of some discoloration on Hades' stomach—a birthmark?—but Hades turned away so quickly that it might've been a trick of the light.

Hades picked up a towel and dried herself before walking toward the lounging area. With her back to Persephone, she set aside her towel and fussed with something out of view. She placed one foot on a bench and leaned over, massaging scented oil into her skin. She worked her way around her calf, up over her knee and along her thigh, then straightened up and repeated the process on her other leg.

Persephone knew she ought to look away, but she did not, even when Hades began turning her attention to the rest of her skin. She watched the way light and shadow played over Hades' body as she massaged the oil all over herself, her hands running over the curve of her hips, dipping in toward her waist and flowing out over her breasts. Hades raised her arms over her head and ran her hand over one wrist and down toward her shoulder before gathering more oil in her palm and repeating it on the other side.

When Hades was finally done, she picked up her damp towel and left, without ever once looking back.

It was as though a spell had been broken. Persephone sucked in a mouthful of air, then stood. The bath water had grown too hot for her flushed and over-heated skin. She went to the showers and blasted herself with a jet of cold water, yelping as the pressure hit her in the chest. She turned off the flow, shivering again as she leaned her forehead against the wall.

Alone at last. What she'd wanted, but there was no peace to be found, not here, not with the scent of asphodels still lingering in the air.

At the front of the bath chamber, the water clock continued to drip, and a small bell rang out to mark the changing of the hour.

Persephone found no rest that night, not with the image of Hades' nude and glistening form seared into her eyes. She shifted uncomfortably in her bed, cheeks pinking as her mind betrayed her, going back over and over again to the slightest of details. The curve of Hades' thigh. The way her shoulder blades shifted as she stretched. The smallest glimpse of the side of her breast.

She settled further down on her pillow and parted her knees under the sheets. Her hand crept between her legs, and she was not at all surprised to find herself already wet, her folds parting at the slightest touch.

She'd thought she'd been cured of this, cured of wanting *her*, but it seemed there was nothing in the underworld that Hades had not spoiled.

Persephone tried to put Hades out of her mind, to think of anything else. The plump pink bow of Aphrodite's lips. The sleek, long legs of Artemis's huntresses. That serving girl who had worked for Demeter one harvest, until Demeter had caught them behind a grain silo, their lips locked in a kiss.

None of it was helping.

Persephone bit her tongue in frustration. The sharp bright tang of ichor flooded her mouth, grounding her. She rocked her hips from side to side, seeking peace, seeking an end to the images that tormented her, but it would not come.

Was Persephone so debauched, so broken to need Hades' touch and hers alone?

She pictured herself in the bathhouse again, but she was different this time. A huntress. She plucked the oil flask from Hades and took over, running her hands over Hades' nude and warm flesh, kissing the surprise from her face. Pushing her onto the bench, pressing on her shoulders until she was at the perfect height. Entangling her hand in Hades' braid, tilting her face upward. Watching the lust smoldering in her eyes. Jutting her hips forward and pulling Hades in to meet her, until her lips were upon Persephone's sex, until her tongue was inside her, until—

Persephone pressed her face into her pillow and silently screamed, her hands fisted in the sheets. This wasn't fair. It wasn't *fair*.

Her knees locked together as she shuddered, her skin feeling alive as though she had touched one of Zeus's bolts. Her fingers stilled between her legs; her wrist ached.

She kicked off the blankets covering her and curled up with her knees hugged to her chest. Demeter had always said there was something wrong with her. Perhaps she'd been right after all, and there was some kind of sickness lurking inside Persephone, a sort of darkness only a mother could see.

No one in her position would want Hades. Would they?

Hades had brought her to ruin, made Persephone unfit for any virtuous marriage. The idea of someone else touching her—gently, lovingly—aroused nothing, no emotion either for good or ill, but left her feeling hollow and vacant. Even if she left the underworld, someday, somehow, she would never truly be free.

She sat up, went to her wash basin and cleaned herself up. She smoothed her tunic down over her hips and ran her fingers through her hair.

A sliver of light shone beneath the door to Hades' rooms. Persephone had no idea what time it might be, though it felt late. She took a deep breath and knocked. Hades made an indistinguishable sound, and she took that as assent, opening the door.

Hades was seated in bed, a scroll in her hands. Her shoulders were bare, her hair lying loose over them, the furs pulled up high to leave her entirely covered.

Persephone wasn't sure if that sudden sharp stabbing feeling in her chest was relief or disappointment.

"What do you want?" Hades asked. "The hour is late."

"I can't sleep," Persephone said, then silently rebuked herself. Sleeping was practically her function, or a part thereof —she'd lost the habit of drifting down into her earth dreams sometime in the last few months because there was so much to do and Xenia always struggled to wake her from them. It hadn't even occurred to her to try.

Hades gave her a long, hard look. "Someone in the kitchens could prepare you a tisane," she said.

Persephone shook her head. "What are you reading?"

Hades glanced down at the scroll in her hands. "A land development report."

"That sounds boring."

"It is."

"Would you read it to me? I'm sure it would help. Put me to sleep." Without waiting for an answer, Persephone walked to the side of Hades' bed. She gestured. "Move over."

Hades lowered her scroll, staring at her with cold and unwelcoming eyes.

If she had to suffer, Hades would too—she had only brought it upon herself. Persephone slid into Hades' bed, forcing Hades to move over or be crushed. Hades moved.

When was the last time she'd been here? That night before her first lesson with Stephanus. An eon ago, now.

Hades had said she would not touch Persephone unless invited. Her words were both Persephone's shield and the walls to her own cage; she had given Persephone the key and set herself as jailer.

Persephone molded a pillow to fit her head and arranged the furs to her liking. The sheets were warm from the heat of Hades' body, with the queen herself clearly naked under the bedclothes. It created a sweet ache in Persephone's chest, knowing she was so close, and yet a cubit of empty bed separated them, forming the no man's land between their opposing wills.

"Are you quite done?" Hades asked.

"Mm." The faint scent of asphodels tickled Persephone's nose. "Go on," she said. "Don't let me interrupt."

Hades continued to watch her for a few moments, her grip

on the parchment so tight it threatened to ruin her report. She glanced down, struggling to find her place.

The report was just as dull as she'd promised. Apparently, the Asphodel Fields only had room to expand in one direction: east, toward Elysium. But it disturbed the shades in the Asphodel Fields to catch even a glimpse of Elysium—so close, yet forever out of reach. The report detailed various options to shape the landscape, to prevent this from happening.

Persephone let the details wash over her and instead studied the shape of Hades' lips, the contours of her face. She had such focus, radiating stillness like the depths of a frozen pond. Hades worked too much. All these clever humans surrounding her, but none worthy enough to read a simple report? Work was her addiction, her crutch. If Persephone remained in the underworld... If she had to stay, she wouldn't allow herself to be put in second place.

Hades finished her sentence, then looked at Persephone. Her fingers creased the scroll. "This is a dangerous game you play. Are you certain you wish to trifle with me?"

Persephone opened her mouth, then closed it again. Certain... Nothing about Hades made her certain about anything, least of all her own feelings.

"Go to bed, Persephone. Your own bed."

Persephone pouted. "Maybe a few more lines—"

"No."

It wasn't always easy to tell when Hades was actually angry with her, or when she was using anger to mask some other, more dangerous emotion. Hades' pupils were dilated, her nostrils slightly flared. Persephone had thought she'd washed herself well, but now she wondered if she still stank of arousal.

Persephone flung back the blankets and swung her legs

over the side of the bed. She was about to leave, then turned, leaning over to kiss Hades' cheek. "Good night, Hades."

Hades said nothing.

Persephone went to her room and closed the door, resting against it as it clicked shut.

She had no idea what she wanted. Not anymore.

Some time later, Hades hosted a banquet to celebrate some obscure piece of underworld history or some forgotten god. Feast days in the underworld did not match those on the surface; Persephone knew she ought to study their calendar at some point, but it had never been a priority.

The fare at her table was noticeably poorer than it had been on previous occasions. Persephone toyed with the food on her plate in a desultory manner. Wheaten cakes, again, with a little fish, but her greens were badly wilted, and there were no other fresh vegetables to speak of.

"Hades," she began, "what season is it in the overworld?"

Hades paused, her chalice halfway to her lips. She set it down. "Summer, I should think."

"Again?" Persephone dropped her knife. She looked down at her hands. She would never be as pale as Hades, but her skin had lost its sun-kissed glow, her freckles faded. She'd been here for more than a year, but she'd scarcely noticed the time passing. There was so much to do—her little infrastructure projects, the care and maintenance of her grove, of course, and the various official duties that she performed in her role as Hades' consort.

She'd become disconnected from the seasons, distant from all the natural cycles. Nothing else could explain her distorted perception of time. If this went on, she'd forget who she once was, just like poor Cerberus, only she wouldn't need Lethe's water to break her mind. Simply remaining here, stranded in a world separated from Gaia's rhythms, would be enough to drive her mad.

"That would mean our wedding anniversary was some time in the past," Persephone said.

Hades eyed her warily over the top of her chalice. "Yes."

"We did not exchange gifts."

"Is there something in particular that you want?" Hades asked, enunciating each word carefully, as if she were dreading the answer.

Persephone played with her wheat cake, tearing it into tiny shreds. "There is only one thing I've ever asked of you."

"Untrue, but you know why I cannot grant your wish." Hades' hand hovered near Persephone's shoulder as though she was going to touch her, but then she must have thought better of it, as she withdrew soon after.

Persephone pushed back her chair and stood. The entire hall went silent, with every assembled person and deity of the underworld turning to glance in her direction. She looked at Hades, expecting some reaction, but Hades did nothing to stop her. She turned and fled from the dining hall, taking the stairs down three at a time.

She didn't have to suffer this, didn't have to bear witness, trapped and silently screaming as she slowly lost herself. She could go to Lethe now, drink of its waters. It was always there as a fallback, in the event that she could not endure this captivity any longer and simply wished to drown her sorrows. But then, if she no longer remembered who Hades was, what she'd done to her, why would she try to resist Hades' silken tongue and her warm hands and warmer bed? No, she couldn't bear that. Lethe was not an option, not unless she wanted to let Hades win.

She was turning a corner when she almost ran into a young scribe, his arms overburdened with scrolls.

"Forgive me," he stammered, dropping a scroll.

Persephone leaned down and picked it up for him. She caught a glimpse of its contents as she handed it back: tallies of the dead, organized by date of arrival. "It's late," she said, not without sympathy. "Is Hades keeping you up all night with work?"

The man's face flushed a deep red, the same red as the acne he had not thought to erase from his self-image, now that he was dead. "The work is an honor," he said, eyes downcast. "I bring news for Hades' attention."

Whatever it was, it couldn't be good. "I found you first," Persephone said. "Let's walk together, and you can tell me on the way."

The man quailed but did as he was told, speaking quickly and walking even more quickly. "The number of new arrivals has almost doubled since the same time last year," he said.

Persephone frowned. "Is there a war?"

He shook his head.

They entered the dining hall together, but Hades was nowhere to be seen.

Persephone hailed a serving girl. "Where is your queen?" she asked.

"She has gone to the Plain of Judgment," the girl said.

Persephone looked to the scribe. "Come on, then."

The man had seemed somewhat relieved to find Hades gone, but now he turned to Persephone and gulped. "Horses make me nauseous."

"We'll just have to manage," Persephone said.

She took a torch and went to the stables, all but dragging the scribe behind her, and borrowed a chariot. The man hugged his scrolls to his chest and hung onto the chariot rails, white-knuckled.

She found Hades on a small rise overlooking the Plain of Judgment. Persephone hopped out of the chariot whilst it was still moving, leaving the scribe to bring the horses to a complete stop, and walked over to where Hades was standing.

Hades did not turn to look at her as Persephone approached. She seemed small against the vast surroundings, the Tyrian purple of her chiton appearing almost black under the night sky. The wind pulled at her skirts and flickered the torch that Persephone held to light her way.

Persephone glanced down at the line of the dead below them. It was not just the very young and old, as was customary at this time of year, but whole families, including adults who looked to be in their prime. All showed some degree of emaciation, their hair falling out, cheeks sunken and hollow, their features lit by the torches they carried.

"A famine?" Persephone asked.

"I knew the numbers were unusually high," Hades said, as though talking to herself. "I should have paid closer attention.

The ranges were consistent with natural fluctuation. But now..."

"Queen Hades," the scribe said, dropping to his knees a few steps behind them. "I've looked at the figures for the last few months, and the deaths keep increasing. The growth seems to be exponential."

"What does that mean?" Persephone asked.

Hades turned to her at last, her eyes completely black from edge to edge. "It means someone up there is not doing her duty," she said, her voice flat, devoid of affect.

Despite knowing she was not the target of Hades' ire, Persephone trembled. She looked down again. There could be no mistaking it; these people had all been starving before they'd died. "There has to be some other explanation," she said. "My mother would not abandon her duty, not when this is the result. Demeter knows that harvest quotas must be met—"

"Demeter is a selfish *malakismeni,* and she always has been!" Hades snapped.

Persephone gasped and pressed her fingertips to her lips in horror. Behind her, the scribe trembled on his knees, his forehead touching the ground.

Hades seemed to notice him for the first time. "You," she said. "Come with me. I must send several missives tonight."

The scribe scrambled to his feet, his head bobbing in agreement.

"What can I do to help?" Persephone asked.

Hades' mouth twisted, the corners down-turned. "Talk to the dead. Confirm their story."

"Of course," Persephone said, grateful to have something to do. "There will be some other reason for this," she added.

"We shall see."

20

NOT WANTED

T he reasons were all the same, just as Hades had anticipated. Crops were failing, grain withering on the stem. Famished cattle collapsing in the fields, the flies thick over their bodies. Last year's stores were long gone, and the price of food had jumped to astronomical heights.

There was nothing else to explain it, save that Demeter had abandoned her worshipers, heedless of their prayers and sacrifices. Persephone could not believe it. Her mother had never seemed so cruel as to look upon a starving child and deny them succor.

The following day, she sought out Hades in her study. It was a large, airy room connected to the library with high, small windows to permit natural light. The walls were lined with scrolls, but there was also ample space to relax on padded klinai.

Hades was not alone.

"Hermes!" Persephone cried upon seeing the golden-haired god. She ran to him and embraced him, clinging to his neck, her feet leaving the floor.

"Sweet sister," he said, laughing and returning her embrace.

His hair smelled like meadow grass, grown beneath Helios's watchful gaze. It brought tears to Persephone's eyes, and she blinked them away.

"Has Hades been keeping you well?" Hermes asked, taking a step back and looking her over.

Hades was right there in the room, leaning against a table, her arms crossed. Her chiton of Tyrian purple seemed rumpled as though she'd slept in it, or perhaps not slept at all.

"Yes, I am quite well," Persephone said. "What news do you bring of my mother?"

Hermes sighed. He glanced at Hades from beneath his long lashes. "Perhaps now is not the time—"

"More humans die every day," Hades said, sounding almost bored. "A season ago was the time, but as we cannot have that, then today must suffice."

"Yes. Well. Demeter sends her regards—"

Hades scoffed, rolling her eyes skyward.

"—and demands the safe return of her daughter. She has regretfully informed Zeus that she will not resume her duties until Persephone is under her care," Hermes said.

"Can she do that?" Persephone asked. "Give up everything, just like that?"

"If your father cannot command her to be sensible, then I suppose yes," Hades said, examining her nails.

"All the gods and goddesses have begged her to come to her senses," Hermes said. "We are all losing followers, more day by day."

"And my fields are swelling with shades. The queues for judgment are becoming unmanageable," Hades said. "What if I were to reject them all, send them pouring back into the mortal world? Demeter is not the only one among us who could bring civilization to ruin."

Persephone's face paled. "But you would never."

"I am sorely tempted," Hades snapped.

"I brought a witness." Hermes gestured toward the door. "If you'd permit me."

"Persephone has already questioned the dead," Hades said.

"All the same. I believe you should hear this for yourself."

At Hades' nod, Hermes went to the door and admitted a mortal, one of the newly dead. He had the brightness of one who still thought himself among the living, and though his frame was gaunt, his clothes were fine and trimmed with embroidery.

At Hermes' prodding, he walked before them and fell to his knees, bowing his head. "O great Hades, Host of Many, Savior of the Dead—"

"On with it," Hades said.

The man bit his lip. "O Queen, my name is Chalcodon. I was the magistrate of Oropus. When the harvests failed last year, we were penitent. We sacrificed our best steers and goats in Demeter's name; we cleaned her temples and had the priests sprinkle sacred water over the barren earth. Everyone went hungry that year, but Poseidon took pity upon us and filled our nets, and we had enough."

Persephone glanced at Hades. Her expression betrayed nothing, and she gestured for Chalcodon to continue.

"This summer has been cruel and scorching. Scarcely half our fields had sprouted, and what grew soon withered beneath the intensity of the blazing heat. We struggled to find enough pasture for our flocks and were forced to slaughter many before their time. My daughters' children were stillborn and tiny, stunted by their mothers' hunger."

Chalcodon paused to take a breath, his eyes glimmering. "We still pray to Demeter, though many say she has abandoned us, but there is nothing left to sacrifice. People clash in the street over a scrap of flour, and even the rats have abandoned our cities, hunted and slain by starving families. Order has collapsed. When a man's wages cannot feed one person, let alone six, what point is there in work? We must have sustenance," Chalcodon said, wringing his hands. "Please, O Queen. It is too late for me, but perhaps the rest in my city can still be saved."

Silence reigned. Chalcodon kept his gaze meekly downcast, his hands on his knees trembling from their combined divine presence.

"I have heard your words," Hades said. "You may go."

Chalcodon gratefully climbed to his feet and left, the door creaking shut behind him.

"You see why you must concede," Hermes said.

"Me? Why should I do anything?" Hades asked. "I have not abandoned all sense of duty, of mercy. I have done nothing wrong."

"One of you must yield," Hermes said. "For all our sakes."

Hades stood very still, save for a muscle twitching under her left eye. Then she exhaled, her shoulders dropping. "You must be tired after your journey. Go avail yourself of my hospitality and rest. My answer will be with you on the morrow."

Hermes shifted from foot to foot, the wings on his sandals fluttering. "Zeus expected me to return this evening—"

"Zeus can wait."

"As you say." He nodded to Hades. "Little sister," he said

by way of parting to Persephone, and then left, closing the door behind him.

As soon as his footsteps receded in the distance, Hades took something from her belt and threw it at the door. It all happened so quickly that Persephone jumped at the thud. The door sprouted the hilt of Hades' dagger at head height, the metal still quivering.

"Damn him. Damn your mother and damn Zeus for letting her indulge in her worst despotic fantasies!"

Persephone's first instinct was to deny it, but she could not. Not after meeting with the dead, not after seeing their tiny babes in their arms—premature, sickly before their time. The adults and older children might remake their images—appearance was malleable among the dead—but the infants? What would happen to them? Would they ever age?

Demeter would see reason. She had to.

Hades ran a hand over her braids, mussing them. She glanced at Persephone, as if surprised to find her still there, and jerked her chin toward a kline. "Sit down. We must discuss your mother."

"I can do so on my feet—"

"Sit. Down."

Persephone sat on the edge of the kline, her back rigid.

Hades remained standing. "Tell me about Demeter," she said.

"She's the goddess of the harvest, of fertility—"

"That is common knowledge. What was she like as a mother? How does she treat her human subjects?"

Persephone fought for something to say. "She looked after me when I was young. She doesn't like soft cheeses. I've never seen her harm a human." She bit her lower lip. "She is my mother. You must know her as a peer."

"Demeter has many faults, but I never once thought she would turn her back on her own progeny."

"She did not neglect me."

"Then why was Stephanus the first person to teach you your letters? Why is your swordsmanship lacking, your mathematics dire, and your knowledge of history non-existent?"

Persephone's cheeks flushed to hear herself described in such a manner. "It's not her fault. I'm simply a poor student."

"Not her fault!" Hades slammed her fist on the table, making Persephone jump. "It is the duty of the parent to prepare their child for the brutality of the world we find ourselves in. And you are not a poor student. If you would take anything from your time here, remember that the world of knowledge lies at your feet. And you are more than capable of grasping it."

Persephone fiddled with the fraying edge of her chiton. "She's always busy," she said in a faint whisper.

Hades looked down at her, studying her expression. "She frightens you, that is plain to see."

Persephone blanched.

Hades paced across the rug, then back again, restless. "I always thought—Zeus claimed—I was wrong, it seems," she said, her face sour. She stopped pacing, hands clasped behind her back, and looked again at Persephone. "You were not wanted, is that so? But a goddess of fertility can hardly deny the seed forced upon her."

Persephone squeezed her hands tight in her lap and looked down at them, willing herself not to cry.

"Yes," Hades said to herself with more confidence. "That

would explain her indifference. But it is wrong to blame a child for the sins of the father."

"I wasn't an easy child—"

"Stop making excuses for her!"

Persephone flinched.

Hades looked at her and sighed, rubbing her hand across her face. "Forgive my tone," she said, more quietly. "It is not your fault—neither your upbringing, nor the situation we find ourselves in. The latter fault lies with me. I should not have underestimated Demeter." She briefly pressed her knuckles against her lips before speaking again. "She has ever been a selfish one. Perhaps you know that."

"She takes pains that others won't see," Persephone said quietly, fighting against every survival instinct that warned her not to speak ill of Demeter.

"Yes. I believe she hates me because I remember a time when she was imperfect." Hades clasped her hands behind her back again, her gaze distant. "At the height of the Titanomachy, it seemed certain that we—the gods—would lose."

It had been before Persephone's time, but every child knew about the War of the Titans. "What did she do?"

"I caught her preparing to broker a deal with the Titans that would save her own skin but doom the rest of the gods. If Zeus had found out, she would have been cast down—chained in Tartarus, or worse."

"You kept her secret."

"I chose to believe that she was sorry. That she repented. I never warned the others of her erstwhile treachery." Hades sighed. "We all make mistakes, after all." She stared pensively into the distance. "If she saw you. If you... returned to her. Would she relent?"

Persephone didn't know whether to hope, the strain of her yearning an ache in her chest. "It would mean she'd won. She likes that. She would be magnanimous in victory."

"Are you sure?"

"Yes," Persephone said with more conviction than she felt. "What should we do? Perhaps if she knew I was safe, she would relent. We could send a token—"

"These deaths demand more than a token," Hades said. She went to the door and pulled out her dagger, sending chips of wood flying. She looked down at the blade, turning it over and over between her fingers. "Go. Pack your things."

"You—you'd truly send me back?" Persephone whispered.

Hades looked up at her. "All your wishes have come true," she said dryly. The dagger sketched a short arc in the air as she gestured. "I shall ask Hermes to deliver you to Zeus, so that he might mediate your return. He sanctioned our union and is obliged to respect it, else be seen as an oath-breaker. You should not meet with Demeter unaccompanied."

Persephone stared at her, open-mouthed. This was what she'd wanted. What she'd begged of Hades, what she'd dreamed of for so long.

So why did it feel like the ground was collapsing beneath her feet?

She ran up to Hades and embraced her, burying her face into Hades' neck. Hades remained still, not moving to touch Persephone of her own accord.

Persephone drew back, her hands on Hades' shoulders. "Thank you," she whispered, tears in her eyes, then turned and fled before Hades could change her mind, before Persephone could let her own doubts overwhelm her.

Home. She was going *home*.

21

AS MY WIFE

There was not much for Persephone to pack, in truth. She visited her grove, touching the trunk of each tree as she passed by. It seemed odd to think that this could be the last time she walked this path, felt this electric hum in the air, the ringing in her ears from the song of the green ghosts all around her. It had never been this intense in the overworld, not when she'd had to share some of her duties with Demeter and all the other minor gods and goddesses of the land.

When she came to the end of the grove, she turned back and plucked a single fruit from the nearest tree. She took it with her to the palace and set it aside with her other belongings.

She folded some spare clothes in a pile, then placed on it her wax tablet and stylus, a few skin creams and grooming implements, and the pomegranate she'd saved from her grove. She wrapped all of her things into a neat bundle and tied them off with a belt, before sitting beside it on the bed and looking around herself.

There were some things she would miss. And she would

always be grateful to Hades for introducing her to the written word—and for granting Persephone her own land and the right to pronounce judgment. She'd learned more in the last year than she'd had in the previous century above ground.

But now she was going home.

She knocked on the door connecting Hades' chambers with her own. "Hades? Are you there?"

Hearing no answer, she opened the door and stepped inside. It felt empty. A chlamys lay on the floor, breaking the almost sterile order of the room. Persephone picked it up and brought it to her face, inhaling the scent of asphodels. She swung it around her shoulders and buttoned it in place.

She could read the labels on the scrolls now. They were sorted by author and time period: poetry, plays, medical texts, memoirs of great generals and human leaders. She looked through them aimlessly, well aware she was not meant to pry, when she glanced at the bottom shelf and found something more interesting.

She crouched down and picked up a scroll. It was one amongst many, unassuming, but when she unrolled it, she forgot how to breathe.

She read it twice. There were two signatures on the bottom: Zeus's and Hades'. She recognized Hades' hand from long exposure: the firm downstroke, the regular spacing.

Her marriage contract. The date was more than a century ago, occurring not long after that fateful celebration at Zeus's palace. The papyrus was not fragile, despite its age; perhaps one of Hades' sorcerers had enspelled it.

Between that time and her descent into the underworld, Hades had never once darkened her doorstep, the asphodels notwithstanding. Why? Why wait so long to claim what—in the eyes of the gods—was legally hers?

She saw no mention of Demeter in the contract, which did not surprise her. Her mother must have been blindsided by the whole affair; no wonder she had retaliated against Zeus and Hades with the only power left to her.

She read it again. In print, she was reduced to a commodity —an expensive one, at that. No dowry for her but a bride price that could have beggared kings. Precious metals and gems from the earth, bales of wool, cattle, and more. Surely it was a sign of how much Zeus disliked Hades and had nothing to do with Persephone's worth. Zeus would not have demanded of Hephaestus a single drachma, had he asked for her hand.

Below all the material goods was a single line: Semele, daughter of Cadmus and Harmonia, restored to her natural lifespan.

Semele. The name sounded familiar.

It seemed so long ago now, but hadn't that been the name of Zeus's lover, the one he'd tried to win away from Hades when Persephone had accidentally overheard their conversation?

Persephone re-rolled the scroll with numb fingers and returned it to its resting place. She tried to tell herself it changed nothing. It didn't matter what Zeus and Hades had decided without her consent—she was going home.

She adjusted the set of the chlamys around her shoulders and left Hades' rooms. The corridors of the palace seemed eerily quiet. Many servants had been reassigned to different duties, with extra bodies needed to process the ever-increasing flow of the newly arrived dead. The few people she saw all looked harried and exhausted, eager to be out of her sight.

Persephone walked through the library, her bare feet silent

against the rugs. She would miss this, too—the smell of papyrus and carbon ink, the way the stylus gave her blisters after too much time spent studying—even Stephanus and his callous indifference to her status.

She stopped outside of Hades' study and knocked.

"Not now," came Hades' voice, sounding muffled.

Persephone opened the door.

"Did I not say—oh."

The study was a mess, by Hades' standards. She sat behind a table littered with scrolls, the index finger of her sword arm stained with ink. Hades ran her hand through her hair; it was loose, tumbling in a riot of curls to the small of her back. She looked like a wild thing, like one of the savage goddesses of Anatolia. It was such a departure from her usual cool, composed self that Persephone did not know how to react.

"Close the door," Hades said, her voice hoarse.

Persephone did so. The gentle click of the door settling into its frame seemed too loud. "Hades, have you... have you been crying?"

Hades set back her chair and stood. She went to a small table beside a set of klinai and poured herself a cup of wine, then drained it in one swallow. "I have not cried since the day Zeus and Poseidon bade me to rule over this place," she said, still holding the empty cup, her gaze on the wine jug as if longing for another. "To show weakness before the gods is to suffer a fate worse than death."

"I'm no god."

"Ah, well." Hades looked at Persephone, her eyes red-rimmed but dry. "I might shed a tear for you yet."

"This melancholy ill suits you," Persephone said.

Hades fluttered a hand in the air. "My apologies, wife," she said mockingly. "Should I bare my breast and pray to Gaia to deliver me of my woes? Or should I put on a smile and behind closed doors punish those left beside me for their crime of following a goddess too weak to hold her own?"

"You are not weak."

"I had not heard." Hades poured herself another cup and drank it, slower this time.

Persephone plucked the empty cup from her grasp. "That's enough."

Hades glared at her. "You have what you wanted. Why are you here?"

Persephone placed the cup and the wine jug on a sideboard, out of Hades' reach. "I came to say goodbye."

"Fine. Goodbye." Hades retreated behind her desk and sat down, picking up a reed pen. "Now, get out. I have work to do."

Persephone could not be moved so easily. "I saw my marriage contract. The one you made with Zeus."

"So?" Hades began to write, her pen scratching out a few short words before she glanced up again. "What?"

Persephone was no longer the little girl who'd been awed by Hades' reputation, who could be cowed by a voice raised in anger. She refused to be that girl. "You traded Zeus's lover for me," she said.

"Among other things."

"You never let the dead leave the underworld."

Hades sighed. "Usually."

"You *never* let them leave."

"Clearly, that is untrue," Hades snapped. "You have seen the evidence."

The enormity of that decision gnawed at Persephone. "Why?"

"Why the moon and stars?" Hades asked dryly. She stared longingly at the wine jug.

"Why break your word... for me?"

Hades wiped clean her reed pen. "I never gave Zeus my word that he could absolutely not have her; I only said he had nothing worth my time."

"But then..."

"After that day... I could not stop thinking of you." Hades crumpled her sheet of papyrus, ruining it. "The echo of your pulse haunted me."

"You signed that contract over a hundred years ago," Persephone said.

"And if I were prescient, I might not have bothered and saved us all a world of pain."

"Why did you wait so long?"

"It matters not."

"It does to me."

Hades threw her hands in the air. "I was not yet certain of my intentions. To condemn another soul to this life—I had to be sure."

"What made you sure?"

"Fortune. You were there, so close to my domain, and for once, without your mother's protection—it was fate. I could not ignore the workings of the Moirai."

"That's not it," Persephone said, biting her lip in frustration.

"What do you want?" Hades demanded. "Do you want a ballad, something flowery and charming in the voice of Erato?"

"I want the truth. You owe me that much."

Hades clasped her hands together and pressed her lips to

her knuckles. She did not speak for some time, but Persephone waited, unwilling to be the first to break the silence.

"You have always had—a light about you," Hades began slowly. "As your powers have matured, it has only grown. It called to me that day I saw you."

"The day you refused Zeus."

Hades nodded. "And if not fate, then what should I name it? There is no death without life and no life without death. Something in each of us yearns for the other. You have felt it, too."

Persephone labeled her fascination with Hades a sick obsession. Her weakness. "I don't know what I've felt."

"I feel..." Hades paused. "You disarm me. I burn in Tartarus each day from your hatred, when all I wish is to have and to keep you and to never allow another person to lay hands upon you again." She leaned back in her chair, her gaze raw with longing. "You stole my heart, and now it beats, fragile and weeping, within your fist. I should despise you for that."

"I don't hate you," Persephone whispered. "Perhaps once, but not anymore. Not for a long time."

The air seemed too heavy, too pregnant with possibilities. She held Hades' heart? What did that even mean for them? "Will we meet again?" she asked.

Hades placed her palms on the table. She had accidentally touched her face with her ink-stained hands, leaving a smudge on her cheek. "Our lives are endless, to a point. I will doubtless see you in the overworld, at one event or the other."

"But not as your consort."

"No. You have made your feelings on that subject abundantly clear," Hades said, pronouncing each syllable with precision.

Persephone's feelings were as tangled as the threads of the Moirai. There was no logic to them, no harmony; nothing to ground her in this swirling sea of confusion.

You stole my heart.

It had never been her intention.

Nothing about this made sense, least of all what she was about to do.

Persephone's hand went to the fastening on her chlamys—on Hades' chlamys. She unbuttoned it and allowed it to drop from her fingertips. "I leave tomorrow, with Hermes," she said, unpinning her fibula on first one shoulder, then the other. "You have given your word." She unhooked her girdle, setting it aside. Her chiton pooled on the floor. "But first, I would have you bid me farewell properly. As my"—she took a deep breath—"as my wife."

Hades remained behind the table, her face an expressionless mask. She did not speak, but her throat contracted as she swallowed.

Persephone took a step toward her, rolling her hips as she'd seen Aphrodite do. She was bare save for her perizoma and strophion, and as she walked, she drew the pins from her hair until her curls hung loose.

She reached the table and swept its contents—scrolls, tablets, pens—to the floor, though she was careful not to move the inkstand.

Hades gasped.

The table was myrtle, stained with ink. Persephone climbed on top of it and crawled the short distance to Hades, keeping her back arched, her movements sinuous as a cat's. She reached out with both hands to take Hades' face.

Hades stared at her, gaze ravenous as her once-impeccable control began to slip.

Persephone leaned in and kissed her.

Hades' lips were soft, like she remembered, and tasted of wine. Persephone drew back and traced them with her fingertips, then brushed her thumb over the ink stain on Hades' cheek.

"If you do this," Hades said, her voice a breathy whisper, "if you do this... I will not let you leave."

She might have felt threatened by that, once. "You gave your word," Persephone said. "And here, your word is law. Not even you can escape it." She kissed her again, her fingers entangled in Hades' hair.

Persephone knew she shouldn't want this, knew there was nothing compelling her to choose this, knew it did not sit well with the old narrative of Hades as her keeper and Persephone her unwilling conquest. This blurred the lines, made it impossible to untangle the scores of who owed what to whom.

It did not mean she forgave Hades. She might never forgive Hades.

But if she blamed Hades, then she blamed herself even more, for needing this, for needing *her*.

When Hades finally touched her it was a blessed relief. She straddled Hades' lap, one hand hooking over her shoulder to cling to the back of the chair, the other fumbling to untie Hades' girdle. Her own underthings were long gone, forgotten like the scrolls she'd swept off the top of the table.

Hades' fingers hooked inside of her, binding them together, her other hand braced against the small of Persephone's back. The stretch was exquisite, and Persephone closed her eyes, her hips naturally rocking back against Hades' hand as she allowed her body to set its own pace.

All those months, those empty nights alone with her poetry and her cold bed, she could have been having this... but no. She hadn't wanted this, not before. Now she was leaving, and everything had changed.

Hades lifted her off her lap and laid her on the table so that her legs sprawled over the edge.

Persephone opened her eyes and gazed up at Hades, taking a perverse joy in knowing that the next time Hades sat down to this desk, she would think of Persephone's body, spread out and pierced by her. She hoped Hades would remember the sight for years to come. Hades worked too much, anyway.

"You will be the death of me," Hades said.

"You'd never lose your immortality for long enough," Persephone said. "The first time your successor tried to change the drapes, you'd be ousting them in a coup."

"You think so?"

"I think"—Persephone sighed, a pleasant shiver running over her skin—"you should concentrate on what you were doing with your thumb."

For once, Hades didn't argue. She lowered her head and sucked one of Persephone's nipples into her mouth, applying enough pressure to make Persephone moan.

She shouldn't be enjoying this. Hades' touch ought to make her cringe, to fester on her skin like a wound, not to make her crave more.

But Persephone had not been born for a pure and virginal life, unlike Athena, unlike Artemis, and if she could not accept Hades' love, perhaps she could accept Hades' fingers on her sex and Hades' mouth at her throat.

She did not think to complain when Hades bit her, bruising her; she was beyond thought at that point, her mind spiraling out, her consciousness bursting into an ocean of pleasure.

She savored the moment, basking in it, for once unencumbered by shame or doubt. She leaned her head against Hades' shoulder, her arms loosely twined around her neck, breathing in the scent of her hair.

Hades clasped Persephone to her as if she'd never let go.

That would not do. "You're crushing me," Persephone said. "You can breathe."

Persephone rolled her eyes and squirmed, flipping them so that Hades lay on the table and Persephone hovered above her.

Hades looked... different. There was a haunted cast to her face, a fragile translucency to her skin. Her hair was atramentous against the myrtle, spilling out around her like a halo.

She was wearing too many clothes.

Her peplos was held at the shoulders by seams, not fibulae. Persephone took no small joy in ripping the fabric, ignoring Hades' anguished gasp.

"It will mend," Persephone said, peeling the fabric down to uncover Hades' strophion. "Your rooms are full of these."

"Coan silk, Persephone!"

Persephone wrinkled her nose. "Why would you want something made from bugs when you could have good, honest linen?"

"It dyes better. Black is difficult to set." Hades sat up and untied her strophion herself, as if to prevent Persephone from destroying more of her clothing.

It was the first time Persephone had properly seen this part of her undressed, in the light. What she'd thought to be a birthmark was instead a long, jagged streak of scar tissue that ran from below her right breast to her left hip, wider and thicker over her hip. It had long since healed, shinier and paler than the surrounding skin.

Divine flesh healed well, and even the worst injuries responded to treatment by sorcery. Persephone had never seen such a scar on another goddess. "What happened?" she asked. She reached out and lightly touched it, her fingertips seeking out the shift in textures.

"A memory from the war," Hades said.

There had been many wars but few terrible enough to leave such a mark. "The Titanomachy?" she asked.

Hades nodded, her features tense as Persephone explored the mark with her fingers.

"Why do you keep it?"

"As a reminder," Hades said, her eyes closed.

"A reminder?"

"That my failures are not simply my own but shape the world around me."

Persephone did not know what to say. "Is that why you work so hard?"

"Harvest comes but once a year. Humans die every day."

"That's no excuse. Your scribes are clever. They could do more, if you let them."

"Our burdens are not for them, Persephone."

Persephone glanced away, a bitter taste filling her mouth. No, those burdens were meant to be held by her, as Hades' consort. Her departure placed them back on Hades' shoulders.

"Come," Hades said, reaching for her. "As you say, we have but one night. Let us not speak of prosaic things."

Persephone leaned over, kissing her. She might not be the

queen Hades deserved, but she could be here, in this moment, and lend her all the comfort she could muster.

It wasn't enough, but she gave it freely. Hades clutched her too tightly, after they'd both been sated, her head nestled against Persephone's neck and their legs intertwined, her arms like a vise. Persephone laced her fingers with Hades' and kissed the salt from her cheeks.

22

THE ASCENT

I n the morning, Hades accompanied them as far as the river Styx. She was serene of face and wore her elegance as armor, nothing like the raw and tender goddess who'd held onto Persephone so tightly the night before. Which one was more true, the ruler or the lover? She'd had more than a year to find out, and yet she still wasn't sure.

Behind them, Hermes waited alongside Charon and his boat. Persephone turned her back on them to say her last farewells.

"Send Zeus my regards," Hades said.

"I will." Persephone leaned in and placed a chaste kiss upon Hades' cheek.

As she turned to go, Hades caught her wrist. "Do not forget me," Hades said, her voice low.

"Never."

Hermes cleared his throat.

Hades released her and spoke to Hermes. "Remember what I asked of you."

"All will be well," Hermes said.

Persephone raised her skirts to climb into Charon's boat. She felt the heat of Hades' gaze upon her, but she didn't turn back as Charon unmoored the boat and pushed them away from the riverbank. She sat perfectly still, clutching her possessions to her chest, until they were almost out of sight.

She waited until she could bear it no longer, then she looked back. There was no one at the dock, not even a wandering shade.

Was that tightness in her chest relief, or disappointment?

"Demeter will be overjoyed to see you," Hermes said.

"I have missed her," Persephone said carefully. "I hope Father will not be too displeased at having to intervene."

"She will set things to rights once you are safely above ground."

The bargain seemed unbalanced, her life in exchange for millions of humans. How could she be worth so much pain?

They reached the other side of the river, and Charon brought the boat to a stop. Hermes hopped out and offered his hand.

Persephone took it, climbing out with her belongings. "Thank you," she said over her shoulder to Charon, but the ferryman was already drifting away.

"How are you with heights?" Hermes asked. "It will be faster if I carry you the rest of the way."

"I'll close my eyes."

Hermes nodded and lifted Persephone into a bridal carry. She wrapped one arm around his neck, the other holding onto her possessions.

"Don't look down," he said, and then he was off, the wings on his sandals beating rapidly.

The Styx was a pale ribbon below them, her grove a faint

smattering of trees in the distance. Hades' palace glittered, a little more coldly than usual, as if rebuking her for her betrayal.

Persephone's stomach roiled, and she leaned her head against Hermes' chest, closing her eyes. She belonged beneath the sun and the rain. When was the last time she'd felt rain on her skin?

"We're nearing the transition point," Hermes said, raising his voice to be heard over the wind rushing past them.

Persephone took a deep breath. There was a fizzing pop in her ears, and her stomach dropped. Even with her eyes shut, she felt the sun touching her skin for the first time in over a year. She opened her eyes but had to immediately shut them again. The sky was too bright, blinding her.

Hermes' feet touched solid ground, and he gently let her go. Persephone clung to him, her eyes still screwed shut.

"My baby!"

Someone pulled Persephone away, forcing her to look up. Persephone gasped in shock, too stunned to plaster a smile on her face. Demeter held her at arm's length. Her face looked cadaverous, her wrists brittle as a bird's. But even as Persephone stared, Demeter began changing, a healthy flush returning to her skin.

Persephone looked to Hermes in confusion. Hades had said —she'd made him promise, hadn't she? How could Demeter be here but not Zeus?

Hermes had landed at one of the highest points around. The sea shimmered in the distance, colored a deep cerulean blue. All around them were rocky cliffs and shrubs, dotted with trees. It would have been beautiful and welcoming, had Demeter not been there.

Hermes glanced aside, not meeting her gaze. "You should be with your mother," he mumbled.

"Hermes!" Persephone said in a whisper.

"What has she done to you?" Demeter cried, placing her hand on Persephone's cheek. "Look at how pale you are, how cold!"

Persephone resisted the urge to move and closed her eyes whilst her stomach roiled. She didn't feel cold. If anything, it was much too hot beneath the sun, its rays burning her exposed skin.

Demeter pinched her cheek, hard, before letting her go. "Thank you, Hermes, a thousandfold, for returning my daughter to her rightful place."

Hermes nodded. "Of course," he said. He glanced at Persephone.

Persephone stared at him, willing him to read her eyes, willing him to change his mind and to do as Hades had bidden.

But Hermes either did not know how to read her or did not care. He leapt into the air once more, waving as he departed.

Once he was gone, Demeter turned a saccharine smile on Persephone. "We must get you home at once." She clapped her hands. "Ladies!"

A trio of mounted nymphs approached, two of them leading additional horses. Demeter took one and nodded at Persephone to take the other.

Persephone remained in place, swaying a little on her feet. She'd wished for this moment for so long, but not like this— never like this! If she didn't move, it wouldn't be real. Perhaps she was asleep, lost in her earth dreams and ready to wake by Hades' side—

"Persephone!"

Persephone snapped her head back up. There was nowhere to run. The nymphs flanked her, and before them Demeter waited, impatiently tapping her nails on her horse blanket.

Each second she kept her mother waiting would only cost her later. But she found herself frozen, unable to summon her old sense of self-preservation. "Where are we going?" she asked.

"Home, of course, you foolish child."

"I want to see my father," Persephone said.

"Zeus has more important matters to attend to than the likes of you."

Persephone glanced around and looked more closely at the nymphs. She could not recall their names, though she could have sworn she'd seen their faces before.

One was tall and lanky, as though she hadn't quite grown into her limbs. She wore a blue chiton, trimmed with yellow. The second had red water fern in her hair and might have belonged to a river nearby. The third looked more like a child of the earth, short with powerfully muscled arms and legs.

If Demeter had chosen them to accompany her here, they would be of no help to Persephone.

"Come now, girl. We've tarried long enough," Demeter said, her tone honey-sweet.

Persephone gathered up her chiton in one hand and hopped astride her mount. Hermes had taken them through an unfamiliar exit of the underworld, and she did not immediately recognize her surroundings—grassy cliffs and weathered paths but no buildings or signs of habitation within view.

"Finally," Demeter said, turning her horse to head down the path. The color had returned to her hair, and she looked much like her usual exalted self. Had Persephone imagined her mother's transformation? No. But then why would Demeter make herself look so sickly? To arouse pity?

The nymphs moved into a diamond formation, with Persephone at the center, unable to break free. They rode for some time, passing through the deserted countryside. Persephone kept looking at all the life around her, from the various grasses forming the patchy scrub to the occasional fir tree. It took her a little while to adjust to the different life signatures, but once she slipped back in touch with her old habits, it felt like she'd never left.

"Stop that," Demeter said.

Persephone jerked to attention. "What's wrong, Mother?"

Behind Persephone's mare, a trail of wildflowers bloomed, their shy heads marking the path they'd taken.

Demeter made a cutting gesture in the air, and as one the flowers bowed over, wilting on their stems.

Persephone gasped, clutching her hand to her chest. A chill ran over her skin. She'd never felt her gifts being overpowered by another's, much less by her own mother's.

"Don't waste fruitful soil on flowers."

"Have you restored the humans' crops, then?" Persephone asked.

Demeter looked back at her over her shoulder. "The mortals will find me a merciful goddess, now that my prayers have been answered."

If they both prayed to Gaia, why was Demeter so favored over her daughter? Would it always be that way?

They had traveled far enough that Persephone began to recognize the shape of the land around them. They were returning home indeed, to the estate where she'd been born and where she'd lived all her life, save for her brief time in the underworld.

This was what she'd wanted, what she'd begged from Hades. But each league felt more like defeat than victory.

Before long, she saw her mother's house in the distance, surrounded by golden fields of grain. She'd kept her side of the bargain, at least. Hades would be pleased.

Hades would not be pleased once she'd heard of Hermes' treachery.

"Our gracious home," Demeter said. She dismounted, and the nymphs followed suit. "Persephone."

Persephone wiped her palms on her knees and slid off her mare. She walked to her mother.

"Thank you, ladies, for your service," Demeter said as the nymphs guided the horses away.

Persephone watched their backs retreating with a pang of loss. She hadn't even learned their names. Not that it would have saved her.

"Come," Demeter said and opened the back door.

Persephone followed her inside and closed the door softly behind her. The walls had been freshly painted, the smell nauseating. Otherwise, it looked much the same—warm and brightly lit with spacious, high ceilings. After the chill of Hades' palace, it should have felt inviting.

"Sit," Demeter said. "Eat with me."

Persephone did as she was told. They dined together, a servant—Kallon—bringing them food and wine. When Persephone caught his eye, his smile for her was strained.

"Tell me everything," Demeter said.

"There's not much to tell," Persephone said. "I'd rather hear about how you fared. You must have been so worried."

Demeter's mouth twisted into an ugly moue. "There'll be time for that later. Let's start with you."

Persephone gave her a sanitized version of events, careful not to cast aspersion on either Demeter or Hades. At times Demeter interjected to comment on what she saw as Persephone's stupidity, or to exclaim how dreadful the underworld must be. At those moments, Persephone repeated her gratitude toward Demeter for saving her, but it seemed like no matter how fervent her thanks, they were never enough.

She had never talked this much about herself in her mother's presence before, and the conversation seemed to drag on for hours until the sun was low in the sky. Demeter wanted to know everything about Hades, much of which Persephone was unwilling or unable to tell her.

"Is she still using that helm?" Demeter asked.

"Which helm?"

Demeter waved a hand. "Before your time. Did she cry over her human souls? The children used to bother her, if I recall rightly."

Demeter's tone made it seem like the prospect of Hades suffering excited her. Persephone was discomfited by the way Demeter watched her over the rim of her chalice, her eyes too bright and cunning.

"I don't think so," Persephone said.

"A pity. Perhaps all those years underground have muddled her brain. Why else would she think to steal my only daughter, my pride and love?"

"It's done now, Mother," Persephone said. "She sent me back."

"Not without some prodding on my part."

"Is that what you call the murder of thousands of innocents?"

Demeter laughed bitterly. "Innocents? Is that what you think? Don't be so naive."

Persephone could feel herself shrinking, made small by her mother's words. She shifted uncomfortably in her seat. "Some of them were infants."

"The Asphodel Fields will be kinder to them than any city made by man." Demeter stood and walked over to the table where Persephone had set down her meager belongings. "Now, let's see what you brought."

Persephone's face flushed and she leapt to her feet. "Those are my things."

Demeter untied the bundle and ran her hand through the folded clothes and trinkets. As she shook out a chiton, Persephone's pomegranate fell out and rolled along the floor.

"What is this?" Demeter snatched it up. "You dare bring this filth into my house?"

"It's... merely a souvenir. I planted that tree from seed," Persephone said, wanting to reach for it but not daring to.

Demeter narrowed her eyes. "Have you eaten the food of the underworld? Tasted its drink?"

"No."

Demeter's face softened a little before she turned on her heel, striding away. Persephone raced after her, following her into the kitchen.

Kallon was cleaning fish, a skinny filleting knife in his hand. He dropped it onto his cutting board as soon as he saw them, trying simultaneously to wipe his hands on his apron and to bow at the same time.

Demeter ignored him and flung the pomegranate onto the cooking fire.

"Mother!" Persephone cried out, searching for a poker or a long-handled spoon.

Demeter blocked her way to the fire. Behind her, Persephone watched as the pomegranate's skin blackened and began to blister. Persephone grabbed a pail of water from near where Kallon was working, and in the pail a severed fish head bobbed up, turning to stare at Persephone with its dead, glassy eyes.

"What do you think you are doing?" Demeter asked.

"Stand aside, Mother."

Demeter folded her arms, tapping her foot impatiently. The fire crackled behind her, the orange flames contrasting with Demeter's white peplos.

Persephone took a step forward, then another. The pail seemed to grow impossibly heavy in her hands, and her fingers slipped, dropping the pail and spilling water and fish guts all over the kitchen floor.

Persephone braced her hand against a nearby door frame, the world spinning around her. One side of her chiton clung wetly to her leg, cold and reeking of fish.

"What have you done to me?" Persephone asked, unable to move as Demeter approached her.

"I've only ever done what was necessary," Demeter said.

Persephone's heartbeat was a war drum pounding in her head, her eyelids too heavy to hold open. Her fingers lost their grip on the door frame, and she fell gracelessly to the floor, her shoulder smacking into the wooden slats and scattering droplets all around her.

23

LIKE OLD TIMES

Persephone woke to find herself on a hard wooden bed, her head aching, her clothes damp and stinking of fish. She instantly felt she was not alone and sat upright, not managing to stem a gasp of dismay as she took in her surroundings.

She'd been taken to a room adjacent to the root cellar, set below ground, though with a tiny grate at the top of one wall which let in air and light. Standing at the door was her mother, her face partially illuminated by a small torch. Demeter set the torch into a sconce on the wall and moved forward, blocking the light, so that her shadow ran long before her.

"Don't you remember what I said the last time?" Demeter asked.

"I haven't been bad," Persephone whispered.

Demeter laughed. "Oh, but you have. And what's more, I said that if you ever humiliated me before the gods, that would be enough to see you back here."

"You sent me away!"

Demeter sniffed. "I did nothing of the sort. I merely said

you were to leave me in peace for a while. You know how your hysterics give me pains in my head. How was I to know that you would run off and get yourself captured?"

"I tried to escape," Persephone said as her gaze roamed the borders of her cell. It felt even smaller than it had as a child.

"You must not have tried very hard, dear. Even mortals manage to leave the underworld somehow, and you have the pedigree of Olympus behind you."

"I tried—" Persephone bit off her words in frustration. It would not matter what she said. It never did. "You poisoned me."

"Don't be so dramatic. A sleeping draught, nothing more." Demeter approached her. "Look at yourself," she said. She grabbed the front of Persephone's chiton, pulling so hard that Persephone staggered up off the bed. Demeter ripped the fabric and then tore at her necklace, the gold one that Hades had given to her on their wedding day, but it would not come undone.

"What witchcraft is this?" she demanded, still trying to wrench it apart. The chain dug into Persephone's neck every time her mother tugged on it, leaving its imprint on her skin.

"I don't know," Persephone said, trying to hold herself apart from Demeter but unable to shy away.

"Spells. Sorcery." Demeter's lip curled as she tightened her grip, removing any slack from the chain, her knuckles digging into the soft hollow of Persephone's throat. "The rumors must be false. You went to her willingly, bound yourself to her like a slave branded by her master."

Persephone's hands went to her throat as she fought to breathe.

Demeter watched Persephone struggling, her pupils large

in the dark. She was radiant in her malice, golden-haired and glowing, her lips upturned.

She twisted her grip on the chain and then threw Persephone across the room. Persephone slammed into the nearest wall before falling to the floor.

She did not have the strength to get up.

"Well? What do you have to say for yourself?" Demeter asked, walking to her, standing over her with hands on her hips.

Persephone wheezed. She planted her palm on the floor, leaning on it to help herself sit up. "...It's complicated," she croaked, reaching up to feel the divots on her throat where the chain had left its mark.

Demeter scoffed. She leaned down and seized her jeweled diadem, ripping out strands of Persephone's hair in the process. She grabbed at Persephone's wrist and broke the clasp of her bracelet, sending a score of beads bouncing across the stone floor, and tore off her belt inlaid with sapphires.

"You reek of filth and excess," Demeter said. "Hades may have made you her whore, but here you are my daughter, and you will comport yourself as such."

Persephone gathered the torn edges of her chiton, clasping them to her chest. Tears streamed down her face. "Why are you doing this?"

"You are not Hades' wife. Zeus had no power to sell you off without my agreement. You are not a queen of the underworld. You are simply my selfish, ignorant daughter, and I am the person with the misfortune to call myself your mother."

"That's not my fault!"

Demeter slapped her across the face, hard. It was nothing in terms of physical pain; Persephone knew the pain in her heart would linger for far longer.

"You have no idea what trials I've been through to find you," Demeter said, her voice dangerously low. "And for what? To be insulted by a mere seedling of a girl?"

"I'm a woman grown. A married woman." Persephone looked past Demeter to the door. It was made of sturdy oak and iron and could be barred from the outside. "I know what you did. During the war. Hades told me."

Demeter froze for a moment, then recovered. "You're speaking nonsense. Hades lies; everyone knows that."

"That's not what they say, *Mother*. I'll tell them. I'll tell everyone how you were ready to betray them."

Demeter laughed, short and harsh. "You think anyone would believe your word over mine? And for what? Some inconsequential bit of ancient history?" She sneered. "The Titans are long gone. Zeus needs my powers. He has no reason to listen to you on this or any other matter. You will stay here, under guard, until I return from Olympus with an annulment for this farce Hades calls a marriage. Until that time, you will see no one and speak to no one. Do you understand?"

"You can't do this to me," Persephone said. "I—I was given to her. Zeus promised. He gave his word. He won't take it back!"

Demeter looked at her evenly. "He'll do what he must." She picked up the torch again, holding the remnants of Persephone's finery in her other hand.

"Wait!"

Demeter slowly turned.

Persephone tottered to her feet. Hating herself with every step, she walked forward and then lowered herself to her knees, bending her head in supplication. "Please forgive my foolishness," she said, the words coming haltingly to her lips. "I have not thanked you enough for all that you did for me, for coming to my aid." She leaned forward and prostrated herself like a foreigner, her forehead almost touching the floor. "Thank you," she said, breathing in the musty scent of old cheese and parsnips.

Demeter left her stewing there for what felt like an eternity. "I'll see you when I return," she said.

"Mother!" Persephone leapt to her feet, struggling to hold the remnants of her chiton over her chest as she rushed to Demeter's side. "If you must keep me under guard until your business is concluded, I will understand. But it has been a year since I've seen the sun. Please, might I stay some place above ground?"

Demeter gestured to the tiny grate. "You have your view."

"But Mother—"

Demeter ignored her and left the cell, closing the door behind her. Persephone flung herself at it, crying out as her shoulder struck the unyielding wood. She heard the bar slide into place, sealing her inside.

She pounded her fists against the door, then pressed her ear to it, striving to hear any sound from the outside. All she heard was her own breath and the too-rapid rhythm of her heartbeat.

She picked up a cushion from the bed and threw it at the door before letting her head drop into her hands. Her chest felt like it was being squeezed by an invisible fist; she took a few deep breaths to steady herself.

The last time she'd been in here, she'd promised herself never again. She had promised to be good and obedient in all things.

That had worked out so well, hadn't it?

Persephone grabbed the end of the bed and dragged it

across the floor, ignoring the hideous noises it made as the wood scraped along stone. She set it against the wall underneath the grate and hopped on top of it, grasping the bars and peering out.

She was taller than she'd been the last time, since she could see outside without needing to jump. It was dark, with few stars visible. As before, the soil nearest her cell was barren, with not even a single blade of grass within reach. In the distance, the wind stirred Demeter's fields of grain, the same breeze caressing Persephone's cheeks.

She hopped down from the bed and went to the door, running her hand over it. She didn't need light to find the marks scored into the wood by the end of a fibula or the point of a buckle. Each slash was one day she'd spent awake; collectively the door bore witness to long months of captivity. For one stretch, a year of her waking life had been spent in this prison. She'd spent many more years in here, unconscious, surrendering to the dreaming earth.

She turned and fumbled in the dark, finding a chest near where the bed had originally been placed. Inside, there was food and water, enough for a few days, and spare clothing. She changed out of her ruined chiton into a fresh one and wrapped herself in a woolen himation.

She sat down on the floor with her back to the wall, facing the door.

She'd survived the underworld. She could survive this.

Demeter could not be angry forever. And then Persephone would...

Would what? Return to acting as the dutiful child? That role had ever been ill-suited for her, and now it did not seem to fit at all.

What other choice did she have?

Persephone curled up with her knees tucked under her chin, her arms wrapped around them. If she'd stayed with Hades...

No. That hadn't been an option, not with Demeter's threats made real. Coming to the surface had been the right decision.

Demeter would never change. A year apart had given Persephone hope, so quickly dashed. She had endured her mother's moods for centuries, knowing nothing else, and had been prepared to live with them for centuries more, but now...

Great Mother Gaia, lend me your strength, your patience.

She crawled into the bed, huddling in a tight ball under the blankets. One hand grasped the frame—it was pine, the dowels made of oak, as familiar to her as her own name. Closing her eyes, she let the dreaming earth carry her into slumber, willing this torment to be over by the time she woke.

24

DEMETER

The shop was small and dimly lit. It took Demeter's eyes a moment to adjust after the blazing glare of the midday sun.

"May I offer some wine? Or ambrosia, if you'd prefer?"

Demeter waved the attendant away. She was not here for pleasantries. She cast her eye on the dozens of swords racked against the walls, at the variety of spears, bows, and polearms on display. The shop stank of oiled leather and metal.

"The game you seek must be quite special, for you to travel all this way," the attendant said. He was a man of small stature, clean-shaven and wiry.

"Quite." Demeter dismissed the rest of his wares with a glance. "I was told you could help me."

"Of course." The man spoke to his servant in rapid-fire Phoenician. The servant set a 'closed' sign outside the shop and shut the door, blocking the slight breeze that had brushed Demeter's shoulders. The heat of the room settled upon her like a shroud.

"Please, come this way," the man said.

Demeter followed him farther into the building and down several flights of steps. She held her skirts in her hand to stop them from trailing behind her. The man held only a rushlight to show him the way, its flame weak and wavering.

The steps leveled out, and the man fished a key from his belt and opened a door before waving Demeter inside.

She found herself in a cellar littered with objects like the site of a battlefield, sans the bodies. There seemed to be no order to the chaos, with shields stacked haphazardly over suits of armor, halberds and pikes propped up against the walls. She was forced to tread carefully to avoid stepping on trinkets. The air held the acrid taste of preservation charms and some other enchantments—protection against theft, possibly, although at first glance it seemed like nothing of value could be stored here.

"I've seen drakon hoards that were better organized," Demeter said.

The man shrugged. "Appearances can be deceiving." He trudged over to a small cabinet, miraculously managing not to touch anything whilst doing so, and moved several pieces of armor in order to uncover it. He took another key from his belt and unlocked the cabinet, then returned the key and donned a pair of thick leather gloves, the type used in blacksmithing.

Demeter rolled her eyes at this theater, but she waited all the same, unable to tear her gaze away from what he was doing.

She was almost disappointed when the man brought out a small clay jar, stoppered and sealed with wax. He gently set it down on top of the cabinet.

"That's it?" Demeter asked.

"The poison of the Lernaean hydra," the man said. "Strong enough to fell the most powerful hero. Even an immortal," he added slyly.

Demeter considered the drab container. "How can you prove this?"

The man brought one gloved hand to hover over his chest, careful not to touch the cloth of his tunic with the glove. "My word and my reputation are all I have," he said. "Strike me down if you find me a liar."

Demeter worried at her bottom lip, calculating. She would have to conduct her own tests, of course—though not here. She had no real suspicion that the man was a fraud. He'd come highly recommended by Artemis herself.

They haggled for some time over the price but eventually settled on an exorbitant fee. Demeter left some drachmae as a deposit and signed a contract to have the rest delivered.

The merchant packaged her goods carefully, wrapping it in three layers of oilskin and placing that into a leather pouch.

Outside the shop it was only slightly cooler than it had been inside, but despite the oppressive heat, Demeter strode along with a spring in her step. Her precious purchase she held cradled in one arm, just like she'd held Persephone once, so long ago.

She couldn't wait to test it.

"It was so kind of you to join me on such short notice," Demeter said, pouring the wine herself.

Monime tittered, her cheeks flushing a pretty shade of pink. "No trouble at all." She looked around the courtyard with wide eyes, no doubt trying to remember every detail in order to lord it over her fellow nymphs when she left. Despite the recent drought, the topiary here were lush and green, the grass soft and inviting. They reclined under a shade cloth attached to the main house, the platters before them groaning with produce. Dining with Demeter was an honor granted only to a select few.

Monime was a safe choice. Few would miss her. Demeter tried to avoid looking down at Monime's chalice, its rim carefully coated with a thin layer of the venom.

Irritatingly, Monime seemed disinclined to drink. Demeter was forced to endure several long minutes of her stories about her fellow nymphs and how she was afraid that her favorite horse required some kind of medical treatment. The girl went on and on, seemingly without needing to draw a breath.

"And then she said—" Monime began.

"You should try the wine," Demeter said at last. "The vintage is from a gentler time."

"Oh, of course!" Monime said. "I feel so blessed." She placed her hand upon the chalice. "Did I ever tell you about the time I almost bought a vineyard in Attica?"

Demeter plastered a smile on her face as if she were interested. "I don't believe so. Tell me more."

Monime did, managing to talk on and on without needing to wet her throat.

As she continued talking, Demeter stood up and snatched Monime's chalice, grinding the rim of it against the nymph's cheek before tossing it, wine and all, into a nearby flower arrangement.

The flowers began to wilt. Monime stared at her in shock and raised trembling fingers to touch her cheek.

"Is this about the wine?" Monime asked. "Because I don't—"

Demeter watched her closely, dropping all pretenses of a smile.

Monime began to shiver, and then she stood, flinging back her chair. "What did you do? What did you do to me?" She looked around, wild-eyed, and then seized a decorative bowl filled with water and floating blossoms and poured it over her head. Sodden petals clung to her hair, whilst the bowl clattered to her feet.

Perhaps that had only succeeded in spreading the venom further. The skin on Monime's cheek began to blister, and she howled like a she-demon, clawing at her face.

Demeter was glad for the loyalty of her servants; everyone a league distant was certain to have heard Monime's cries, terrible as they were. Monime sank to her knees, still screaming and tearing out her own hair in her agony.

"What does it feel like?" Demeter asked.

"Burns... it burns!" Monime whimpered, her words difficult to distinguish. "What did I do... what did I do to offend you?"

Demeter considered it. "Your stories were awfully dull."

Monime wordlessly screamed.

The sounds were giving Demeter a headache. "Would you like it to stop?"

"Yes!" Monime screamed again. She had succeeded in ripping out a chunk of her cheek, and blood ran down her neck, staining her chiton. Still she writhed on the ground, her scuffles making an uneven set of marks that the servants would need to carefully rake over on the morrow. "Yes—I'll do anything!"

"As you say." Demeter waved her hand, and Monime was gone, replaced by a young oak. Some of the bark formations on its trunk almost looked like a face, the mouth gaping wide in perpetual horror.

Demeter looked around at the mess Monime had left, from the fallen bowl and strewn flowers to the chalice nestled under her dying plants. The servants would have to burn it all to avoid contamination, but it was a small price to pay for her successful trial. She made a note to herself to send Artemis a gift basket for her fruitful advice.

That night, Demeter left her home and made her way to the old barn, some distance downhill. Once inside, she went downstairs to the cellar, holding a torch to light the way and humming a few bars from a marching song as she walked.

She nodded to the drakon positioned outside Persephone's room. It had been no small task to get the enormous beast down the stairwell, but they had managed, somehow, emptying the cellar of almost all its foodstuffs in order to make space for it. Persephone's room took up the other half of the floor.

Demeter transferred the torch to her left hand and unlocked the cell door before sliding back the bar that held it shut. Once inside Persephone's room, she set the torch in a wall sconce and dusted her palms on her skirts.

The room stank of fish, and Demeter wrinkled her nose. She glanced at the discarded chiton that was the source of the smell and resisted the temptation to simply burn it on the spot.

Persephone was sprawled on her side on the bed, seemingly still asleep. Demeter was struck, not for the first time, by the girl's resemblance to her father. She had his lips. Sensuous. Cruel. A bruise still marked her throat, a sign of her degeneracy, not quite covered over by the other, fresher marks made by the chain around her neck.

Demeter raised the hem of her gown and delicately prodded the girl with her foot.

Nothing.

"Persephone," she said.

Not even the flicker of an eyelid.

Demeter brushed back the hair from Persephone's face and slapped her cheek. The sound echoed in the small cell.

Demeter watched the imprint of her hand fading rapidly from Persephone's skin, and still the girl did not wake. She placed her hand on the back of Persephone's neck and pinched, hard.

"By root and stem, bestir yourself."

Finally, she saw some changes. Persephone's breathing quickened, and her eyelids fluttered before she roused herself sufficiently to sit up. "Mother," she said, her voice hoarse.

The girl was still confused, half-asleep. Demeter saw the depths of the world in her eyes. She sniffed. As if anyone of consequence had the time to spend in hibernation.

"I've come with great news," Demeter said. She sat down on the end of the bed, as there were no other soft furnishings, forcing Persephone to move to accommodate her.

"What news?" Persephone asked. She blinked and glanced at the door. "What day is it?"

"I've found the perfect wedding gift for your new lover."

Persephone flinched as though she'd been struck. "You said you would have my marriage annulled."

Demeter shrugged. "I've sent my messengers, but you know how busy your father is. He'll be pleased when he sees this matter resolve itself."

Persephone went very still. "What is the gift?"

Demeter smiled. "It's a special treatment for my arrows. I

had my doubts, but Artemis truly came through for me this time."

"You can't mean to attack one of our own."

Demeter scowled. "And why not? She attacked me first, her and your father both, scheming behind my back to take you from me!" She calmed herself with a deep breath. "It will be self-defense."

"And you mean to go to the underworld to give her this gift?" Persephone asked, not even trying to hide her disbelief.

Poor, sweet, simple child. "Of course not."

"Then—?"

"She'll be coming here," Demeter said.

"Here?" Persephone echoed, wide-eyed and open-mouthed. She glanced at the door as if expecting Hades to walk in at any moment.

"I sent back your borrowed finery, along with an invitation. It's time she came here to atone for what she's done." Demeter sniffed. "I expect she'll be making the arrangements as we speak."

Persephone clutched the blankets to her chest, as if they could shield her. "She can't come to the overworld," she said, in part to convince herself. "Not without permission."

Demeter airily waved her hand. "I'm sure she will find some way to bend the rules; she always does," she said, her eyes narrowed. She hooked her fingers under Persephone's necklace, yanking her forward. "And you, my dear, will be the perfect daughter when she comes, won't you?"

Persephone grabbed Demeter's wrist and pried it away from her. "Don't touch me."

Demeter smacked her. "Never forget where you came from. Never forget who gave you life."

"This is not living!" Persephone said, pressing her palm to her cheek.

Demeter looked at her and thought about how much more pleasing she would be as a poplar. Her children of the earth were never so disappointing. "You've always been ungrateful."

Persephone let her hand drop. "It's true. I have neglected my duty to you, as a daughter. But then that fault is mine, isn't it? It's mine. Not Hades'."

She'd changed. Her sweet and stupid girl, grown thorny like a weed. The underworld had ruined her, planted ideas of rebellion in her mind which had lain fallow for so long.

"Your punishment will come, be not concerned about that." Demeter stood. She had wasted too much time here.

Persephone remained on the bed, her hands clasped in her lap. "Mother," she said softly, mumbling as she so often had in the time before the underworld.

"Yes?"

"You cannot... You would not truly harm Hades, will you? There must be three. Zeus, Poseidon, and Hades. The underworld needs its ruler—"

"It shall have a ruler," Demeter snapped. "That is no concern of yours."

Persephone stared at her with her dirt-brown eyes, set in her too-pale face. "I was named queen-consort of the underworld. Its ruler is my concern."

Oh, the airs! Demeter could not believe what she was hearing. "You may cling to that fantasy as much as you like." She snatched the torch from its sconce. "Good night."

When she shut the cell door, she slammed it with more force than was strictly necessary. The drakon glanced briefly in her direction, its forked tongue flicking, but otherwise paid her no heed as Demeter stormed out of the cellar.

A year of solitude would not be enough to teach Persephone humility. She could see now that it would be an uphill battle.

Well... enough of that. There was still the matter of Hades and the annulment. Demeter held all the cards; the gods could do nothing to stop her, not when she'd discovered the extent of her hold over them. Not even Zeus could stand against her now.

Demeter smiled in relief to herself. Yes, a few more decades and she would have back her sweet, pliant Persephone. No more talk of the underworld, no more pining for power beyond her station; that would be forgotten, like a bad dream. Demeter could scarcely wait.

25

THE DRAKON

Her mother had gone mad, Persephone was sure of it. A weapon? Or some kind of poison? What was she thinking?

Demeter could not harm another goddess, surely. And yet she'd seemed so certain...

Persephone paced back and forth in her cell, staring at the marks on the door. She hadn't made an imprint this time around, though she had the means to do so—a rusty nail, pried from the boards of the chest. Perhaps it was hubris, but she hadn't yet felt the need. She wouldn't be here long. Someone would think it odd for her to be absent from daily life, now that she was an adult, and shower Demeter with difficult questions. Wouldn't they?

She wondered if Zeus's true-born daughters were treated as such, whether Hera locked up her children for years on end.

Probably not. They probably weren't as wicked as Persephone—

No. She had to stop thinking like that. In all the plays and poems she'd read in Hades' domain, the children were never locked up like this, save by a villain, or an evil step-parent. That meant it wasn't right.

But what were those tales except mere stories and allegories? Maybe Demeter was right and she was in the wrong. Maybe—

She reached the end of the cell, the tip of her sandal stubbing the wall. This could not be right.

She went to the door, pressing her ear against it. "Hello? Can anyone hear me?"

No response.

Persephone slid down until she was sitting with her back against the door, one knee bent. She looked at the slender lines the moonlight cast on the floor, reaching in through the bars. At least she had moonlight now.

No! She could not sit here and bear this, whilst Demeter hatched her schemes and threatened the very order of their pantheon. She could not wait for Hades to rescue her this time. Persephone simply had to rescue herself.

Easier said than done.

She stood up and pressed her hands against the door. It was oak, ancient and worn. She closed her eyes and listened.

It had been a seedling in the days of Kronos and Rhea, its years beyond measure. It scarcely remembered the touch of the sun, its bones scattered into pieces and trapped here for all eternity. Its spirit rested in Elysium, providing shade to mortal heroes and a home to an unkindness of ravens.

Persephone gasped and drew back, her fingertips trembling. She never would have gained such depth of feeling from an unliving thing before—glimpses and sporadic images, perhaps, but not this. And never would she have known of its presence in the underworld.

It was another sign of how the underworld had changed her, and that might have disturbed her once, but now she only looked around herself with new eyes. Demeter might have burned all the vegetation within spitting distance, but the door, ceiling, and furniture were all made of wood, though the walls were brick. The floor was stone, edged in lime mortar to prevent even a sliver of earth from being accessible. That left Persephone with few options.

She jumped onto the bed and stretched her hands up to the edge of the rafters. Oak as well, though not as ancient as that of the door. She'd transplanted its spirit into her grove, from elsewhere near the palace. She'd tended and watered it and read beneath its branches.

She clambered down from the bed and went once more to the door, placing her hands upon it. "Hello?" she called out again, her ear pressed to its surface.

Demeter had never bothered posting a guard on her before. Why should she? With no seeds and no dirt, she must have thought Persephone defenseless.

Persephone stepped back from the door. "Please," she said. "I know it may be... strange," she continued, struggling to word her request. "This was your body. These planks were your branches, your trunk. Remember what you were. Help me."

For a while, nothing happened. She stared expectantly at the door, and it remained just that.

She was asking too much. A kind of spirit possession—trees did have spirits, no matter how coy Hades had been upon the subject—but Persephone had no idea whether her request was even feasible. She trailed her fingertips over the surface of the door, hoping to feel something, anything.

She had begun to wonder if she'd gone mad with delusions

of grandeur when the door exploded outward, away from her, its wooden frame collapsing and taking a few of the bricks down with it. Persephone jerked back and covered her eyes with her arms, then slowly lowered them, blinking in the faint glow of torchlight that now flooded her cell.

The light should have been brighter. It took her a few moments to realize it was being blocked by an enormous beast, large enough almost to fill the entire space in the cellar. Its scales glittered blue and silver, and it watched her with two slitted, yellow eyes. The ridge above its brow bone was bleeding, no doubt from the shrapnel of the exploding door.

The door might have formed part of her cage, but it had also been her protection against this creature. How fitting that Persephone could prove to be the source of her own destruction —not Hades and not Demeter.

"Easy," she said, both hands extended in what she hoped was a placating manner. "You're here to protect me. From intruders." She wondered where her mother had found such a beast and how she could have possibly compelled it to serve in such confined quarters.

The drakon sniffed the air, then slithered forward, its nails clicking on the stone floor. It worked half its length into her cell, completely blocking the doorway and most of the light. Behind it, she heard the ominous rustling of its tail sweeping the cellar floor.

Persephone slowly moved sideways, and it turned its head to follow her movements. Several horns protruded from its rigid bone plate, their tips looking wickedly sharp.

Too nervous to take her eyes from the drakon, Persephone felt around on the floor with her foot until she bumped into a discarded waterskin. She slowly crouched, watching the creature the whole time, and picked it up.

Some drakons had poorer night vision than others; she did not know enough about this one to tell, but she hoped it was diurnal. She threw the waterskin to the other side of the room, where it bounced against the wall with an audible smack.

The drakon swiveled its head toward the noise, and Persephone ran toward it, hoping to leap through the small gap in the doorway between the drakon's body and the ceiling.

The beast struck Persephone with its front leg, sending her flying across the room. She struck the far wall and groaned, falling to the floor. The drakon advanced, its claws gouging marks in the stone. She raised her head to see its jaws yawning open, exposing its muscular tongue and the red lining of its mouth.

Persephone rolled to the side as fire spurted from the drakon's mouth, toasting the spot where she'd just been. The hem of her chiton caught alight, and she swatted at it frantically whilst climbing to her feet.

Heat radiated off the bricks behind her; she backed into them as close as she dared, as the drakon stared at her with its gleaming, yellow eyes. She didn't know when she'd turned from its treasure into its adversary—whether it was due to Demeter's command or simply that the beast was not terribly bright. She had nowhere to run.

The drakon took a step toward her, and its mouth parted.

There was no time for conscious thought. Persephone reached up into the air with a grasping motion, then brought down her hands into fists by her sides, summoning the ghost of the oak tree that had been felled to create the rafters. She didn't wait to gauge the outcome of her command, but ran toward the bed. She slid the last few cubits on her stomach, then crawled until she was completely underneath the bed, her belly flat on the floor and her hands clasped over her head.

The rafters creaked, then buckled. The drakon closed its mouth for a moment, angling its head upward as though puzzled.

One beam snapped and then another. The drakon inhaled. Persephone whimpered.

The drakon exhaled upward toward the rafters, bathing the room in garish orange as flames spread across the ceiling. The ancient oak screeched as it fell, burning beams scattering across the room. The floor above must have been used for storage, as amphora fell down, too, the flames hissing as wine and pickling juice splashed against them.

Persephone screamed when a beam fell onto the mattress above her, causing the bed to sag. She heard the drakon roar and could not help but feel pity for the suffering in its voice.

After that, she heard only the crackling of the fire. When she breathed, she tasted smoke in the back of her throat.

Persephone uncovered her head and crawled out from under the bed. Her fingers touched something sticky, and she recoiled.

The drakon's glassy eyes stared at her, accusingly, its head lolling on the floor. A massive truss crushed it to the ground, blood pooling all around it.

Persephone held her himation over her face, coughing. Sweat rolled down her back as she stumbled toward the door, skirting pottery shards and flaming beams. She heard another crash behind her as she entered the cellar proper and found the stairs, taking them two at a time.

The floor above was completely gone, except for the stairwell area. Persephone fumbled at the door that she knew from memory would lead her outside. It was locked.

She coughed again, her throat searing. She did not have time for this. Ash and elm—she raised her palm, and the door...

Did nothing.

She slammed her fists against it. "Help," she croaked. She coughed and tried again. "Help!"

She closed her eyes, her questing fingers fumbling around the door's edges. Had she missed something? Was she just too exhausted to make this new ability of hers work, or had the first two times been some kind of fluke?

She banged on the door until her knuckles bled. "Help!"

Tears sprang to her eyes, trying to wash out the smoke, to no avail. Persephone coughed and yelled and knocked until her vision grew hazy and dark and she could no longer do any of those things.

"**H**elp me understand," Hades said. "You left her there. With Demeter." With Demeter the oath-breaker; Demeter the traitor.

Hermes ran a hand through his blond locks, too craven to meet her gaze. "With her mother, yes—"

"Precisely what I told you not to do!"

"For Zeus's sake, Demeter is her mother! She has a right!"

Perhaps Hermes had a right to keep his organs on the inside, and yet Hades longed to run the point of her blade from his neck to his navel. Still, even through her rage she could not forget that psychopomps were few and far between. The underworld needed him, even if Hades could no longer see any point to his existence.

"Go," she said. "Get out of my sight."

"I can still help—"

"Go!"

Hermes scuttled away like the lackey he was. Hades no longer had eyes for him.

Her gaze drifted down to the paperwork scattered across

her table. Her mind flashed back to the sight of Persephone's bared breasts, her knees spread and overhanging the edge of the desk—

Hades picked up Demeter's letter of invitation and scrunched it into a ball. She held it out on her palm, and the papyrus ignited, burning with a blue flame that shot a cubit's length into the air before extinguishing itself. She turned her hand, and the remaining ash gently floated toward the floor.

She so dearly misliked walking into a trap, but could see no way around it. She took a fresh piece of papyrus and began to write, her pen making short, sharp motions, the lines blurring slightly in her vision until she blinked. She dropped the pen and pressed the tip of her dagger to her thumb until ichor welled to the surface, then rolled a golden thumbprint at the bottom of the papyrus.

Hades scattered powdered bone over the wet ink to dry it, then shook it free. She tugged on a bell pull by her table, then re-read her document as she waited.

Xenia appeared, her face drawn and pale. "My queen?"

"Take this to Cottus," Hades said, handing her the parchment. "Tell him to hurry. I intend to depart before he sees this."

Xenia briefly looked down. "A release order? Surely you do not intend to leave here alone?"

Hades strode out of her study with Xenia trailing closely behind. "I must. An armed retinue would cause a diplomatic incident. I cannot let Demeter paint herself as a victim." She went to her armory and stood in the anteroom devoted to her personal effects, considering her options.

Xenia reached for Hades' cuirass.

"No," Hades said. "No armor. No provocations."

Xenia lowered her hand. "Except when you took her."

Hades slowly turned her head toward her, and Xenia quailed. "I gave you a task, did I not?"

Xenia pressed her lips together, then dropped her gaze and left Hades alone.

No armor, but... she could not go defenseless. Her hand hovered over the hilt of her favorite sword, then moved across to another blade, shorter and lighter, its scabbard inlaid with gold. She could always say it was ceremonial. A wafer-thin defense, but she intended not to draw it, if that were at all possible.

She strapped the sword around her waist, already missing the comforting weight of her leathers. She had made the right decision—the only one, she told herself, as she led Alastor from the stables and swung herself over his back. Emerging from the depths with all the deities of the underworld at her side would bring a reprisal she was not prepared to face, not even for Persephone's sake.

If Demeter hurt her, though...

Hades took the exit into the cave nearest Demeter's estate, gritting her teeth as the air coalesced and then thinned as Alastor emerged on the other side. She inhaled, breathing in the dry heat. And they called her realm unbearable.

Alastor snorted, tossing his head. Hades held onto an enspelled lantern, using it to light their path through the cave. The naturally phosphorescent lichens seemed much smaller in number compared to the last time Hades had passed by.

She'd known even then that Persephone was something special.

Hades felt the siren song of Persephone's necklace calling to her as a faint itch at the back of her neck. She nudged Alastor onward, trusting him to find his own way in the semi-darkness.

For miles she rode, pushing Alastor as hard as she dared. His flanks heaved for breath under her knees, but she didn't dare stop.

She knew she had to be close when she could almost hear the necklace singing, like a hum running through her teeth. A building loomed in the distance, its thatched roof catching the light of the half moon.

She slowed and dismounted, briefly running her hand through Alastor's mane. "Thank you," she said and continued on foot, glancing around for any sign of Demeter's guards.

Wait. That smell. Fire?

Hades broke into a run, heedless of the noise it caused. She reached the building, where smoke billowed out from a small grate set close to the ground.

She circled around the other side to reach the door, relieved to find it still felt cool to the touch. "Persephone?" She rapped on the door but received no answer.

She stepped back. A locked draw bar stood in her way, placed across the door to hold it secure. Hades unfastened the fibula on her left shoulder and stuck its pin in the keyhole, using the edge of the hole to bend the tip of the pin. She crouched down and inserted her makeshift pick further into the lock, bringing her ear close to hear the click of the tumblers.

It had been some time since she'd picked a lock. Centuries, perhaps. Fortunately, human development in this area had not progressed significantly since the last time she'd tried. That, or Demeter simply had not bothered to secure her valuables more carefully.

There was one final click as the lock disengaged. Hades moved the bar, sliding it free and flinging the door open. Her heart stopped cold. She'd tarried too long.

Persephone lay on the floor like a corpse, her pallor ghastly in the light of the orange flame flickering from the back of the cellar. Her hair fell loose around her head in an arc, her eyes closed as though in slumber, her long lashes dusted with soot. The folds of her chiton clung to her like clouds veiling the perfection of the night sky.

She looked so beautiful.

Ichor was smeared across her knuckles, and a line of bruises encircled her throat, but a second glance confirmed those injuries were superficial. Far more concerning was her lack of consciousness.

Hades crouched down and scooped Persephone into her arms, bringing her out into the fresh air. She carried her past the dirt ring encircling the building and laid her down on a patch of dry and yellow grass. The moonlight cast shadows upon Hades' face as she kneeled, Persephone's body sprawled as though lifeless upon the ground before her; the keeper of the dead cradling the herald of life. An image for the Muses.

Perhaps this was her punishment for finally wanting something, for needing something for herself alone; not because it bettered her realm or her people, but because she desired it. Desired *her*.

She brushed the hair from Persephone's face to observe her breath, her fingers alighting on Persephone's wrist to feel her pulse. She was not breathing and lay still, so still, as if the Moirai were mocking Hades for her vices.

Hades would know if she were dead—even now, with her hands trembling and a ringing buzz in her head so loud that it could not possibly be due to the necklace's charm—but even the gods needed air.

She would have to breathe for them both.

Hades sealed off Persephone's nose with her thumb and forefinger and pressed her lips to Persephone's, exhaling into her mouth. She repeated this three more times, then paused to see whether it had done any good.

Nothing yet.

Hades pressed her palms against the grass, their dried-out husks snapping as her fingers dug into the dirt. "Gaia, I beseech you, return your child to the waking world. Keep her from the unending gray. It is not yet her hour."

There was no time to wait and see if her prayer had been heard. Hades wiped off her hands on her chiton and leaned over Persephone once more, sharing her breath. Persephone's lips were turning blue. Hades silently projected her prayers, promising anything of worth to the Mother Goddess—devotion, libations, temples—anything, just to see Persephone smile once more.

She lost track of how long she'd been there, praying and breathing and not pausing to think, when she heard a sound.

Persephone inhaled.

27

CONFRONTATION

Persephone's throat ached, as though she'd swallowed live coals. She coughed, then blinked, seeing stars.

The night sky was so lovely, so vast in its splendor. She relaxed to feel the living earth beneath her fingertips, and a contented smile crossed her face for a few moments.

"Persephone."

She found Hades hovering near, wild of eye, her braids all in disarray, her chiton hanging loose from one shoulder.

Persephone sat up in alarm. The drakon. The fire. "How can you be here?" she croaked, then coughed, burying her face in her arm. She swallowed and tried again. "Am I dreaming? Am I dead?" she asked, her voice rising on a note of hysterical terror.

Hades placed her hands on either side of Persephone's face. "I am here, truly. We are in the overworld, and you are most certainly not dead."

Persephone embraced her, pressing her face against the crook of Hades' shoulder. Her hair smelled of smoke, or perhaps the wind was still bringing smoke toward them. "You came back for me," she said, closing her eyes. No one had ever done that before. They might've seen something, heard something, but few dared defy Demeter.

"Always," Hades said.

Persephone could have stayed like that forever, but her legs started to cramp, and it dawned upon her that they were still not safe. She drew back, brushing her hand across her eyes. Hades was missing a fibula. Persephone smoothed out the loose edges of Hades' chiton and tucked them into the top of her strophion, turning her gown into a one-shouldered masterpiece. Aphrodite would've been so proud of her. "How are you here?" she asked as she adjusted the fabric.

"I gave Zeus something he wanted. His son, Pirithous."

Persephone blinked. "But his judgment—"

Hades sighed. "He will be mine again, soon enough." She shook her head, releasing Persephone. "I thought you would be safe. I never suspected—I should have—"

Persephone's eyes welled with tears. "It's not your fault. I'm to blame. I—"

"No!" Hades took a deep breath. "Do not cast aspersions upon yourself. You alone are blameless in all of this. Demeter has fallen further than I had ever imagined." She gave Persephone's hand a squeeze, then released it. "Can you stand? We must go." She hesitated. "If you would accept my help."

Persephone climbed to her feet, with Hades following suit, watching her carefully as though she thought she might fall. Persephone wasn't that fragile. "Will you take me back to the underworld?" she asked.

Hades clenched her jaw. "If you would so desire."

"And if I don't?"

Hades glanced aside. "I will not compel you."

Persephone breathed out a sigh. That was a good start, but it wasn't enough. "I have your word?"

"It is yours."

Now, after everything, Persephone finally had an inkling of what she wanted—no. What she needed. She had to have them both—Hades and the world above. She would not survive without either of them, not anymore. But now was not the time to voice her thoughts. "Then yes," she said. "We should go."

"Why? Hades has not yet enjoyed my hospitality."

Persephone slowly turned from Hades to see her mother approaching on horseback, her nymphs in tow—only two of them this time. As Demeter drew near, she pulled hard on the reins, and her horse reared, pawing at the air before falling back to the earth with a thump.

Hades moved slightly so that she was standing in front of Persephone. "Demeter," she said, her hand never far from the hilt of her sword.

"Hades," Persephone whispered. "My mother, she's found some kind of weapon, a poison—"

Hades' fingers briefly entwined with hers, silencing her. Persephone worried at her bottom lip, her eyes only for her mother. Only she knew what Demeter was truly capable of. How low she'd stoop to get her way.

Demeter smiled but did not dismount. She wore no armor, but she had brought her bow and a quiver. The orange glow from the torches held by the nymphs illuminated an almost manic gleam in her eyes. "You've come for a fight," she said, glancing at Hades' sheathed sword.

"I would prefer to talk," Hades said. "Like rational adults."

In the distance, the cellar continued to burn, smoke

pouring out into the air. The structure groaned as it collapsed in on itself.

Demeter laughed. "A talker would have approached me for my blessing upon Persephone's marriage."

"You would have kept her under your thumb for eternity, given the chance," Hades said.

"As is my right!"

Persephone stepped forward. "You forfeited all rights to motherhood the first day you brought me to that cellar. I decide my fate now." She inched closer to Hades. "And I choose to be wed to Hades."

Hades glanced at her, eyes wide.

Demeter sniggered. "How sweet. It sickens me."

Persephone watched Demeter's hands. "Let us pass, Mother. Zeus blessed our union."

Demeter narrowed her eyes. "And that should mean what, exactly? Did he carry you for nine months? Did he nurse you at his breast, watch over you as you slept?"

"You gave me life, and I will always be grateful for that." Persephone held out her palms placatingly as she took a step toward Demeter. "But I must make my own choices now."

"You would truly choose her?" Demeter asked in disbelief.

Persephone took her gaze off Demeter for a split second to glance at Hades. "Yes. I would."

When she turned back, Demeter had an arrow nocked. Its metal head gleamed with an oily liquid. "So be it," she said.

"Persephone—" Hades said.

Persephone didn't think but simply threw herself in front of Hades. She felt a whoosh of air and heard a thump in the scrub behind her. Then she was falling, her limbs paralyzed, her face upturned toward the sky. She heard shouting, as if from a great distance away, or as though she were underwater.

Her arm burned like it was devouring itself from within. Someone was screaming. She wished, distantly, that they would stop.

"You there!" Hades' voice. "Find Hermes, tell him to fetch Asclepius—hurry!"

Apollo's son? She had no need for a healer. She just needed to sleep.

Hades' face hovered above her, her forehead creased with worry. Persephone longed to reach out and touch her cheek, to reassure her. "Sleep, dearest," Hades murmured. "The way you used to. That would be best. It will slow the poison."

Poison. Yes, Demeter had said something about tipping her arrows. But this could not be so; it felt as though her flesh were melting. Surely her mother would never have done something so cruel.

The pain spread from her arm, through her shoulder and down across her chest. The screams abruptly stopped as her lungs felt like they were being squeezed dry of air.

Oh. She had been the one screaming.

Hades took her hand, the one on her uninjured side, and pressed her palm against the dirt. "Return to Gaia, my precious flower," she said. "Just for a while. You have my assent."

Persephone drew a long, shuddering breath, and her fingers clenched in the dirt, digging deep to find the smallest speck of moisture under the surface. She closed her eyes, and darkness engulfed her. No fear, no pain, no memories. Just her and the dreaming heart of the earth.

28

WAKING

Persephone woke to find herself in a real bed, though the light pouring in over her body was actual sunlight and not the glow of the underworld. The air was dry and warm. Summer. Someone had dressed her in a simple tunic and wrapped a bandage around her arm. She pressed lightly over the bandage and felt no pain. Her fingernails picked at it until she found its end and unraveled it.

A puckered white scar ran across her arm where Demeter's arrowhead must have grazed her skin. She ran her fingertips over it, frowning, then flinched when she looked properly at her own arms: gaunt, the muscle wasted away. "No, no, no," she murmured, her hands trembling.

She tried to leave the bed, but her legs refused to support her weight, and so she stumbled, finding herself on the floor. The ceiling swam above her, and she closed her eyes, counting petals under her breath.

Two women rushed into the room and exclaimed over her, tutting. They wore Hades' colors, a strip of black sewn into their clothes, an insignia that resembled a three-headed dog stitched over their left shoulders. Persephone looked at their faces but saw only strangers. She missed Xenia and her kind smile.

"Where am I?" Persephone asked.

"You are in Epirus, mistress, and this estate is owned by Hades," said one of the women. The servants plied her with nectar and ambrosia and bade her to remain in bed. Persephone would not have allowed them to confine her thus, save that her legs simply wouldn't obey her. She was forced to stay, fuming, and eventually drifted off into a restless slumber.

She dreamed in images, for the first time since the night of the fire. In her dreams, the poisoned arrow struck her not in the arm but in her heart, and her ichor flowed freely over the soft loam of the earth.

The next time she woke, she was not alone.

It was mid-morning, judging by the angle of the light. Persephone looked over to see Hades seated by a window, the sunlight streaming over her pale face. She had a few new freckles on her arms, as though she'd been spending more time in the sun. Hades wore gray; the color was so uncommon on her that Persephone had to blink to make sure she hadn't been mistaken.

As though sensing Persephone's gaze, Hades turned and smiled. "You're awake. Thank Gaia."

"What day is it?" Persephone asked.

Hades paused for a moment before responding. "In the time you've been unconscious, babes have grown into men."

"What?" Persephone leapt out of bed, or tried to. Her weakness had not yet left her, and she still wasn't used to her new limitations.

Hades hurried over and took her arm. "Easy."

Persephone had to lean on her, the simple effort of getting up leaving her breathless. Hades guided her to sit back on the bed and sat beside her, ready to catch her again at the first moment of weakness.

"I spent the years wondering if you would ever wake," Hades said. "Thinking you might die at any moment."

"Wouldn't I have been guided to the underworld, then?"

Hades' gaze was full of misery. "I don't know."

That had to gall her—this sliver of ignorance about her own domain. There was no precedent. No god had ever lost their immortality—Ares had come close, once, and the centaur Chiron had been placed among the stars, but that was all.

Persephone's scar itched. She massaged it with her fingertips, cringing at how strange it felt. She would not keep it. She wanted no mark from Demeter etched into her body.

"Asclepius believes you will make a full recovery," Hades said.

"Is he here? I should thank him for saving me."

"He managed to incur Zeus's ire, and thus he is one of mine now. But he should not receive all the credit. He said you may not have recovered, had you not been able to... hibernate." Hades' fingernails picked at the embroidery on Persephone's coverlet.

"To dream," Persephone said. She raised a hand to her head, finding her hair twined into a loose braid. Even that simple motion was exhausting, and she dropped her hand back into her lap. "What happened to Mother?"

"When Demeter hurt you, she violated her own function as the personification of motherhood. As with Medea, that crime could no longer be ignored," Hades said.

"What about all those times she locked me in a cellar?"

Hades looked at her. "It was never specified that she had to be a *good* mother."

Persephone knew in the eyes of the other Olympians, the petty crime of neglectful parenting was so mundane as to not attract censure. But Hades knew. She had seen the cellar and inferred the rest. Persephone wasn't crazy. "Was it not sufficient that she had already once abandoned her duties as goddess of the harvest, leaving so many to die?"

"Humans die all the time, whether through divine intervention or their own folly. But to harm another god..." Hades shrugged. "Her transgressions became too great for appeasement."

"Meaning?" A chill ran through Persephone. "They didn't hurt her, did they?"

Hades sighed. "No. But they confiscated the rest of the Lernaean hydra's venom and executed the mortal supply chain involved in procuring it. Demeter has been told in no uncertain terms not to make contact with you, unless you so desire it."

It was too much to take in all at once. "I don't and won't desire it, at least for a century or so. But she's my mother."

"Yes, and she almost robbed you of your immortality," Hades said.

"I'm fine," Persephone said, trying to stand again.

Hades bit her lip and watched Persephone as she clutched a side table, leaning on it heavily. Persephone remained in that position for several moments, resting, before she summoned the strength to grope her way to a set of klinai, holding on to the walls and other furniture along the way.

She dropped down onto a kline, breathless with exhaustion. Hades followed and sat opposite.

"I'm fine," Persephone said, glaring at her.

"As you say."

Despite her words, Persephone had to rest for a few moments, her eyes closing. The urge to sleep was almost overwhelming, but she brushed it aside—she had been doing too much of that, it seemed. It was time to return to the real world.

"Who did you release from the underworld to be here this time?" she asked.

"No one. Your role as my consort has been accepted by the gods, and I am within my rights to visit you after your convalescence." Hades' gaze softened. "I have missed you."

"And I you."

Something unreadable passed across Hades' face. "I confess, you surprise me."

Persephone pressed the back of her hand to her forehead. The light was too bright here, again. She knew she would grow accustomed to it, but part of her felt a yearning for the cool gray and brown sky of the underworld and the way the mists rose over the rivers. "I'm full of surprises," she mumbled and pinched the bridge of her nose.

Hades watched her with a concerned expression. "I brought you a gift, if you would permit me."

"Is it another severed head? I can't promise I won't throw up."

"I have murdered no demigods as of late. The administrative fallout was bad enough the last time."

Persephone tried to summon her anger and failed. She couldn't quite bring herself to make light of the events that had led to her flagellation, but neither could she continue to resent Hades for it. "As you like, then."

Hades walked to the other side of the room for a moment, out of sight. Persephone watched dust motes dancing in a beam of sunlight. It seemed nice here. Epirus. She wondered what the soil was like outside and whether the hot, dry summers would wither all her fruit on the vine.

Hades returned and set down a pomegranate on the table between them. "Your grove has been faring well, despite your absence. But I sense that the land, too, misses you."

Persephone looked at the fruit. Its skin was smooth and even, colored wine red. "If it's been as long as you say, my trees must be tall now."

"You could see for yourself, if you wished." Hades took out her dagger and cut the pomegranate open, revealing its jewel-like interior. Each seed shone wetly, prettier than any ruby. Their facets caught the light, almost glowing.

Hades lowered herself to her knees before Persephone. "I have not always treated you with the courtesy you deserve. But if you choose to return to my home, to return to me, it will not be as my slave but as my queen." Hades took a deep breath, her eyes never leaving Persephone's. "I offer you my faith and my heart."

Persephone smoothed the hem of her tunic over her knees, taking a moment to compose herself. "You have done me ill, it's true. At first, I could not stand the sight of you. I had nightmares," she said, her voice growing cold, "for months." She held up a hand when it looked like Hades might speak. "But you came for me when no one else would. When others willfully turned away, because it was Demeter; because she was my mother and the keeper of the grain. You saved me. I'll never forget that."

"You saved me, too. When you took Demeter's arrow in my stead."

Persephone ran her fingertips over her scar. "I had to. I couldn't stand by and watch you suffer."

Hades bowed her head. "Why not?"

"Because..." Persephone trailed off. "You know why." Her voice trembled. For Hades, that night had been half a mortal lifetime ago, but for Persephone, it might as well have happened yesterday. She remembered the heat from the fire, the scent of burning, the way the fumes stung her eyes. "I saw Demeter was going to take you away, forever, and I couldn't—I couldn't stand the thought of living in a world where you weren't—where you no longer existed."

"Oh, Persephone," Hades whispered.

Persephone reached for the pomegranate, holding it in her lap. "In the overworld, I'll always be in Demeter's shadow. She will never let me forget that. Below... I've made a difference." She briefly closed her eyes. She *had* changed things, made circumstances better for some—it was the truth and not conceit to say as much. "To the souls you care for and to the land itself. I don't wish to leave you again—at least, not forever. But I belonged to the earth long before I ever met you. I must have the sun."

"If I could capture a piece of it and bring it down with me, I would," Hades said.

"I know." Persephone counted out six shining seeds from the pomegranate, freeing them from the white pith, and held them on her palm, placing the rest of the fruit back on the table. "I'll dwell with you for half the year—six months. For the other six, I'll reside in the overworld. Will you accept?"

"I would have you by my side, always. But if I cannot..." Hades sighed. "Yes. I accept."

Persephone placed the six seeds on her tongue, all at once.

Hades' gaze never left her face. She watched, enraptured, as Persephone sucked the juice from her fingertips.

The seeds were honey sweet, cut through with an acidic tang. When Persephone swallowed, she could taste their bitter edge.

"Is it done?" she asked. She didn't feel any different. Hungry, perhaps, longing for more of that tart sweetness.

"It is done," Hades said and smiled, her expression uncharacteristically tremulous. "May I?"

In response, Persephone leaned down and kissed her, wrapping her arms around Hades' neck. Hades kissed her back, and for the first time, it felt like coming home.

EPILOGUE

Summer ended, and Persephone returned to the underworld to sit by Hades' side and to be her wife in all respects. When the land above had grown cold and bitter, she journeyed once more to Epirus to make a home worthy of a queen.

The cycles continued, each parting bittersweet, each reunion joyous and passionate. She trained herself not to pine for the other world after every transition, knowing she would return soon enough.

During one blisteringly cold winter, she lounged in Hades' artificial solarium, nestled on a fur-lined kline. Daedalus and Perdix had entered a kind of arms race for architectural glory, each seeking to outdo the other in scope and prestige. The solarium had been Daedalus's project, a glass-sided chamber built on the rooftop along the east wing. From here, one could see the rolling green hills of the Elysian Fields, whilst being warmed by the enchanted 'sun' that hung above. Whilst it boasted a few shelves lined with scrolls, Hades had agreed not to bring her work into the room.

The drakon's ghost huddled at Persephone's feet, its head on its forearms, its serrated tail curled around its body, yellow eyes shut in a state of semi-hibernation. In winter, it seemed to prefer the false sun to the warmth of the Phlegethon, and she'd not had the heart to dislodge it from the solarium.

Persephone leafed through her correspondence. Few gods bothered to write to her in the underworld, choosing instead to make their presence known during the warmer months. She worked her way through a pile of letters a hand's width deep, throwing each one to the side once she had glanced at it.

From the kline opposite her, Hades set down the scroll she'd been reading and looked up. "May I ask why you are making such a mess?"

Persephone scrunched up the final letter and threw it against the wall. It bounced and slid close to the drakon's face, but the creature did not stir. "They're all from Mother. Well, her scribes, anyway. More than one. I don't think she even bothered to sign these herself. All the handwriting is different."

"A century has not yet passed."

"She knows that, I'm sure."

Hades leaned forward, resting her head on her palm. "What do you intend to do?"

Persephone was due to return to the overworld a few days hence. All her things were packed. She traveled light—her estate at Epirus was well-established, and her household knew her preferences. "If I don't see her, she'll keep harassing me, and it'll be worse up there. She might even show up in person." Demeter hadn't thus far crossed that line, but her missives before hadn't been quite so insistent, either. "What do you think I should do?" Persephone asked.

Hades shrugged. "I cannot say."

"You must have an opinion."

"In this case, it is irrelevant."

Persephone looked around at the mess she'd made, at the letters fallen to the ground like dry leaves. Bitter, nasty leaves. If she'd had Hades' abilities, she'd snap her fingers and turn them all to ash.

"What will you do?" Hades repeated.

Persephone rubbed at her temples. "If I go, she'll see she can breach the rules I've set at any point. But if I don't go, I'll always be afraid during my time in the overworld. I'll always dread that knock on my door."

"Did you find a sorceress to renew the wards around the estate?" Hades asked.

Persephone sighed. "Not one whose skills pleased me. Sorcery is a dying art among mortals, it seems."

"A pity."

Persephone fingered the chain around her neck. She might never be free of it, not unless she asked the immortal Circe for aid. The thought did not bother her unduly much. "I should give her a chance. To apologize." Demeter's letters had hinted at such a possibility, but whether it was her mother's words or her scribes' presumptions, Persephone could not tell.

"If you must," Hades said. "But prepare yourself for disappointment."

Persephone smiled, the muscles in her cheeks feeling overly tight. "Always, where she's concerned."

The late winter air was mild by the underworld's standards, and yet Demeter had led her near a crackling fire, trapped indoors with nowhere to run. Persephone held her clasped hands in her lap and tapped a finger against her wrist, unable to keep still.

Demeter's house had grown over the years, with rooms added and walls demolished so that her receiving room no longer matched the images of Persephone's childhood. Still, some things were familiar—a large tapestry of a threshing floor on the wall, and the table in the center of their klinai.

Pleasantries had been exchanged and then some. Demeter looked much the same as ever, agelessly beautiful. She had changed something about her hair, her golden braids looped in intricate knots like the snakes of the Erinyes.

A servant came by to pour more wine. Persephone didn't recognize his face.

"I expect you'll be wanting to celebrate the Mysteries this year," Demeter said.

"The what?" Persephone asked.

Demeter's teeth glittered in her smile. "The Eleusinian Mysteries, dear. Have you not been reading your letters? The mortals like to celebrate your return to us with a festival."

Persephone rubbed the spot on her arm where her flesh sometimes still ached. "Do you shoot an effigy of me at the finale, or is that part conveniently forgotten?"

Demeter scoffed. "That little thing. Are you still obsessed about it? Why, there's not a mark on you."

Not on her skin, not anymore, but her arm still ached during the heat of high summer. She'd never forgotten the look of anguish on Hades' face, from a fear so deep it still remained lodged in her heart. "Your letters implied that you wanted to apologize," Persephone said.

Demeter's eyes widened. "Apologize? Whatever for?"

"Well—"

Demeter jabbed one ring-studded finger in her direction. "You ran off with your chthonic lover, a match I did not approve. Hades robbed me of your presence. And Zeus stole my parental rights. All of you should be apologizing to *me*."

Persephone realized her hands were clawing into her thighs. She forced them to relax. "You shot a poisoned arrow at Hades. The same poison that killed the centaur Chiron."

Demeter scoffed. "That again?"

"You stole decades from my life! Then and before. When I was a child," Persephone said. She forced the words to leave her mouth. "You locked me in a cellar for years on end. What you did to me wasn't right."

Demeter shook her head. "You don't know what it's like to be a mother, dear." She smiled slyly. "And now, I suppose you never will."

Persephone was losing the thread of her sanity. "So it was fine then, everything you've ever done?"

"Everything I've done?" Demeter tilted her head slightly. "Everything I've done was to protect you from people like *her*."

"Well, it didn't work."

"It's not my fault you grew up to be a little slut."

Persephone stood, pressing her knees together to stop them from shaking. "I see. In that case, I believe we should part. Thank you for your hospitality. Please don't write to me again; I'll ask the servants to burn any letters." She took a deep breath, steadying herself. "Goodbye, Mother."

"That's it?" Demeter asked, the legs of her kline screeching across the floor as she stood. "After all the sacrifices I made for you, all the tears I shed—for you!"

Demeter spoke to her departing back. Persephone forced

herself not to turn around, putting one foot in front of the other. She was done. No more listening to her mother's fervent rantings, no more accepting her distorted vision of the truth.

Demeter followed her to the door, continuing to screech, but Persephone refused to listen. She kept on walking, the frozen ground crunching underfoot. A door slammed. Persephone glanced back but saw no one behind her. She shook with relief.

She wrapped her himation more closely around her shoulders, walking down to the stables where she'd left her horses. The groom nodded to her and helped hitch her chariot.

He seemed like a nice boy. Too nice for Demeter's moods. "If you ever need a job, come to Epirus," Persephone said.

He bowed his head. "Thank ye, mistress."

Persephone left her mother's estate for the last time, driving down the old, familiar roads. Tears stung her eyes, freezing on her cheeks. The ground was ready to thaw, but she wasn't. Not yet.

The day was late by the time she returned to the underworld. She knocked on the door to Hades' chamber and waited.

"Come in."

Hades was seated at her dressing table, brushing out her hair. She glanced at Persephone's reflection in her bronze mirror. "I take it Demeter gave you no satisfaction."

Persephone closed the door behind her and shook her head. She couldn't speak.

Hades rose and went to her, enfolding her in her arms. She was her sanctuary, her shield against the storm. Persephone clung to her and cried, digging her nails into Hades' skin. Her wife did not seem to mind, stroking her hair until Persephone's tears subsided.

"It's over. I'll never see her again," Persephone said, sniffling.

"'Never' is a long time."

"If she changes—but she won't. It's pointless to keep hoping she will." Persephone wiped her eyes and gazed up at Hades. "Don't be mad. I'll leave again, in seven days. I just can't bear to be on the same plane of existence as her right now."

"You are welcome here, Persephone. Always."

Persephone pressed her lips to Hades' neck and buried her face against her skin, relishing the familiar scent of her. They both deserved a rest; why not.

Spring would simply have to come late this year.

ENJOYED READING?

Thanks for joining Persephone and Hades in *Captive in the Underworld*. If you loved the book and have a moment to spare, I would really appreciate a short review on the page where you bought the book. Your help in spreading the word is gratefully appreciated and reviews make a huge difference to helping new readers find the novel.

Go here to find a store page:
https://go.lianyutan.com/underworld

Thank you!

DOWNLOAD YOUR BONUS SHORT STORY

If you loved reading about Hades and Persephone, you can get the sexy bonus chapter, *Breathless*, for free now when you sign up to join my mailing list. You'll also be notified of giveaways, new releases, and receive personal updates from behind the scenes of my books.

Breathless: An F/F Hades and Persephone short story

Hades steals her breath away.

A few weeks into their marriage, Persephone is still learning how to please Hades, dreaded goddess of the underworld. As her fear wars with desire, Persephone must learn how to satisfy her captor and steel her own heart in order to survive.

Go here to get started: https://go.lianyutan.com/subscribe

MORE BOOKS BY LIANYU TAN

- Unnamed standalone F/F gothic horror vampire novel set in 1920s Singapore — coming 2022
- Breathless – a sexy Hades and Persephone short story, available exclusively to newsletter subscribers

ACKNOWLEDGMENTS

A book is a labor of love, and this novel was no different.

To my loving wife, I owe a debt of gratitude. Thank you for leading me to the gravity well of authordom, for nurturing my fragile writer's ego and for believing in me, always. You have my heart.

My utmost thanks to my beta readers, Anders and Juliana, for pushing me to do better. Hades has blossomed under your thoughtful input.

Thank you to Wicked Words and Christa Cooke for your help in editing and wrangling my words into shape. I appreciate all of your insightful comments and kind feedback.

Thank you fellow authors Rae D. Magdon and Lexa Luthor for your kind words of encouragement and advice. I appreciate your support, so generously given.

And for everyone who's followed me from my Sylvanna/Morrigan days, thank you for your trust in my work.

Sule sal harthir.

ABOUT THE AUTHOR

Princesses in towers. Heroines in chains. Tales of abduction, suffering and smoldering passions. Those stories have captured Lianyu's imagination since forever.

In her dark lesbian romance novels, fear can turn to love, monsters can find redemption, and beauty always succumbs to the beast.

Lianyu was born in Malaysia, but now lives in Australia with her wife and two cats. She loves to hear from readers. You can reach her as follows:

- Email: lianyu@lianyutan.com
- Website: https://lianyutan.com
- Subscribe to newsletter:
- https://go.lianyutan.com/subscribe
- Facebook: https://go.lianyutan.com/facebook
- Twitter: https://go.lianyutan.com/twitter
- Insta: https://go.lianyutan.com/insta
- Goodreads: https://go.lianyutan.com/goodreads